Sweet Revenge

Meaghan Pierce

Pierced Soul Publishing

For Caoimhe. Without your love and encouragement this book simply would not exist.

Chapter One

S tealing was getting boring. Something she considered both annoying and inconvenient, considering she was on her way to another job. This one in—she checked the file she'd been sent on her tablet—Atlanta.

She'd been tasked with stealing a small, hideous gold statue. It didn't look like much as she swiped through the photos, but who was she to say what rich people with too much money and not enough sense should want? Especially if they were willing to pay her to acquire it for them.

As the private jet descended toward the runway, she turned her tablet off with a click, sliding it into her bag. This would be a quick trip. The plan was to be in and out during the house party her unwitting mark was throwing tomorrow evening with the statue carefully tucked into her handbag and no one the wiser.

Maybe that was the problem—this one was too simple. It had been almost a year since she'd had an assignment that really excited her. She'd taken it too easy since that close call with the cops in Morocco, and now she was bored.

It was her own fault, really. Morocco had shaken her confidence, made her wonder if she'd lost her edge. As a result, she'd laid low, taken simple jobs here and there to keep her feet wet. Staying out of the game too long made it hard to get back in. No matter how good she was at what she did, it didn't take much to be replaced by someone newer and younger.

Once this job was done and the money securely in her account, she'd put some feelers out for something a little more high stakes. Something to shake this restless feeling that had settled into her bones in the last few months.

The plane taxied to a small hangar where a black town car waited, and she climbed into the back of the vehicle, tossing her bag on the seat beside her. They drove out of the airport and wound their way to a hotel downtown, the steel and glass spearing up into the inky black of the starless sky.

The hum of conversation drifted into the lobby from the bar at the other end as her heels clicked across the polished marble floor to the front desk. To any casual observer, she might be a businesswoman coming into town for work.

She made eye contact with the concierge, a man in his early twenties who took a moment to look her up and down before locking his eyes on her face, smiling wide.

"Checking in?"

"Yes. The King's Suite."

His fingers flew over the keyboard. "Carolyn Walsh?"

For today, anyway. "That's what they tell me."

He tapped a few more keys, then turned to grab her keycard. "Do you need any help with your bags?"

She flashed him a flirtatious smile. "I think I can manage. Thank you." Her eyes dropped to his name tag. "Charles."

As she walked toward the elevator, she felt his eyes following her and grinned. Men made such easy targets. Distract them with thoughts of sex, and they'd never notice you lifting something out of their pockets.

She let herself into the hotel room with a mechanical whir of the automatic door lock. Bypassing the bedroom with its luxurious king-sized bed and jetted tub, she dropped her bag onto the coffee table and pushed open the sliding door to the balcony.

The noise of traffic drifted up from the street, and she leaned against the balcony's railing, eyes drifting closed as the breeze teased her curls off her face. She'd lived in eight different countries in eight years. Visited so many more on jobs or just to travel that she'd lost count.

Early in her career, she'd loved the freedom to pack up and move on whenever she wanted a change. To go wherever the wind blew her, knowing she had no one to answer to. It had thrilled her once, that freedom. Now it was just lonely.

She hadn't intended to come back to the states after spending so much time in Europe, but when she packed up in Prague and headed to the airport, she booked a one-way ticket to New York without thinking. Being back in the states and so close to home had stirred up something else inside her. Longing. For what she wasn't sure, but the pang of it was getting harder to ignore.

The money currently sitting in her bank account was enough to live on for ten lifetimes. She had everything she could ever want or need, the ability to live anywhere in the world, to be anyone she wanted to be, and still, it felt like something was missing.

On a sigh, she pushed away from the balcony and stepped back into the suite, closing the door behind her with a soft thud. Might as well unpack and test out that jetted tub. She had a busy day tomorrow. She was going back to her roots and charming her way into a country club so she could snag a last-minute invite to that party.

∼

"I swear I dropped it in here this morning." She rifled through her oversized handbag, some of the contents spilling out on the glass-topped reception desk.

"I'm sorry, Ms. Walsh, I can't let you in without ID."

She pressed her fingers to her eyelids, waiting until tears formed before looking up again. "Of course. I understand." She began shoving things back into her bag, hands shaking. "It's just that we had an issue with our luggage, and I still can't find half of my things. But"—she waved a hand in the air—"none of that is your fault."

"Is everything all right here, honey?"

She peeked over her shoulder at the petite blonde standing behind her, wrapped tightly in a deep purple sheath dress. Bingo. Right on time. "I'm sorry, I'm getting out of your way." Dragging her bag off the counter, she knocked over a stack of business cards and watched them flutter to the ground, mortified.

"Oh God, I'm so clumsy." She stooped to pick up the scattered cards as the blonde and the receptionist hurried to help her. "We're supposed to be on vacation, and now my husband is away on business, and he swore he bought me a week-long pass, and now I can't even get in for a mimosa and some pampering and—" She blew out a shaky breath. "You don't care about all that."

"That sounds like a rough time," the blonde agreed.

Her southern twang sounded more like Texas hill country than Atlanta society. Rocksprings, Texas, according to her file.

"You should come on in with me. You can join me as a guest."

"Oh, no. I couldn't impose." Standing, she offered the business cards to the receptionist, hitching her bag up on her shoulder.

"It's not an imposition at all. Really. I'm Melody."

She shook the hand Melody offered. "Carolyn, ah, Carrie."

"Well, Carrie, how about we go get us one of those mimosas?"

She offered a grateful smile and followed the blonde inside past a dining room buzzing with activity, several private meeting rooms, and the hallway that led to the tennis courts and out onto the pool deck. Melody greeted staff and other patrons by name as she led them back to a reserved cabana.

"How long have you been in Atlanta?" Melody wondered, signaling a waiter.

"A little over a week. Visiting from Seattle on what was supposed to be our second honeymoon. Something fun to celebrate our fifth anniversary, you know?" She made a show of twisting the gaudy diamond ring she wore around her finger. "But every time I think we're going to get more than ten minutes alone together, he gets called away for work. And then yesterday he just up and left for a business trip! Now I'm on a honeymoon by myself in a city I've never been to before."

"Aren't men something else? My fiancé always seems to be gone more than he's home some days."

"Does he work in finance too?" she wondered, sipping the mimosa the waiter left.

Melody smiled. "Real estate."

They chatted about men, places they'd traveled, Atlanta society gossip, retreating into the shade of the cabana as the hour dragged on to lunch, and it reminded her how much she hated small talk. Especially with other women, when she couldn't flirt to get the info she wanted faster. Usually, anyway.

She made a big show of checking her watch. "Oh, goodness, I should probably get going." She pushed back from the table. "I really appreciate you helping me get in. It was nice not having to spend my entire vacation alone."

Melody tipped down her sunglasses and offered a sympathetic smile. "It was my pleasure. I really enjoyed our chat. You know"—Melody stood to leave—"we're having a party tonight, and you should come. As my guest."

"Oh, well," she flushed as she slung her bag over her shoulder. "I don't think I could impose on you twice in one day."

Melody waved a hand in the air. "It's not an imposition at all. Besides, it sounds like you could use a little bit of fun while your husband is away. We would love to have you."

"It's been ages since I've been to a good party." She chewed her bottom lip. "As long as you're sure…"

"I'm definitely sure." Melody rummaged around in her bag for a card and a pen. "This is the address. It's black tie."

"Looks like I might need to go shopping."

Melody grinned and handed over the card. "Party starts at seven. Maybe you'll meet someone who can show you a good time in Atlanta after all."

She accepted the card with a sheepish grin. "I'll see you tonight."

Stepping away from the table, she dropped the card into her bag and strode out of the club. The cab she signaled rushed to a stop at the curb, and she climbed in with a triumphant grin.

At eight, the town car pulled up to the gate of the towering mansion in Atlanta's wealthiest neighborhood, and the driver gave her name. Once they were waved through, he pulled around the circle drive, and the valet helped her from the car.

The driver pulled away with strict instructions to stay close in case she wanted to leave early.

She climbed the stairs in her navy blue sheath dress, stilettos clicking against the stone. It flattered her curves and showed off her cleavage, but it wasn't flashy like some of the sequined numbers a few women were wearing. The goal was to blend in, to go unnoticed.

The house was teeming with people dressed in their finest, white-jacketed waiters carrying trays of hors d'oeuvres and champagne weaving among the guests. Soft music floated through each room, and she grabbed a glass of champagne off a passing tray and took a sip. Dom. Classy.

Garrett Wells, Melody's fiancé, did indeed work in real estate. At least enough to cover for his side hustle of stolen artifacts. There was a precious Ming vase she recognized on a side table in the family room because she'd stolen it three years ago. And that's the way her world worked.

She wandered through the rooms, eyes sharp though she'd already memorized the layout of the house from the plans she found online. The statue was in the library on the first floor. Once she had it, she'd have to make her way past the kitchen, through the family room, and down the long hall to the foyer.

As long as she didn't run into Melody and get sucked into conversation and introductions, she calculated she could be in and out of the house in under fifteen minutes. As if on cue, she heard Melody's slow southern drawl from somewhere behind her and pivoted away and down the hall.

The door to the library was open, which was good for her. It wasn't an off limits room she might get caught in and have to explain her way out of. Sconces highlighted paintings on the walls, and a gaudy chandelier hung down from the ceiling. Wells didn't have taste so much as a preference for expensive things. Money couldn't buy everything.

The statue, no bigger than her palm, sat on the edge of a bookshelf. It was even uglier in person. A little golden gargoyle with its mouth twisted in a grimace, claws poised to scratch. She couldn't imagine why anyone would pay such a hefty sum to get their hands on it.

She pretended to study the titles of the books on the shelf above it as she casually reached for it. When her fingers closed around the cold metal, a buzz shot up her arm. However easy the job, stealing was always a rush. Of power, of skill, of control. Unhooking the clasp on her bag, she shifted so her hands were hidden from the couple examining the paintings and dropped it inside.

She moved one of a trio of paperweights into the spot where the statue had been so the space didn't look empty. Stepping back from the bookshelf, she wandered slowly toward the door. Once in the hall, she danced between the waiters that came and went from the kitchen. The key here was to leave quickly, but not in a rush. Rushing made people suspicious.

A few people sat on the plush couches in the family room, and the hallway was mostly clear of guests, though some still drifted in through the set of double doors left open to the evening air. Pulling her phone out of her bag, she texted the driver and waited for his signal of acknowledgment.

When she heard heels on the stone followed by Melody's lilting accent, she flicked the phone to silent and pressed it to her ear.

"It's only a party, Brad," she hissed. "I just got here. I haven't even been inside!" She waited a beat. "Well, it's not like you cared about leaving me on my own before jetting off to God knows where for work," she sneered the last word as she turned, letting surprise then embarrassment flit across her face when she met Melody's gaze.

"And that's a low blow. I have to go, Bradley. Fine! And

thanks for making sure I have a terrible time no matter what I do. Happy anniversary to me," she snapped. "I'm sorry," she said to Melody.

Melody reached out to rub her arm, squeezing it gently. "It's okay. To hell with Brad. Did you want to come in for a drink?"

She looked past her at the guests, the music drifting out into the night, chewing her lip as she considered. "It'll just make him angry if I stay, and then that'll be a whole thing. I already called the car." She held up her phone. "The house is beautiful, Melody."

Melody gave her a pitying smile, flipping her sleek blonde hair over her shoulder. "If you need a good divorce lawyer, I know a few."

She smiled sadly as the car pulled up and the valet opened the door. "I'll keep that in mind just as soon as I have evidence to beat the prenup. I'm sorry I can't stay."

Climbing into the car, she settled back against the seat, shooting off a quick text to let her contact know that the job was done and she expected him to meet her at the airport. By two in the morning, she was safely tucked in bed in her sprawling New York apartment, sleeping like a baby.

Chapter Two

Before even getting out of bed the next morning, she checked the balance on her offshore account. She'd watched her contact make the transfer, laptop propped on the hood of the SUV he drove, before she handed over the statue. But it never hurt to make sure you didn't get screwed.

She'd made that mistake before, when her first international job in Berlin hadn't gone exactly as planned. Even though she'd narrowly evaded the police, her contact had taken the jewels she'd acquired for him and vanished, leaving her high and dry. It had taken a week of cozying up to a diplomat to get back home, but she'd learned a valuable lesson. Never leave a handoff without watching the money hit your account.

Padding down the hall to the kitchen, she put coffee on, eating a banana over the sink while it dripped and hissed into the pot. When it finished, she filled a mug and took a greedy drink before adding a splash of cream and taking another, slower sip.

Leaning back against the counter, she watched the light

play over the balcony as clouds flitted across the sun in the spring breeze. Today would be the perfect day to call up a couple of girlfriends for brunch and maybe some shopping. Too bad she didn't have any.

Grabbing her bag off the edge of the counter, she carried her coffee into the office. She crossed to the desk and slid open the bottom drawer, lifting out the heavy safe she kept inside. She keyed in the code and raised the lid on a neat stack of passports and driver's licenses—one for each state and country she'd lived in so far.

In ten years, she'd never lived in the same place twice. At least not until she'd finally given in to the pull of New York and left Prague to return to the States three months ago. Even William had been surprised to hear she was back.

Still, the restlessness she'd hoped to shake loose with the move clung on. She'd have to fix that with a visit to Will and a job more complicated than stealing trinkets from house parties.

She shuffled through the IDs, exchanging the one she had in her wallet for the one she'd been using since moving back to New York. When she moved to set the stack in the bottom of the safe, one bounced onto the table, landing face up. She picked it up, rubbing her thumb over the photo of herself, over the name.

Evelyn O'Brian. She'd left that girl and that name behind a long time ago. Placing the ID back in the box, she flipped the lid closed with a thunk and set it back in the drawer. Downing the rest of her coffee, she set the mug in the sink and retreated to her bedroom for a quick shower.

Maybe she'd treat herself to brunch and a little shopping after all. Just because she didn't have girlfriends didn't mean she had to live like a hermit. She preferred being alone anyway. Other than the occasional lover, she mainly kept to herself. People asked too many questions, caused too much of a distraction.

As she towel dried her hair, quickly running mousse through her curls, her phone buzzed on the counter, and she smiled.

"Hello?"

"Evie." She could hear the smile in her mother's voice.

"Hi, Mom."

Evie didn't know what had prompted her to reach out to her mother a few months ago. When she'd called to wish her a happy birthday, she'd expected to get the machine, but her mother's soft voice, full of surprise, had answered instead. Panicked, she'd nearly hung up, but there had been no judgment in her mother's tone, no anger.

They'd talked for nearly two hours that first time and every week since. Her mother didn't push, didn't demand to know where Evie had been or why she'd left. Those weekly calls had become a tether that kept her grounded when she worried she might lose herself.

"You'll never guess who I ran into today at Mass."

Evie grinned. "Who?"

"Helen Maguire!"

"From high school?" Evie wriggled into a green sundress, contorting herself to tug up the zipper.

"Yes, I was surprised she didn't catch on fire just from being inside!"

Evie laughed as her mother's cheerful voice chirped in her ear. God, how had she survived so many years without this? She didn't recognize half the names her mother mentioned as she weaved her story, but it didn't make it any less entertaining. Gossip had always been her mother's favorite hobby.

Every week she unburdened her soul at Mass so she could start burdening it again by sharing all the bits of news she'd collected. Who was getting married, who was pregnant, who was cheating, who was pregnant and cheating. If you wanted to know anything about anyone, all you had to do was ask Mary Elizabeth O'Brian.

"And what have you been up to?"

She asked that question every time she called, and Evie always gave some vague response about work being crazy or life being hectic. If Mary Elizabeth wanted to know more, she didn't pry.

"Just got back from a work trip. Quick turnaround."

"Oh, good. I hope it went well."

"Yeah, it was great."

There was a long pause. "Evie?"

"Yes?" Evie prompted when her mother didn't continue.

"Well, I was just wondering if—" Evie could hear a shuffling noise in the background. "Never mind. I think your father's home, so I've got to run. Hey. I love you, sweet girl."

Evie's frown melted into a smile. "I love you too, Mom. Talk soon."

Feeling considerably lighter, she took the elevator down to the lobby, whistling happily, and pushed out into the early spring sunshine. The noise of the street rolled over her as she weaved between meandering tourists with their faces tilted up to admire the towering stretch of glass and steel and hurried locals with eyes down on their phones or the pavement.

When the light changed, she crossed the street with the throng of people and turned the corner. Stepping into a restaurant, she pushed her sunglasses onto the top of her head and returned the hostess's kind smile as she led her back to a table for one. The dining room bustled around her, and she filtered through the conversations while studying the menu.

The couple to her left was trying to decide where to spend their summer vacation. The wife wanted to recreate their

Parisian honeymoon while the husband wanted to spend the summer boating in Greece. Evie's money was on the wife getting her trip to Paris when she caught the husband staring at the waitress's ass.

A table of twenty-somethings in front of her lamented about how unfair it was that their fathers actually expected them to get jobs when all they wanted to do was enjoy their summer and work on their tans. Evie snorted into her mimosa when one girl called her new allowance child abuse.

Beyond the entitled whining of the table of spoiled little rich girls living off daddy's money, another couple caught her eye. They were younger than the married couple still arguing over Paris or Greece, too comfortable with each other to be a first date, but not jaded enough to have been dating for years. A young love where she still laughed at his jokes and he brushed his fingertips over her arm just to be close to her.

A memory she'd buried a long time ago of a boy who used to look at her with eyes full of love and promises, whose fingers brushed her arm just to feel her surfaced, and she shoved it down again. That chapter of her life was closed. She'd cried enough tears over what could never be, and she wouldn't waste time doing it again.

As the brunch crowd faded and the buzz of conversation died, Evie pushed back from her table and took the long way back to her apartment past some of her favorite boutiques and shops. The French bakery paled in comparison to an authentic French patisserie, but she couldn't resist the macarons and a beautiful mini lemon tart piled with fresh raspberries.

She wasn't much for fashion other than when she could use it to start a conversation with a banker's wife to learn more about her husband's habits or run into a mark in a dressing room to make a copy of her house key. But she bought a couple of dresses and a new blouse at a boutique that produced only unique, handmade pieces.

Clouds rolled over the sun and darkened to a petulant gray. She could smell rain just under the exhaust and sweat, and she quickened her steps. She barely made it inside the lobby of her building before the skies opened up, and she heard the yelp of people as they raced for cover or simply kept walking in their brisk New York fashion. Nothing fazed New Yorkers.

The doorman nodded as she crossed to the elevators. While unlocking the door, her phone beeped from the inner recesses of her bag, and she set her shopping bags on the kitchen counter to dig it out. Bringing the message up with a few taps, she frowned.

Hi, sweetie. Can't talk today. Will call some other time. - Mom

Evie set her phone down on the counter, eyes scanning the message a second time. Not once had her mother ever texted her. Evie wasn't even sure she knew how. And why would she say she couldn't talk today when they spoke earlier?

She turned to put the bakery box in the fridge and pulled out a bottle of water, taking a sip to cool her throat, which had suddenly gone hot and dry. There was probably a perfectly rational explanation for the sudden message. Maybe she'd intended to call back since their call had been cut short and couldn't now. That was probably it. Nothing to worry about.

She read the message again, wiping her palms on her thighs. Something else about it struck her as odd, but she couldn't quite put her finger on it. She tried to stuff down the worry that shuddered through her. She was being ridiculous.

Shaking her head, she reached for her phone and dialed her mother. If it was a mistake, Mary Elizabeth would pick up even if just to say she couldn't talk right now like she had a few times before, and everything would be fine. Voicemail.

Evie tapped her fingernails against the back of her phone. She didn't even have anyone in Philly she could ask to check on her mom. When she'd resumed communication with Mary Elizabeth, she asked her to keep their weekly chats a secret. From her father, her sister, her friends. Everyone. Her mother hadn't liked it at first, but it was the only demand Evie made of her, so she agreed. This was the first time Evie wished someone knew.

Rereading the words, her eyes narrowed in on what seemed off. Sweetie. Never once in thirty years had her mother ever called her sweetie, only sweet girl. In that moment, she didn't care if she was overreacting or if someone spotted her in Philadelphia; she had to drive down to Philly to check on her mother. She'd much rather get there and find her mother asleep and her father out than do nothing. Grabbing her keys and bag off the counter, she left her apartment, letting the front door slam behind her.

Chapter Three

Declan Callahan ruled Philadelphia with an iron fist. His reputation had been earned in blood. There was never a question that he would take over the syndicate after his father's death. A Callahan had sat on the throne for over a century. But if his father had been building a kingdom, Declan was building an empire. Empires required constant vigilance.

He'd done a lot of work bringing the vision he had for the syndicate to life. He didn't merely want to make money and maintain the status quo; he wanted to build wealth and amass power. He was insatiable.

In the two years since his father died, Declan had molded the syndicate in his own image. He'd left the drugs to the Italians—not that they'd managed to make much success from the gift he'd offered to them—and set his sights on bigger things. Arms dealing, among other things, had proven to be a very lucrative investment.

Rising from behind the desk, he slipped off his tailored suit coat and hung it on a peg in the corner. Through the window, he could see the packed restaurant parking lot in the golden glow of street lamps. Converting the old whiskey distillery into an upscale restaurant and event space had been one of his first investments when his father had given him some leeway in handling business dealings.

Patrick Callahan had never understood the need for a high-end bar and steakhouse. Or the commercial real estate Declan had bought for a steal when the economy dipped. Both times. He'd been skeptical of the nightclub purchase and complained about the cost of renovations despite how much and how often he'd enjoyed them.

His father hadn't been able to see it, but all of it had served a greater purpose. Declan had carefully built a successful, legal facade that allowed him to move hundreds of millions of illegal dollars through Philly's docks under the watchful eye of loyal syndicate men who were strategically employed around the city. His aboveboard businesses and generous political contributions afforded him a great deal of respect and access.

He liked money. No, that wasn't true. He liked winning. And money was just another game to play. A game he excelled at. As a result, the empire was thriving—in every way but one. Crossing back to the desk, he picked up the heavy, gilded invitation and frowned at the curling script that cordially invited him and a guest to the wedding of James Callahan and Maura Kelly.

All anyone had been able to talk about for weeks was his cousin's fucking wedding. Which meant renewed gossip about his own relationship status. Or lack thereof. Mainly people wanted to know when he would finally settle down with his own wife and spawn the next generation. By the time his father turned thirty-one, he already had three sons and one on the way. A fact no one failed to mention in his presence.

If things had worked out differently ten years ago, he had

no doubt he'd have his own gaggle of kids by now. But they hadn't, and he'd made the syndicate his baby instead. A fruitful way to focus his time and energy, if nothing else.

At a knock on the office door, he dropped the invitation back on the desk and turned to see his brother Finn poking his head through the opening.

"Got a minute?"

Through the open door, he could hear his assistant still typing away on her computer. He probably should have sent her home hours ago. Declan motioned Finn inside and moved to the bar cart he stocked with his favorite whiskey. Pouring a finger into two glasses, he dropped into one of the chairs that faced his desk and took a sip.

"Long day?"

"All the days are long."

He could sense Finn studying him, but if his brother wanted to nag him like his wife, Cait, often did, he thought better of it. "Have you heard from O'Brian today?"

Declan frowned, trying to remember the last time he'd spoken to his father's best man. "Not since yesterday. Maybe the day before." He downed the rest of his whiskey and set the glass on the edge of the desk. "Why?"

"He was supposed to run a surveillance op on DiMarco today, and he never showed."

That wasn't like him.

"The op?" Business always came first.

"Rory McBride stepped up. It went fine. Brogan is reviewing everything as we speak, but no one's been able to reach O'Brian, house or cell. McBride did a drive-by of the house on his way home, said all the lights were out."

Declan adjusted his watch on his wrist, checking the time. "I've got a key. I'll swing by on my way to the club."

"Not going home?"

Declan shook his head and pushed to his feet. Slipping his

arms into his jacket, he adjusted the collar and cuffs of his shirt. "There's always something to do."

Finn flashed a quick grin. "Or someone."

"I'll leave the whoring to Aidan. Besides, how would you know? We both know you're madly in love with your wife."

Chapter Four

It was dark when Evie pulled up in front of her parents' house. It loomed behind the flower garden that teemed with new life, windows black and ominous. Dread pooled in her belly. She couldn't remember a time when her mother hadn't left at least the porch light on at night.

She cut the engine, plunging the yard into darkness. Picking her way up the bricked path in the faint, sickly green glow from the street lamp on the cross street, she peered in the windows that ran the length of the door on either side. Nothing.

She jiggled the handle, but the door was locked. Checking the street for cars or nosy neighbors, she moved further down the porch into the shadows of the shrubs that lined the railing and stopped in front of the living room window.

Carefully removing the screen and leaning it up against the side of the house, she braced herself and elbowed out the window, hissing as a piece of glass scraped along her forearm when she reached in to unlock it.

Her first thought as she climbed in, stepping over the broken shards, was that it was freezing. Far too cold for early

April. Rubbing warmth into her arms, she crossed to the thermostat on the opposite wall. Forty degrees. When she cut off the air conditioning, the house fell into eerie silence.

"Mom?" Her voice was thin, tinny to her own ears as she called out into the emptiness.

The living room was pristine. No drawers left hanging open or papers thrown around. Throw pillows were tucked neatly into the corners of the couch, a blanket draped across the ottoman. She could make out the shape of photos that hung on the wall in the dark. Resisting the urge to cross the room and inspect them, she followed the hallway back toward the kitchen.

The formal dining room she remembered using for holidays and special occasions looked untouched, except for one chair that sat askew, as if someone had pulled it out to sit down and forgot to tuck it in when they got up. Her mother always insisted they tuck their chairs in.

"Hello?"

She turned toward the kitchen and noticed a faint golden glow that spilled out into the hallway. Probably from the light over the stove or kitchen sink. Relief washed through her, and she quickened her steps, rounding the corner into the kitchen.

Relief melted into terror when she saw her mother collapsed on the floor behind the kitchen table. Oh God, please. Please still be alive. She didn't notice the blood until she dropped to her knees, fingers searching her mother's neck for a pulse. Nothing. A sob escaped her lips and she tried again, fingers slipping as she desperately willed her mother's heart to beat.

She drew her hand back, staring numbly down at the thick, sticky blood that coated her fingers. Another shape on the floor drew her gaze up, and her father's body came into focus.

"No," she sobbed, throat tight. His eyes were open, staring, and blood dripped from a single gunshot wound to his temple.

She looked from her father to her mother in horror, hands trembling. Desperate for some air, she bolted to her feet and out the back door onto the deck. Gulping in the fresh night air, she leaned over the railing and threw up into her mother's hydrangeas.

When headlights swept over the side yard and she heard a car pulling into the driveway, her body went rigid. Shit. She'd left the .22 she always carried in her purse in the car. She darted back into the kitchen, carefully stepping around her mother's body, and grabbed a cast iron skillet off the stove, wielding it like a bat as she peeked around the doorway and down the hall.

She moved quickly into the living room as keys jingled in the lock. Nessa? Footsteps receded, pausing as if whoever it was had noticed the window she'd broken. They moved back to the door. Too heavy to be her sister. Who else would have a key?

Holding her breath, she waited for the door to swing slowly in. It was a man, tall and broad. She could just make out the outline of his body and the gun he held low at his side.

He stepped in off the porch, shutting the door behind him, and she pressed her back against the wall. She was trapped. Should have left out the kitchen door when she had a chance. If she rushed him, she might be able to take him by surprise before he had a chance to fire.

Gripping the cast iron tighter, she poised to leap, but he threw her off guard when he flicked on the lights, and she blinked against the unexpected brightness. When his hand gripped her wrist, she yelped, but he'd already tugged the pan free, setting it down next to the TV.

"Evie?"

His voice was deeper than she remembered, but no less familiar. She risked a look at his face. He didn't look angry; he looked…confused.

"Declan." It came out a whisper.

"What in the fuck are you doing here?" he demanded as he slid the gun into the holster at his back.

"I…" She shuddered, hugging herself only to remember that her hands were slick with blood. Pulling them away, she looked down at them, and Declan's gaze followed her own.

He stepped back, and she could feel his eyes travel down the rest of her body.

"What happened? Are you hurt?"

Evie shook her head. Christ, why couldn't she make her brain work?

"Evie?" He waited until she met his gaze. "Where are your parents?"

"They're…" Her eyes drifted to the hallway.

He pulled the gun out of its holster again, saying nothing as she followed him down the hall. When he reached the kitchen, he calmly turned on the lights. It was worse in the light. Blood spattered the cabinets and counter tops. It pooled under their bodies in dark puddles and oozed its way under the table.

She wasn't sure what reaction she'd been expecting from him, but the measured control on his face when he turned to her surprised her. So different from the boy she had known.

Gripping her upper arm, he led her back to the living room, waiting a beat before he said, "Who did that?"

"I have no idea. I only got here a few minutes before you did."

He studied her, and she had no idea if he believed her or actually suspected her of murdering her own parents. He pulled out his phone, dialing and pressing it to his ear.

"What are you doing?"

"I found O'Brian," he said, ignoring her. "I need you to meet me over here. Now."

He hung up before whoever it was had time to respond and slipped his phone back in his pocket. "I didn't know you still spoke to your parents."

"My mom, and no one did."

He nodded. "Did you check the rest of the house?"

"No."

"Stay here."

He climbed the stairs, and she could hear his footsteps creaking through the floor, hear the click as he opened doors to all the bedrooms, the scrape of closet doors opening and closing. Her lower lip trembled as another car pulled into the driveway, and she bit it—hard. She would not break down here.

More heavy footfalls on the stairs, and the door swung in on Finn, the second Callahan son. Finn stopped abruptly when he saw her standing in the middle of the living room alone, hands, arms, and knees smeared with blood.

"Kitchen," Declan said as he descended the stairs, and she clenched her hands into fists to keep them from shaking as they paced down the hallway.

"Fuck me," she heard Finn say. "Who?" he demanded when they were both back in the living room, and Evie wasn't sure if he was asking her or Declan.

"I don't know. Yet," Declan said, eyes never leaving hers. "Call McGee to come get them and get Aidan and James out here to knock on doors. This whole block is syndicate families. Maybe somebody saw something."

"They might not want to talk."

Declan's voice was a threat. "They don't have a choice." He waited until Finn left to make his calls before speaking again. "Where are you staying?"

"Nowhere. I just…" She huffed out a breath.

Her whole body tingled, like daggers stabbing at her skin from the inside out. She had to get the fuck out of here.

"I just got here."

He was silent for a minute. "You can stay at Glenmore House tonight then."

"No." She shook her head. "I can stay at a hotel."

"You can't."

Her head snapped up, eyes narrowing on his face. Why the fuck was he so calm when she felt like she wanted to crawl out of her skin?

"And why the hell not?"

"Because you're covered in blood."

The simple sentence deflated her, and she looked down at herself. Hands caked with dried blood, more of it smeared across her arms and soaked into the hem of her dress. A fresh wave of nausea swamped her.

"Not Glenmore House, then. I have an apartment I keep in Center City. It's closer than the house. Private access so no one will see you. You can shower and sleep. We can figure out the rest in the morning."

"Okay." She'd sleep in her car if it meant she could get out of this fucking house. "My car's out front."

"I'll drive you."

She could feel the tight hold she had on her control slipping. Too tired to argue, she nodded and climbed gingerly into the front seat of his Range Rover. They drove through familiar streets, past homes and shops she recognized. Somehow everything managed to look exactly the same and completely different at the same time.

He pulled into an underground parking garage, punching in a security code and waiting for the gate to roll up. After parking in a reserved spot, they followed the signs to the penthouse elevator. Declan swiped a card on a black pad, and the elevator doors opened with a ding.

He held his hand against the door when she stepped inside. "It'll open right into the apartment. Use whatever you need."

When he stepped back, the doors slid closed, and the elevator rose without a sound. She stepped off onto polished black marble that gleamed in the city lights. The kitchen sat to her right, and she could see the living room beyond, so she followed the hall to her left past an office and a room with a pool table until finally finding one with a bed.

This was his room. It had to be, with its king-sized bed and dark mahogany furniture. It smelled like him. She crossed to the bathroom in the dark and turned on the lights. Avoiding the mirror, she turned on the water as hot as it would go, stripping out of her dress and dropping it into the trash can before stepping under the spray.

She stood under the punishingly hot water, frantically scrubbing her skin until the water ran clear. Satisfied that she'd gotten all her mother's blood off her body, she sank down to the cool tile floor and wept.

Chapter Five

I t was early when Declan let himself into the apartment the following morning. Setting the coffee and food he'd picked up on his way over on the counter, he listened for movement. Hearing nothing, he headed for his bedroom. The door was closed but not locked, so he eased it open.

She was sprawled out in the center of the bed on her stomach. Her mass of chestnut curls spilled down her back and over the pillows. He'd had her in his bed before, albeit under vastly different circumstances, and damn it all if he didn't like the look of her there now.

Shaking that thought from his head, he stalked back to the kitchen, slamming cabinet doors and drawers as he pulled plates and utensils out for breakfast. When he turned, she was framed in the archway to the kitchen, hair still tousled from sleep.

She wore only one of his button-downs, sleeves unbuttoned and pushed up to her elbows. It skimmed the tops of her thighs, fluttering around her when she crossed her arms over her chest. Even after all these years, she could still send lust coursing through him with a look.

"I brought breakfast," he said, gruffer than he meant to be.

He set the plates on the island and pulled containers out of the paper bag. "Coffee," he added, sliding one of the to-go cups toward her when she crossed to the counter.

He watched her take a sip before sliding onto one of the high-backed chairs. She looked steadier this morning. Her hazel eyes were clear of the haze of shock he'd seen in them last night, and she wasn't as shaky as she'd been. Bringing his own coffee to his lips, he sat, leaving some distance between them. She flipped the lid on the box he handed her, and her head jerked up, eyes meeting his.

"You don't like french toast anymore?"

"I do." Her eyes flicked to the logo on the bag. "This is french toast from Nicky's. Extra crispy with lots of raspberries and chocolate chips. My favorite," she added, studying him with an expression he couldn't read.

He shrugged. "It was on the way." It wasn't, not since Nicky had moved to a bigger location five years ago, but her groan of pleasure at the first bite made the extra twenty minutes worth it.

"Tell me what happened last night."

She paused with the fork halfway to her mouth, her expression sobering. "The house was dark when I pulled up. I didn't have a key, so I broke the front window." Her fingertips brushed at shallow scratches that dotted her left arm. "The house was freezing. The AC was on and set really low. I turned it off."

She took another bite, chewing slowly. "I called out for Mom, but nothing. It was quiet. Really quiet," she whispered, swallowing. "I saw her on the floor. I thought heart attack at first, but then I noticed the blood when I felt for a pulse."

"And your father?"

She looked up at him, eyes shimmering with tears that

tore at his heart. Even after all this time, he wanted to protect her.

"That's about when I noticed him. I didn't touch him. I knew he was already dead." Shoving her food away, she sat back. "You showed up a few minutes later, and you know the rest."

"What are you doing in Philadelphia?"

Her spine straightened, chin ticking up, and his lips twitched in amusement. So her fire still sparked under that rigid control.

"I don't see how that's relevant."

He quirked a brow, leaning forward. "One of my best men is dead and his wife on top of that. Then I find my ex-fiancé, who I haven't seen in ten years after she practically left me at the altar, covered in their blood. I'd say everything's relevant. So?" he prompted when she didn't continue.

"I got a text message from my mother."

"That doesn't seem like something that would cause you to rush here from...wherever," he said with a dismissive wave.

She took a slow sip of coffee. "Well, it was."

He sighed. She was determined to be difficult, it seemed. "Any idea who might've done this?"

"You'd know better than me, I think. Piss anybody off lately?"

He chuckled. "No more than usual. Preliminary thoughts from McGee are murder/suicide." He noted the anger that flashed in her eyes. He took it as a good sign.

"There's no fucking way. Why would he think that?"

"Because your mother was stabbed several times, but your father was found with a single bullet wound to the head."

She flinched, fingers flexing on the coffee cup. "He wouldn't do that." She cleared her throat. "He wouldn't."

"I agree. We should have the results of the autopsy in a

few hours. I told him I'd bring you by to discuss funeral arrangements. And I called Nessa."

Evie nodded, eyes focused on a spot over his shoulder before sliding to his face. "How did she sound?"

"Devastated. With a million questions I can't answer for her. I told her to meet us at McGee's."

"Yeah. Okay. Hell of a family reunion," she mumbled, taking a sip of coffee.

"Where have you been, Evie?" The question slipped out. He'd thought to give her more time before asking questions like that, but he had a right to know where she'd gone. And why.

"I left. Does it really matter where I went?"

"That's your answer? That it doesn't matter? That we didn't matter? That you leaving didn't matter?" He spat the last words, barely leashing the anger simmering just below the surface.

"That's not what I said."

"Maybe, but it's what you meant. If you expect me to help you, the least you could do is be honest with me."

She snorted, shoving to her feet. "I didn't ask for your help, Declan, and frankly, I don't want it. The fact that it's got strings means not a damned thing has changed anyway. Where's my car?"

"What the hell does that mean?" His grip tightened on the coffee cup in his hand, and he forced himself to relax it.

"It means I want to change my clothes and bury my parents and get the hell out of here. I'm not here to dredge up the past. It's done. My car. Where is it?"

Declan wanted to push her, wanted to know that she'd hurt as much as he had over the last decade, but he couldn't bring himself to. Not with the way she looked last night covered in blood fresh in his mind or the way her voice broke when she talked about her parents.

He reached into his pocket and drew out her keys, setting them on the counter between them. "Finn drove it over last night. I imagine he's already trying to talk Cait into buying one."

She frowned. "Cait? Why?"

"Because they've been married for about eight years now."

That one caught her off guard. Whatever Evie talked about with her mother, Mary Elizabeth had never mentioned that Evie's childhood best friend married Declan's brother. She'd said last night that she only spoke to her mother and that no one else knew. He wanted to know more about that, more about everything, but he was patient enough to wait for the right moment.

"Where are you going?" he demanded when she scooped her keys off the counter and headed for the elevator, jumping up to head her off.

"I keep a bag in my car with extra clothes. Unless you want me to go to McGee's looking like this." She gestured down the length of her body.

"I don't want you going anywhere like that. I'll get it," he added, ignoring the annoyance that flitted across her face.

"I thought the elevator was private."

"It is, but the parking garage isn't." He held out his hand, palm up. "Keys."

She hesitated, eyes darting past him to the elevator as if she was gauging whether she could make a run for it. When she scowled, he knew he'd won, and she dropped the keys into his outstretched hand.

"It's in the trunk."

"Great." He barely suppressed a grin. "Wait here."

He watched her until the elevator doors hid her from view. If he had his way, no man on earth would ever see her dressed like that again. No man but him.

Chapter Six

Evie took her time getting ready. Under the harsh bathroom lighting, she looked pale with shadows under her eyes from last night's tears and restless sleep. She massaged lotion into her skin, using makeup to ease the paleness and disguise the shadows. Unwilling to fight with her unruly curls, she swept them up in a messy bun and decided it was good enough.

Rummaging through her bag, she pulled out a pair of dark wash skinny jeans and a plain black t-shirt, tugging on both. She gave herself one last long look in the mirror before loading everything back into her bag and carrying it into the bedroom.

The room fit him, with its dark, imposing furniture and deep navy linens. Sleeping in that bed last night with his scent wrapped around her had been a comfort as much as a torment. She didn't know what to make of his generosity. He was probably eager to keep her close so he could keep an eye on her.

She wouldn't be his problem much longer. As soon as her

parents were buried, she was getting the hell out of here and never looking back. There was nothing in Philadelphia for her anymore except painful memories.

He was seated at the kitchen counter, intently watching a video on the tablet in his hand, but he tapped the screen to pause when he noticed her standing in the front hall. His eyes dipped down to the bag in her hand and back up to her face.

"You can stay as long as you need to."

"Thanks, but I'm going to check into a hotel until the funeral."

"And then?"

"And then I'm going back to New York."

He gave a curt nod, sliding the tablet into a case and tucking it under his arm. Rounding the counter, he stopped in front of her. Their height difference hadn't changed much over the years. He still had about five inches on her five foot eight, but he was imposing in his dark gray, tailored Italian suit and crisp white button-down with the collar open.

The angles of his face were different, harder, chiseled with a decade of age and experience, and the dark sweep of his hair made his blue eyes even brighter. Those eyes had captivated her once. Drawn her in and consumed her. She had to be careful it didn't happen again.

"Ready?"

"No," she followed him into the elevator, "but let's get it over with."

He'd parked her car in a second reserved spot for the penthouse, and she tossed her bag into the trunk before climbing behind the wheel. She knew the way, so she didn't wait for him to follow her before peeling out of the garage. It was warm for April, so she rolled the windows down and let the breeze tease the curls that had fallen loose from her bun.

Pulling into the parking lot of an unassuming gray building, Evie cut the engine. To anyone driving by, it would be overlooked as a suite of office buildings rather than a makeshift funeral home and morgue. McGee had operated as the Callahan syndicate's coroner and funeral director for as long as she could remember, though she'd never been closer to death than the occasional funeral before now.

Declan's Range Rover and another car she didn't recognize pulled in behind her. Nessa. Evie watched her twin sister climb out of the silver BMW. Her hair was shorter than she'd kept it in high school, and she wore it straight down to her shoulders with auburn highlights that caught the light. They weren't identical, but it had been easy enough to fool people from a distance when they were kids.

They paused to speak next to Declan's SUV, and when he gestured to Evie's car, she had the sudden, overwhelming urge to flee. Just throw the car into drive and never look back. If she'd never yearned for home, never called her mother to wish her a happy birthday, none of this would be happening. She could be in New York or Seattle or fucking Timbuktu. Literally anywhere but here with the memory of her mother's blood smeared on the kitchen floor and the devastated look on her sister's face.

When they started toward her car, she forced herself to get out and face her sister for the first time in ten years.

"Oh, Evie," Nessa said as soon as she saw her, wrapping her up in a firm hug. "It's all so awful."

Evie's eyes widened in surprise as she looked at Declan, who only shrugged. She had no idea how to respond or what to say, so she gave her sister an awkward pat on the shoulder.

"What happened?" Nessa looked from Evie to Declan and back again.

"McGee's finished the autopsies, and he's got some theories." Declan gestured toward the door at the side of the building and held it open for them both.

The inside was nicer than she'd anticipated, nothing like

the cold, sterile place she'd always pictured. But not even the polished hardwood floors and soothing blue paint could mask the smell of death. Funeral homes always smelled like death. Death and sadness.

McGee appeared from a side door, a little grayer than she remembered him, but with the same kind eyes. He took Nessa's hand, gripping it tightly.

"Your parents were good people," he said. The thick brogue of his Irish accent hadn't faded in the three decades since he moved to America. "And I mean to lay them to rest well."

When he reached for Evie's hand, she crossed her arms over her chest, remembering what Declan said about his suspicions.

"Ah, yes. Declan must have told you about my initial report." McGee shot a quick look at Declan. "My apologies. I meant no disrespect."

"What initial report?" Nessa wondered.

"He thought Dad murdered Mom and then shot himself," Evie replied, voice clipped.

McGee inclined his head. "I did, but I don't think that anymore. Come, sit."

He gestured to a small round table ringed by four chairs and waited until they all took their seats before producing a folder from a stack and flipping it open.

"I don't want to get into all the details," McGee began, eyes on Nessa before moving to Evie, "but after getting a better look, your father inflicting these wounds on your mother doesn't make sense. They're too frenzied, hurried. Some shallow, some deep, like first there was some hesitation, and then there wasn't. Your father probably surprised whoever it was, and they shot him."

"Why would they stab her and shoot him?" Evie wondered as Nessa wiped at tears with the back of her hand.

"Weapon of opportunity, I think. Then more time to react to your father coming home. I can give you the full report." McGee turned to Declan, who glanced up from his phone and nodded. "Later. For now, let's discuss the funeral arrangements."

McGee closed that folder and opened another one, pulling out brochures. Nessa nodded intently, eyes wet with tears, but Evie couldn't stop thinking about who could have done this. Probably an attempted burglary. That kind of thing happened all the time in a city like Philadelphia, and while it was a nice neighborhood, it wasn't impervious to crime.

"Evie?" McGee called, and she surfaced from her thoughts to everyone staring at her.

"Yes, sorry."

McGee smiled softly. "Not at all. I said the priest will be here shortly. Why don't you two take a look at the caskets in the next room over there, and when he arrives, I'll bring him out to discuss the service."

Evie blew out a breath, rising from her chair when Nessa did. The room was set up like a display case, and caskets in varying colors and wood grains lined the walls like a macabre parade.

"Pick a casket," she mumbled, watching Nessa circle the room to inspect each one.

"You okay?" Declan asked softly in her ear, making her jump.

She hugged herself tightly. "Of all the ways I used to picture myself coming back to Philly, this didn't make the top ten." She sighed. "I would've had to do this at some point. Or Nessa would have. Children bury their parents; that's how it goes. She just turned fifty a few months ago."

"Your father threw her a big birthday party at the restaurant."

Evie smiled, rubbing a hand over the deep pang in her

chest. "She told me about that. That's why I called. To wish her a happy birthday."

"I—"

"The O'Brian girls."

Evie turned at the croaking voice of Father Michael as Declan quickly stepped away from her. The priest had been ancient when she was a girl; he must be held together with prayers and luck at this point.

He used to take her confession and warn her of the carnal sins of the flesh. Little did he know what she got up to in her spare time. Her gaze drifted to Declan. Or with who. Father Michael was supported by a younger priest with dark hair and dark eyes who looked vaguely familiar.

"I was so sorry to hear about your parents. They were good people. Generous," Father Michael added, his breathing strained.

Evie wondered how many times over the next few days she was going to have to listen to platitudes about how wonderful her dead parents were. It made her want to bolt again.

"If you'll excuse me, this is Father Charles, newly ordained."

The younger priest offered his hand, and recognition dawned. She blinked in surprise. "Charlie? Charlie Ryan? I never would have figured you for the cloth," she added. He'd run wild with Declan and his friends as a boy in a way that would have made the saints blush.

Father Charles smiled affably, ignoring Father Michael's disapproving grunt as he shook her hand. "Declan and God saved my life years ago. I felt I owed them both."

"Let's sit," Father Michael said, shuffling over to the table. "Discuss what you'd like for the service."

Nessa folded herself neatly into a chair, hands clasped on her lap so the wedding ring on her finger glinted in the overhead light. Evie slid a look to Declan, brows raised. She was going to have to ask about that later.

Father Michael opened a big book that Father Charles passed across the table with shaking hands, pages whispering as he flipped through them. Evie hadn't attended a funeral since her grandfather died when she was fifteen, so she let Nessa take the lead when it came to choosing the prayers, the music, the benediction.

There was an endless litany of choices that had to be made. Everything from choosing the flowers to the caskets to the pallbearers. And Evie didn't know the right ones for any of it. When McGee asked them to bring outfits their parents could be buried in and photos they could frame for the service, Evie shivered. The thought of going back into that house made her nauseous.

"I have to get out of here," Evie said once the priests and McGee disappeared with their notes.

She shoved away from the table and pushed out into the fresh air, leaning back against the side of the building and closing her eyes, tilting her face up to the sun.

"Thank you," Evie said when she sensed Nessa step up beside her.

"For what?"

Evie looked at her sister. They had the same eyes. "For making all the decisions in there. I didn't...I couldn't..."

Nessa laid a hand on Evie's arm but dropped it quickly. "It's okay. Do you want to come with me to the house? To pick out their clothes and things?"

She wanted to say no, to tell her sister to pick out whatever she thought was best, but she couldn't be that heartless. She was no coward. "Yeah, I'll go with you. Tomorrow?"

Nessa smiled sadly. "Tomorrow. You can get my number from Declan," she added when he joined them.

Evie dropped her head back and stared up at the clouds.

She could feel him staring at her, and it warmed her in a way the sun could never. She couldn't get out of this city fast enough.

"She's married?"

"She was."

She met his gaze then, brows knitting together. "She's got a wedding ring on."

Declan nodded, checking his phone when it signaled and then slipping it back into his pocket. "She was widowed two years ago."

"That's sad." She blew out a breath. "Did they have kids?"

"No."

She looked over at the unexpected softness in his tone. For the first time, she wondered if he had kids, if he'd gotten married after she left. She didn't remember seeing a wedding ring, but she hadn't been looking for one. That possibility stung more than she wanted it to.

Shoving away from the wall, she slid sunglasses onto her face and dug out her car keys. "She wants me to go to the house with her tomorrow to choose their clothes and whatever."

"Do you want me to go with you?"

He really needed to stop throwing her off balance like that. "No, but thank you. Do you have her number?"

He pulled out his phone and keyed up Nessa's contact information, passing it to Evie so she could copy it down. "Here, take mine too." He tapped the screen and brought up his own number.

"Declan," she said when he turned to go. There were so many things she wanted to say to him but couldn't. "Thank you. For last night, for this." She gestured to the building behind her. "I know they would be grateful. I'm grateful."

"It's no more than I would do for any of my men."

This time when he turned to go, she didn't stop him, but the unexpected sting of his words served as a reminder that though they had meant something to each other once, they didn't anymore. And it was better that way.

Chapter Seven

Declan watched Evie stare after him in his rearview until he turned the corner and she disappeared from view. Tossing his phone on the seat beside him, he headed back to Glenmore House to meet his brother for a full debrief.

He tried to go over the details in his mind of the op they'd run on DiMarco from the quick rundown he'd gotten from Finn last night, but his thoughts kept drifting to Evie.

He didn't recognize the woman she'd become. This cool, calculated woman who carefully measured her words and didn't wear her heart on her sleeve. But he could catch glimpses of the girl he'd known underneath, the one he'd loved since before he even really knew what love was.

Her hair was the same wild tumble of curls he'd loved to bury his fingers in, loved to feel splayed out over his chest. Her eyes were the same hazel flecked with gold, and they were still quick to flash with anger. She still tilted her head to one side when she was annoyed and chewed her bottom lip when she was upset. And she still looked damned good wearing one of his shirts and nothing else.

Pulling into the driveway, he punched the button for the tall, wrought iron gate and waited for it to swing in before pulling around the circular drive and into the garage beside his brother's Jag. Reliving the past was pointless. She'd made her choices and he'd made his, and now they were both living with them.

Ignoring the mail one of the staff had left on a table by the door, Declan climbed the wide, carpeted stairs to the third floor. Glenmore House had been in the Callahan family for generations. Some great-great-grandfather had built it before the stock market crash of the '20s, and it had been passed down to every first son and heir ever since.

Like everything else about the Callahan name and legacy, Declan took his responsibility to this house and its upkeep very seriously. Which is why he'd recently paid an exorbitant amount to restore the third floor from unkempt old servant's quarters with peeling paint and drafty windows to updated staff rooms, a library his mother would have loved, and a sprawling tech lair for Brogan.

Indulging his brother's natural affinity for technology had been another of his moves to drag the syndicate into the twenty-first century. His father had wasted Brogan's time and talents on old-school listening devices and wiretaps. Why risk planting a bug for anyone to find when you could hack directly into a security camera for a live twenty-four-hour feed?

Rounding the corner toward Brogan's windowless lair, Declan could already hear the hum of the machines. He didn't understand how half the shit worked, but Brogan did, and that's what mattered.

"What did we get?"

Brogan barely spared him a glance as he finished typing neon letters into a black box. When he was done, a black and white video popped up of cars rolling through an intersection. A traffic camera. Brogan dragged the video feed onto another screen and brought up a series of stills on the monitor closest to Declan.

"We confirmed his pattern, and it's exactly what we expected." He clicked through the images of DiMarco disappearing into a restaurant in Little Odessa.

"So he's playing both sides with the Russians and the Italians."

"Seems to be. Couldn't prove anything for sure, though. Maybe the asshole just likes borscht."

Brogan shrugged when Declan raised a brow.

"I want dirt on this guy in case he becomes a problem."

"For the Italians or the Russians?"

"For my city. Where's my dirt?"

"McBride swears he carries a little flash drive around with him everywhere." Brogan blew up an image where it looked like DiMarco was holding a small silver lighter. "Apparently he never lets it out of his sight. If that's true, I imagine he's got some pretty incriminating shit on there."

"Yeah, but how do we get it from him without him knowing?"

"That's the million-dollar question. I'll keep working on it."

"Good." Declan checked his watch and rose. "Keep me posted."

"So, Evie's back."

Declan paused in the doorway, slowly turning to face his brother who was staring intently at his screens. "Until the funeral."

"Huh." His fingers flew across the keyboard. "And you're okay with that?"

"Get back to work, Brogan."

Declan left his brother alone with his expensive toys and

headed for the stairs. He debated going into his office over the restaurant or working from home the rest of the day. Pulling his phone out of his pocket to text his assistant, he stopped in front of the library and, against his better judgment, wandered inside.

His great-grandfather had drawn up plans for this room for his great-grandmother who loved to read and write—one of her original poetry books was preserved in a glass case in the far corner—but hadn't been able to build it before he died. When Declan meticulously described the renovations to the architect, he told himself it had been to preserve the history of his ancestors for future generations.

But bringing this room back to life had never been his dream. It had been the dream of a girl with wild curls and hazel eyes flecked with gold. The girl who had walked back into his life but was still impossibly out of reach.

On second thought, maybe he'd work from the restaurant.

Helen was waiting for him when he stepped off the elevator with a stack of folders and a cup of coffee. He finished the text he was sending to his youngest brother Aidan about a delivery they were expecting and pocketed his phone, accepting the cup of coffee from Helen.

"The realtor sent over some property options for the inquiry you made last week. She said they've all got flexible zoning depending on your plans, and she's available next week to show you whichever ones you choose. I moved the ones I think you'll like best to the top."

She waited until he slid into his chair before laying the folder on his desk. He flipped it open and quickly looked through the options. She was right; the top three were more along the lines of what he had in mind. When he closed that folder and set it aside, she laid another one in front of him.

"First quarter numbers are in from all the tenants. Revenue is up, and one of them wants to talk about a renovation."

"Which one?"

"The bakery. She wants to add outdoor seating. I scheduled her into your calendar for a meeting later this month."

Her sales numbers were impressive. Who knew cupcakes turned such handsome profits? "Pull the numbers on her lease. I want to see what she's currently paying in rent."

"Of course. Nothing exciting in the mail today except for an invite to the mayor's fundraiser for his next run." She handed over an embossed envelope, opened with a precise cut down the fold.

Declan tapped on the stationery, running his thumb over the gaudy gold filigree. He wouldn't turn down the invite. If he was going to bother lining a politician's pockets, he wanted to be photographed with them. Often. That way if he went down, they went down with him. DiMarco often operated the same way, which meant this party might serve two motives.

"Can you get me the guest list for this?"

Helen frowned. "Probably. Any particular reason?"

He pinned her with a look. "I want it."

She bobbed her head, clasping her hands in front of her. "I'm sure it won't be difficult. McGee sent over the final report about the O'Brians." She handed over the final folder.

"And?"

"I didn't read that one." She squeezed her fingers together tightly, lips pursed.

"Anything else?" he asked, looking up when she didn't move.

"I heard Evie O'Brian is back in town," she said in a rush of breath.

There it was. He sat back in his chair, his face neutral. "She is. People tend to do that when their parents die."

"I heard they were murdered."

Declan glanced down at the folder that sat closed in front of him and back up at Helen's face. "I thought you didn't read this."

She shifted, brushing at the skirt of her dress. "I didn't. I was having dinner with my parents last night and my brothers. They were…speculating about what might have happened."

"It's not really their job to speculate, is it?"

"No. Will that be all?"

He nodded and waited for her to close the door behind her. Swiveling in his chair, he looked out the window at the street below. From this vantage point, he could just make out the traffic on the opposite side of the street. It would start to pick up soon as the day ticked into the lunch hour and busy executives emptied out of their skyscrapers for a quick bite.

There was always talk. The Callahan syndicate consisted of twelve families, so it was impossible to squash gossip. Especially about something like this. Helen was a Maguire, one of the original five families, so if they were talking, then others definitely were.

It would have to wait until after the funeral, but he'd call a meeting with his lieutenants and set the record straight on exactly what did and didn't happen so they could all stop gossiping like old ladies and get back to their jobs. He shot a quick message to Finn to put the word out and flipped open the folder on McGee's report.

It was pretty much a written version of what he'd told Evie and Nessa this morning, except with diagrams of the stab wounds and photos of the crime scene and bodies. He'd make sure Evie got a copy of this if she wanted one.

Having McGee had certainly made their lives easier. It got harder and harder every year to keep good cops on the payroll. He had a few left, loyal syndicate men, but not nearly enough were willing to play the game anymore.

So he provided McGee with whatever funds he needed to handle shit like this, and they kept their deaths and their investigations internal. It was much easier to dish out your own justice when you could get answers without having to deal with the cops.

Once he had his dirt on DiMarco saved for a rainy day, he'd get Brogan to use whatever tools he had at his disposal to find the bastard who'd killed his people. Just because it was random didn't mean someone wasn't going to pay. No one fucked with the Callahan syndicate and walked away clean.

Chapter Eight

When Evie pulled into the driveway of her parents' house the following afternoon, a knot tightened in her belly. Nessa was already there waiting for her, and when she climbed out of her car, Evie did the same.

The house looked different in the light of day with its happy yellow siding and blue shutters. The flower beds were just starting to wake up, and in a few weeks, they'd be a riot of colors and scents. Her mother loved to get her hands in the dirt and tease life out of it.

She wound her way up the brick path and reluctantly climbed the stairs. The window had been boarded up and the glass swept off the porch. They'd have to see about getting that replaced. Nessa slid a key into the lock, and the door swung in on silent hinges.

Cold pricked her skin when she crossed the threshold, even though the air conditioning was off. Everything looked normal, just as it had been when she arrived two days ago. Throw pillows and blanket neatly arranged. Not even a speck of dust glittered on the TV.

Closing her eyes, she could almost hear her mother's cheerful greeting from the kitchen, her father yelling at a baseball game on TV. A moment frozen in time.

She could make out the faces in the photos that hung on the living room walls, and it was almost like a timeline of her childhood. A string of memories her mother kept up as a daily reminder.

She turned to see Nessa staring down the hall to the kitchen, and she hugged herself tightly against the chill that washed over her.

"That was where—"

"Yes."

Without a word, Evie crossed to the stairs. She would not go back to the kitchen. No matter how well McGee and his men cleaned up, she'd never get the image of all that blood out of her head.

The fifth step creaked as she climbed, and she smiled softly. When she was sixteen, she'd broken her arm skipping that step. She'd been trying to sneak out to see Declan, but it was almost impossible to get one over on Mary Elizabeth O'Brian.

She was running late, and in her rush to miss that creaking step that would most definitely wake her mother, she'd slipped and fallen down the stairs, landing the wrong way on her forearm. Her mother hadn't even been sleeping; she was lying in wait in the living room.

Mary Elizabeth had flicked on the lamp, clucked her disapproval, and taken her to see Doc. Somehow, though, losing her virginity to Declan with a cast on her arm had made the experience even more memorable.

Shaking her head to clear it as she crested the stairs, Evie turned left down the hall. She gripped the knob to her parents' bedroom door tightly, steeling herself before pushing into the room. Like the rest of the house, it was neat and tidy.

The bed was made, the ruffled comforter tugged up to cover the pillows and tucked carefully in at the corners. It smelled like her mother's perfume, and the scent brought tears to her eyes.

Nessa crossed to the closet doors and slid them open. Everything was arranged by season and then by color, as her mother liked. Mary Elizabeth O'Brian had always been a stickler for order. Evie willed her feet to move and joined her sister, who was already scraping metal hangers against the wooden rod.

Nessa pulled out their father's best black suit, brushing at a spot of lint on the lapel before laying it on the bed and moving back to choose a tie. Their father didn't own many, but he had some for formal occasions or when he let his wife drag him to Mass or confession.

"How's everything been since..." Evie asked softly, leafing through her mother's collection of Sunday dresses.

"Since you left?"

Evie flinched. "Yeah."

"They were sad, obviously. Confused, I think. Your note didn't explain much."

"No, it didn't." Evie pulled out a sea-green dress and held it up for Nessa's approval. "I don't think I really knew what I was doing or if it would be permanent." She crossed to the bed and laid the dress out next to her father's suit, smoothing out some wrinkles in the skirt. "After a while it just got easier to stay away."

"When did you start talking to Mom again?" Nessa wondered, lifting the carved lid of their mother's jewelry box and poking through the pieces.

"About six months ago."

Nessa looked up, smiling sadly. "For her birthday. Will you stay?"

"In Philadelphia? No," she added when Nessa nodded.

51

"There's nothing here for me anymore." Nessa's head jerked up. "I didn't mean that."

"Yeah, you did. But that's okay. I know how you feel." She twirled her wedding ring around her finger. "I feel the same way sometimes. But I guess we all move on in our own ways, right?"

"Do you miss him?"

"Only every day. I think Mom would just want something simple, don't you?" She held up a delicate gold crucifix on a thin chain.

"Yeah." Evie smiled. "That one's nice."

Her eyes dropped to the jewelry box, and she reached in to pull out their great-grandmother's strand of pearls, running her thumb over the glossy bulbs. Evie remembered her mother clasping them around her neck for her first communion, whispering in her ear that she'd wear them at her wedding someday.

"Would it be okay if I took these?" She looked back at her sister, who was carefully setting the clothes and shoes into bags, holding up the pearls.

Nessa's eyes dropped to the necklace, and something flitted across her face that Evie couldn't quite read. It was gone again just as fast, replaced by a serene smile.

"She'd want you to have those," she said before turning to finish zipping the clothes into the garment bags.

"You're sure?"

"Of course."

They descended the stairs, that creaking step greeting them as they reached the bottom. Evie waited at the base of the porch steps for Nessa to lock the door and walked with her to their cars.

"Are you busy today? Maybe want to grab coffee?"

"No, I'm good. I've got to get this to McGee and take care of some other stuff. Sorry."

"No." Evie waved a hand in the air. "Don't be." She tried to ignore the guilt that squirmed just under the relief. "What are we supposed to do about the house?" Evie cast a long look over her shoulder.

"Let's get through tomorrow. Then we can worry about everything else."

With a nod, Evie waited for Nessa to climb into her car and pull away from the curb before turning back to the house. Looking up at the only home she'd ever truly known, grief settled like a weight in her chest. This was the last time she'd ever see it, and now her memories of this place would be forever coated in blood.

Chapter Nine

Evie stood in the middle of her third store in as many hours. Christ, she hated shopping. It was even easier to loathe it when spring made it impossible to find a suitable black dress for a funeral she didn't even want to go to.

She hooked the navy dress back on the rack with a frustrated sigh. She'd missed so much already. She couldn't—wouldn't—miss their funeral too. But what the fuck was she supposed to wear?

"Evie?"

The soft, familiar voice made her tense, and she forced herself to relax. In less than forty-eight hours, she'd be back in New York, and this would all be behind her. She could handle anything for forty-eight hours. She turned slowly.

"Hi, Cait."

She expected the same awkwardness she'd gotten from Nessa, but there was nothing but warmth in her old friend's smile. Evie's eyes dropped to the enormous diamond on her finger, and Cait's bawdy laugh rang out. She'd always been amazed at how someone so small could laugh so big.

"I know, it's obscene. Finn said you were back, but I didn't think I'd believe it until I saw it with my own eyes." Cait smiled again, blue eyes crinkling at the corners. "You look good."

Warmth spread through her chest, and she wasn't quite sure what to make of the sensation. Like Declan, Cait had always felt like home.

"You look better. So you married Finn? What could you possibly have seen in him?"

Cait laughed, and Evie smiled. "Tall, dark, and handsome. What's not to like?" she replied, using an old adage from their childhood. "Plus, he makes pretty cute kids."

Evie's heart squeezed in her chest. She'd dreamed about children once. They'd sit up late into the night with their friend Maura whispering about what their kids would be like and how they'd grow up playing together. They'd been so convinced that everything would be perfect. Cait, at least, had found perfection.

"How many?"

Cait's smile softened as if she was also remembering their late-night dreams. "Just the one, but more eventually. Want to see him?"

"Absolutely."

Cait dug her phone out of her purse and moved to stand next to Evie, swiping through pictures of a tow-headed boy with rosy cheeks and the Callahan blue eyes. He was triumphant at the bottom of a slide, fists raised in the air, sweet in sleep with his thumb half hanging out of his mouth.

"He's beautiful."

"Thank you." Cait beamed, slipping her phone back into her purse. "I can't believe he'll be four this winter. Do you have any?"

"Kids?" Cait nodded. "No." Her dream of having children evaporated when she left Philadelphia.

Cait laid a hand on her arm, squeezing gently. "I've missed you, and I'm glad to see you even if I hate the reason. And since you hate small talk, I'll skip over the clichés about how amazing they were and instead say that it fucking sucks."

Evie barked out a laugh. Cait had always known her better than she knew herself. "You can say that again."

"Do you have time to catch up?" Cait checked her watch. "The nanny is usually good for another hour or so. We could grab coffee."

"Oh, I…" Evie looked at the racks of brightly colored dresses around them, reality dragging her back to the reason she was in this damn store in the first place.

"I interrupted." For the first time, Cait looked unsure of herself, twisting her bracelet around her wrist. "I didn't mean to make it weird."

"No, you didn't." It surprised Evie just how much she wanted to get that coffee. "I need to find a dress for tomorrow, and I'm not having much luck."

"Oh." Cait stopped fidgeting with her bracelet, brow unfurling. "I probably have something back at the house you can borrow. You're still miles too tall, but a few longer ones should hit you right at the knees. Or," she added when Evie hesitated, "I could have someone deliver a few options to wherever you're staying."

That seemed silly. More than that, she couldn't ignore the bittersweet tug of the friendship that had always been uncomplicated and easy. Keeping distance between them would be best. Opening herself up would just make leaving again harder. She should definitely say no.

Instead she said, "I can come over. My car's out front."

Cait's smile was infectious. "Perfect. You can follow me. I won't run any yellow lights this time."

Evie laughed, following Cait out onto the street, where she

watched her expertly climb into a black Escalade. She tailed her from the outskirts of Center City and toward the Main Line. When Cait turned onto a tree-lined drive with stately mansions set back on massive estates, Evie's fingers tightened on the steering wheel.

Declan lived in this neighborhood. His family had for generations. New money occasionally moved onto the Main Line, but many homes were passed down from one generation to the next as Glenmore House had been. She caught a glimpse of it through the trees as they drove.

A fountain rose from the center of the circular drive. Behind it stood imposing gray stone covered with ivy that snaked across the east wing and out of view. It looked exactly like she remembered it. There had been a time when she'd been a welcomed guest there. Now the gate would likely never swing open for her again.

When Cait slowed, Evie panicked. Did they live with Declan at Glenmore House? She hadn't prepared herself for that possibility. The tightness in her chest eased, and she let out the breath she'd been holding when Cait turned into the driveway across the street.

This house was newer construction. The whitewashed brick dotted with wide windows flanked by black shutters rose into view from behind the trees as she pulled through the gate. It was imposing but still nowhere near as big as Glenmore House.

She parked in a flat, shaded spot next to the garage and followed Cait inside. It was quiet, and Cait motioned her back to the kitchen, picking up wayward toys on her way and dumping them into a basket.

"Finn is out, and the nanny has Evan at the park, so we're all alone in here. Coffee?" Cait pulled open the refrigerator door and disappeared behind it. "Tea? Margaritas?"

Evie shook her head and smiled. "Water is fine."

Cait handed her a chilled bottle and leaned against the edge of the counter, studying Evie with her clear blue eyes.

"You're not staying, are you?"

There was that tightness in her chest again. "No, I'm not."

Cait's lips curved into a sad smile. "All right then. Let's find you something to wear."

And that was that. It had always been that simple between them. They'd known each other all their lives. Their own mothers had been friends since childhood, so becoming friends had never been a question. Evie had been closer to Cait than she'd ever been to her own twin. Cait never asked her for anything she couldn't give.

The double staircase curved up to the second floor, and Cait led her down another hallway dotted with toys. Evie found something oddly comforting about them. Like they were evidence of a happy life well lived. She liked knowing her friend seemed to have everything she wanted. When they turned into the room, Evie stopped short, mouth hanging open.

She'd been expecting a bedroom with a nice closet, but this was an entire room dedicated to clothing. Shoes on special display shelves lined an entire wall. Double racks of clothes were stacked one on top of the other in three, no, four lighted cubbies.

In the spaces in between were drawers that ran from floor to ceiling. There weren't even any men's clothes in here. This all belonged to Cait.

"Jesus, Caitlin."

"I know," Cait all but groaned, running her hand over the brightly colored clothes. "Finn built it for me after Evan was born."

A huge square ottoman sat in the center of the room, and Evie couldn't help but smile when she noticed a small stuffed dog sitting on the edge of it. She brushed her fingers over its soft fur while Cait crossed the room.

"We look like we're about the same size still. So this one should work." She pulled out a long black dress with lace cap sleeves and hung it on a hook. "This one too. Although it's pre-baby when my boobs were smaller, so it might be a little tight. This one might be a little too casual, but I probably have a jacket you could wear over it. What?" she asked when she turned and caught Evie's smile.

I've missed you. "Nothing."

"I'll step out," she said when Evie hesitated.

"No." Evie stripped off her shirt and laid it across the ottoman. "It's fine. It's not like you haven't seen it all before." Wriggling out of her jeans, she stepped into the second dress and struggled to hold it closed over her breasts so she could tug up the zipper. "Maybe not this one."

Cait giggled while Evie replaced it on the hanger and reached for the next one. "Are you happy, Cait?"

Her hands froze. She had no idea where that question had come from, but it's not like she could take it back now.

"I am. I have an amazing husband, an adorable son, and a good life. Are you happy?"

Evie studied herself in the mirror. The dress was a little tight across the ass, but not unwearable. Her mother would probably click her tongue at the cap sleeves that showed her shoulders through the lace, but it hit below the knee, so at least she'd approve of that.

Besides, it was this or nothing. Even Mary Elizabeth would have to forgive her. She met Cait's eyes in the glass. Was she happy?

"I'm not sure."

Cait helped her out of the dress and slipped it into a garment bag while Evie got dressed. When she turned, her eyes were sad.

"I'm not going to ask you why you left because I don't want you to lie to me. But I will say that you deserve to be happy. So," Cait held out the dress. "If you really aren't, maybe you can figure out a way to be."

Evie took the bag, draping it over her arm. She wasn't so sure. "Thanks, Cait."

They descended the stairs in silence, and Cait waved from the front step while Evie climbed in her car and backed down the driveway. Refusing to spare a second glance at the house across the street as she sped away, Evie captured her bottom lip between her teeth.

One more day, and then she could go back to her real life. She'd gotten over the pain of loss the last time she left Philadelphia. She could do it again. She'd have to.

Chapter Ten

Evie came awake with a gasp, heart thudding thick and heavy in her chest. Scrubbing her hands over her face and through her hair, she inhaled slow and deep, willing her heartbeat to slow. She'd pay any sum to erase the last image she had of her parents from her mind.

Collapsing back against the pillows, she squeezed her eyes shut and tried to recall the last good memory she had of them. The one she'd used often right after leaving Philadelphia. It had kept her alert when she'd stay up all night in cheap hotel rooms in bad parts of Manhattan, too afraid to sleep.

Slowly her mother's face came swimming into view. She had kind eyes. That was always the first thing Evie noticed when she thought about her mother's face. Her kind brown eyes that crinkled at the corners whenever she smiled or laughed.

Mary Elizabeth had been nothing but smiles when she'd celebrated her daughters on their twentieth birthday. Evie and Nessa insisted that twenty was nothing special to be celebrated, but Mary Elizabeth wanted to mark the occasion as the last year her whole family would live under the same roof. Evie was to be married six weeks later.

She decorated the house in their favorite colors, made all their favorite foods, rented their favorite movies. And they'd watched them, the three of them, cuddled up on the couch together, talking and laughing like nothing bad could ever happen.

Two weeks later, Evie was gone with only a note on her pillow as explanation, and she hadn't seen her mother's smiling face since. Now it lived only in her memory. She opened her eyes and blinked against the burn of tears. It was going to be a long day.

She glanced at the clock on the bedside table. Seven. Two hours until the funeral. Twelve until she was back in New York and figuring out how to get as far away from Philadelphia as possible.

She slid out of bed, crossing to the blinds and pulling them back across the window. She could see the sky just beginning to lighten on the horizon, the inky blue of night fading into shades of purple and orange as the stars winked out.

Turning from the window, she moved into the bathroom and cut on the spray for the shower. She'd shower, pack, and then grab something quick for breakfast before heading over to the church.

The hotel provided his and hers toiletries, and Evie opened the men's shampoo, inhaling its scent. It smelled faintly like her father's aftershave. She could remember waking up from nightmares cradled in her father's arms, surrounded by the woodsy smell of his aftershave as she buried her face against his neck.

She replaced the bottle on the counter and took the rest into the shower. Tilting her head back, she let the water rush down over her face and hair. When tears threatened to bubble over, she shoved them back. She wouldn't cry again. She'd learned a long time ago that dwelling on the past was a waste of time. They were gone, and all she could do was move forward.

She scrubbed herself clean and gave her curls a quick wash. Wrapped in a towel, she applied a light layer of makeup—just enough to hide the toll the last few days had taken on her—and swept her hair back into a low bun. Mary Elizabeth would never have tolerated loose hair at a funeral Mass.

The air pumping out of the AC unit pricked over her skin as she exchanged her towel for a bra and panties. The sun cast long shadows, its rays peeking between buildings as it continued its climb, deepening the sky to dramatic reds and oranges.

Evie carefully folded her clothes and laid them in her bag, tossing her toiletries on top just as her phone rang from its place on the nightstand. Her eyes darted to the clock. Who was calling her at barely eight in the morning? She scooped it up off the table, frowning at the name that flashed.

"Hello?"

"Evelyn, my darling, how are you?"

William's posh English accent floated through the phone. He was the only one besides her grandmother who ever called her Evelyn.

"I'm fine."

"Hmm. You don't sound fine."

Casting her eyes to the ceiling, Evie crossed to the closet and unzipped the garment bag. "How would you know? I talk to you maybe once a year."

"That hurts," William replied, and Evie could imagine him clutching his chest in mock insult.

"I'm a little busy right now, Will. Did you need something?"

"I need you to come see me."

"Why?" She straightened from her crouch to retrieve her shoes from the shopping bag she'd left them in, instantly suspicious.

"Because we have something I'd like to discuss in person."

"We haven't had anything to discuss in person in years."

"Well, now we do. How soon can you come?"

Intrigued, Evie sank onto the edge of the bed. It was rare for William to demand an audience. He may have given her the start she needed in New York all those years ago, but since she started stealing for higher profile clients, he kept his distance. He preferred to do all communication through burner phones or encrypted servers. Which suited her fine. The man was obsessed with the sound of his own voice.

"Tomorrow."

"Oh, you're in town then. That's good. I can't tomorrow, but I could on Friday. Noon?"

"Sure. Noon on Friday is good."

"Perfect. And Evelyn, darling, get some sleep. You sound exhausted."

He didn't wait for her reply before hanging up, and Evie tossed her phone on the bed with a shake of her head. Even through the phone, she apparently sounded like a mess.

Zipping her bag closed, she went to the closet and slipped Cait's dress over her head, tugging it into place. A small smile ghosted her lips at all the times she and Cait had swapped clothes over the years. She imagined if she looked hard enough through her childhood bedroom, she'd find at least one piece of clothing that didn't belong to her.

Fastening her great-grandmother's pearls around her neck, she stroked them gently. Now she'd have her memories and these to remember her mother by. Stepping into her shoes as her alarm buzzed, she slapped at it and then waited the extra five minutes for the wake-up call from the hotel's front desk before slipping out the door and taking the elevator down to the lobby.

The smell of coffee and eggs drifted from the restaurant entrance on the far side. No time for breakfast now. She wasn't sure her nerves would be up for the task anyway. Instead she pushed out into the cool spring morning and let the crisp air raise goosebumps over her bare arms.

It wasn't until she heard her name over the rush of morning traffic that she registered the black SUV parked across the street. Cait climbed out of the back, and Declan stood by the driver's side of his Range Rover dressed in a tailored black suit with a dark gray shirt and black tie, sunglasses hiding his eyes.

Evie stood rooted in place as Cait quickly crossed the street and stopped in front of her.

"I know you have a car, but I thought you might appreciate some familiar faces. And maybe a ride."

The stranglehold Evie had on her control loosened ever so slightly. "A ride would be nice."

Chapter Eleven

Declan watched their exchange and knew Cait had won her over in the way that Evie's tense shoulders relaxed before they both waited for the light to change and crossed back. He held the door open for Evie while Cait jogged around to where Finn waited on the other side. Her jaw was set but her eyes were sad, and he had to resist the urge to wrap her up in a hug and run a comforting hand down her back.

When they pulled up outside the church, Declan could feel the anxiety rolling off her, noting the way she clenched her hands in her lap, lip caught between her teeth. He shot Finn a telling look and waited for him to help Cait out of the car.

"I just need a minute."

He nodded. "We'll wait."

"What if I need a minute alone?"

"Do you?"

Her eyes met his in the rearview mirror, and he watched her adjust the skirt of her dress with trembling fingers. "No."

They sat in silence a bit longer, and when her hand

reached for the door, he got out and held it open for her. He watched her spine straighten and her chin tick up as she inhaled long and deep.

The crowd gathered outside the church fell into a hushed silence when they saw her. He waited as she paused to speak to people she recognized, shake hands, accept condolences. The mood inside the cathedral was somber; conversations were traded in soft whispers that reverberated in a low hum through the vaulted ceilings and archways.

He hadn't been to Mass in ages. After a childhood spent in Catholic school and the confessional, Declan decided to save church for weddings and funerals instead, maybe the occasional christening.

Bouquets of the purple and white flowers Nessa had chosen crowded around a large framed photo of O'Brian and Mary Elizabeth, and he saw her stare before deliberately turning to greet Rory McBride and his wife, Bridget.

He watched her carefully, but his ears were tuned for snatches of conversation. He wanted to know what the gossip was. The meeting with his lieutenants was set for tomorrow morning, but it didn't hurt to know what they were saying so he could head them off as much as possible.

Most of the gossip today, however, seemed to be about the long-lost O'Brian daughter coming back to town and exactly what that might mean. He wanted answers to that question as much as anyone.

As they neared the front of the church, they both spotted Maura at the same time, and one look at his cousin's fiancé told Declan this was not going to be a happy reunion. He exchanged a glance with James, who gave the slightest nod and stepped up beside Evie.

"Maura," Evie said softly.

"You really are back. I heard as much." Maura's gaze

drifted to Cait, who stood at Evie's other elbow, then snapped back to Evie's face.

"I'm glad to see you."

"Are you?"

Evie's expression hardened. "I'm sorry I hurt you, Maura. But we all make choices."

"Yes," Maura spat. "And I'm making one right now."

Pinning Cait with a look of disappointment, Maura stepped around Evie and moved to the back of the church, taking a seat in the last pew. James looked to Declan and waited for his nod of approval before joining his fiancé.

"She's just upset with everything that's happened, stressed about the wedding," Cait soothed.

Evie peeked over her shoulder, the hurt clear in her eyes. "I'm not so sure. It doesn't matter anyway."

They took their seats in the first pew beside Nessa, who shared a quick, awkward hug with Evie. Evie and Nessa had never been close, even as children, and time had driven them even further apart. Evie, Cait, and Maura had always been an unstoppable force, though, getting each other into and out of trouble as girls.

Hell, they'd roped him and his brothers into their schemes more often than not. Declan knew Maura's icy reception hurt Evie more than she would let herself show, and the fact that he couldn't fix it pissed him off. Not because he couldn't, but because he knew she wouldn't let him.

When Father Michael appeared from a side door, robes swirling around him, the congregation stood silently. The priest took them through the processional of the caskets, the scripture readings, and the prayers, and Declan glanced around the cathedral to check in with men he'd staged around the perimeter.

He always had security at big syndicate gatherings, no matter the occasion. He never left his people vulnerable to attack. The Callahan syndicate stood as the most powerful in the city, but that didn't mean other crime families didn't like to test his boundaries and his patience when they thought they had something to gain.

You'd think the simple fact that anyone who tried ended up dead would discourage people, but sometimes hubris knew no bounds. Like DiMarco and his moonlighting gig as an accountant for both the Russians and the Italians.

Either DiMarco was trying to infiltrate the Russians on behalf of the Italians, or he was playing both sides. Declan didn't much care either way. He cared only about keeping order in his city, and he'd do so by whatever means necessary.

The brush of Evie's hand against his arm as she stood for the hymn startled him out of his thoughts, and he rose beside her. Her voice was as clear and beautiful as he remembered it. She used to sing along to whatever was on the radio, volume all the way up. He'd pick her up from her parents' house in his Mustang, top down, and let her pick the music. Didn't matter what it was as long as he could listen to her sing it.

When Father Michael began the homily, Declan followed Evie's gaze to the framed photo of her mother and saw the tears gathered in her eyes. When one fell, he reached out without thinking to brush it from her cheek, and she surprised him by leaning into his hand for the briefest of moments.

She looked at him then, and for a split second, he could read all the sadness and longing in her gaze. Then the shutters came down, and she was lost to him again. She pulled away, and he dropped his hand as Father Michael resumed the prayers, inviting them all to sit.

When the service ended, they led the procession to the private cemetery in silence. Father Charles offered up his own prayers this time, and Declan could sense Evie's growing desire for this all to be over in the way she couldn't stop fidgeting.

Her fingers plucked at the edges of the program, twisting and tearing it into tiny pieces that the wind whipped away. He reached out to lay his hand over hers, and she turned her palm upward, lacing her fingers through his as if by habit, and he ignored the warmth that spread through him.

When the priest called for them to stand for the final prayer, Evie pulled her hand from his grasp, staring down at her fingers and then up at Declan before moving to drop a handful of dirt on top of each casket.

As the crowd dispersed, Declan kept his distance but watched her closely. When the last person said their goodbyes and moved away, he stepped in front of her, shielding her from the view of the lingering crowd.

"Let me take you back to the hotel."

She dragged her gaze up to meet his, eyes unfocused. "Isn't there a family thing? I should go to that."

"It'll just be people talking and eating and drinking."

"Is it really an Irish party if there isn't any booze?"

He grinned. She'd said the exact same thing about their wedding. "That's why we always have lots of it."

She looked at him then, and he saw the recognition in her eyes. Her mouth opened, then closed again, and she shook her head, looking at a distant point over his shoulder.

"Let me take you back."

"Yeah. Okay," she replied softly.

They drove back to the hotel in silence, and to Declan's surprise, she let him walk her to her room without arguing. He waited for her to slip the key into the slot and the door to swing in. He was just about to speak when she bit off a curse and rushed inside.

He slapped a hand out to catch the door, curious as she bent down to examine her bag where it sat on the edge of the bed. She peered inside without touching it and then stood up to take a better look around the room.

"What is it?"

She turned from the front of the closet and glanced down at the bag. "That was zipped when I left."

"Maybe you just thought you zipped it and forgot."

She pinned him with a hard stare. "This door was closed, not open. Did I forget that too?"

Probably not. But why would someone break into her hotel room? "Maybe the maids got nosy, poked around a little."

"But didn't make the bed?"

His eyes followed her hand to the rumpled covers and haphazardly placed pillows. She crossed to the bathroom without a word while he studied the closet. The hangers had all been pushed to one side, not exactly evidence that someone had gotten in, but if she said she'd left it closed, he had no reason not to believe her.

When she didn't emerge from the bathroom, he joined her, frowning at the look on her face. Then he caught a glimpse of the mirror out of the corner of his eye and turned. What the fuck.

YOU'RE NEXT

The words were scrawled across the mirror in bright red lipstick, the tube left sitting, uncapped, on the edge of the counter. He moved closer to examine it, and when he focused on her reflection, he noted how the words fell over her body. The thought that someone was threatening her incensed him, and his hands curled into fists.

"Who knows you're in Philly right now?" he demanded.

"No one."

"You're sure?" He moved to stand in front of her. "Then who would know to threaten you here?"

"I'm guessing the bastard who killed my parents."

He whipped his head around to study the mirror again. *You're next.* Meaning her parents had been first. Before he could respond, his phone signaled, and he held it up to show her who it was.

"Nessa. What? Slow down. What happened?" His eyes held Evie's as he listened to Nessa's hysteric ramblings. "Don't touch it. I'm going to send Brogan over to take some photos. Okay, that's fine. Go wait for him downstairs."

He disconnected the call and tapped out a quick text to Brogan before meeting Evie's curious gaze. "She found the same message on her mirror."

Evie sucked in a sharp breath. The thought of her going, knowing someone was actively hunting her, made his stomach tighten. If she insisted on leaving again, he wasn't going to let her go easy this time.

"What are you going to do now?"

Her voice was hard when she spoke. "I'm going to stay and figure out who the fuck murdered my parents."

Good. "I'll help you clean up."

Chapter Twelve

After trying and failing to talk Evie into staying at Glenmore House or even his penthouse, he'd helped her clean up the bathroom mirror and seen her safely to another hotel. She didn't need to know it was one he owned, just like Brogan didn't need to know why he wanted 24/7 access to the surveillance footage on his tablet.

Declan would prefer she was safely under his roof, but either way, he'd make sure anyone who threatened her again would not escape his notice. Or his wrath. Whether she liked it or not, she was his responsibility until they found out who did this.

Which is why he'd insisted on going with her to New York to pick up some supplies until she relented. He didn't care if she hated him as long as she was alive to do it.

He'd briefed his brothers on the update last night. Brogan reported that the message on Nessa's mirror matched Evie's exactly, down to the use of red lipstick. The handwriting looked similar, but it was hard to tell, considering the medium.

This morning's meeting was hardly going to quiet the

rumors that had been swirling through the syndicate. Now Declan wanted to know what truth there might be to them. Other than Evie's broken window, there was no other visible forced entry into the O'Brian house, but he wanted to send one of his people who worked as a forensics tech for the city to look the place over.

For now, he'd debrief his men, gauge their reaction, and see if they had any information on beef O'Brian might have had with someone. They'd want blood, and he was obliged to give it to them.

He pulled into the parking lot of Reign, his nightclub, parking in his designated space next to the employee entrance, and let himself in. At night the club pulsed under neon lights and pumping music. Metal and black marble gave it an edgy feel, and liquor bottles lined shelves backed by glass. During the day it looked cavernous, empty, but at night it came alive.

He nodded to the cleaning crew that came in each morning to clean up anything the night shift missed before buzzing himself into the security door that led down to the basement. The club itself, already big with its sprawling layout and VIP balconies, sat on top of a concrete basement that had been converted into a series of large rooms.

This is where he preferred to do the bulk of syndicate business. It was far more secure than his suite of offices above the restaurant, and he liked to keep the two as separate as possible. Up there, he was Declan Callahan, successful businessman and billionaire. Down here, he was king.

Motion sensors caught his movement and filled the basement with light as he made his way to the biggest room at the back that was most often used for a meeting space. He'd had Brogan rig it with tech that killed cell signals and listening devices so their private conversations stayed private.

He stepped inside and flipped on the light. A large cherry

wood table sat in the center, surrounded by chairs. It looked out of place among the plain drywall and concrete floors, but it served its purpose. Optics didn't matter down here, only orders.

"You're earlier than I expected."

Declan turned from his inspection of the room to face his uncle, his father's half-brother. Sean had struggled with Declan's leadership style after Patrick died, but he'd eventually come around. Declan may have been raised to take over the syndicate, but Sean had lived it longer, and the men respected him.

"I couldn't sleep."

"Aidan told me what happened with the notes."

Declan kept his face neutral. "Did he?"

"What do you make of it?"

"I'm not sure yet," Declan replied honestly. "But I don't like it."

Before Sean could reply, Finn strode in, and Brogan wasn't far behind.

"Where's Aidan?"

"He was still asleep when I left the house. Stayed up late with some chick who stumbled out at 3 a.m.," Brogan said. "I told him to get his ass moving."

"Just when you think he's plowed his way through all the girls in Philly, he finds one more," Sean muttered.

"We'll get started without him if we have to," Declan said.

"We're not really thinking it was one of our guys, are we?" Finn wondered.

"No, but somebody's got to know something, and if they do, I expect them to tell me. We've got two people dead who didn't need to be. I won't have two more."

Declan checked his watch. "Brogan, they should be arriving by now. Go let them in. And," he added when Brogan started out, "tell Aidan if he's not here in five minutes he'll be stuck doing whatever scut work I feel like dishing out for as long as I feel like dishing it."

Brogan snickered as he left to open the basement door and threaten Aidan with his fate.

They filed in, the heads of the twelve families that made up the Callahan syndicate. Well, eleven families now, since Evie had no brothers, no surviving uncles. They were a mix of old and young. The older ones acknowledged Declan first and then Sean, while the younger acknowledged Declan and then Finn in turn.

A subtle but meaningful shift in loyalty and the hierarchy of the Callahan clan. As Declan moved to stand behind his chair at the head of the table, he caught Aidan sliding in at the last minute, barely thirty seconds to spare, and sent him a warning glance.

"I know the rumor mill has been churning over what happened to O'Brian and Mary Elizabeth," he began. "I was planning on telling you this was all a random burglary so we could put the rumors to bed. Turns out there might be more to those rumors after all."

He waited for the murmurs to fade. "I want to know what you've heard. Then I'll tell you what I know."

Colin Maguire spoke first. "My youngest, Kevin, cleaned the crime scene. Said it looked like murder."

"Why?" Declan's tone was level. He didn't want to give anything away.

"Too much blood."

Not exactly foolproof logic. "And if I told you it was a murder-suicide?" He could see the disbelief on their faces.

"Was it?" Rory McBride asked.

Declan spread his hands, palms up. "Hypothetically."

"Then I'd have to say bullshit," Mick Donahue spat. He and O'Brian had been close. "O'Brian loved Mary Elizabeth and his girls, and he wouldn't hurt any of them."

"I agree," Declan said and watched some of the tension visibly drain from the room. "Because yesterday both Nessa and Evie found these messages on their bathroom mirrors."

He pulled up side-by-side photos of the big red letters on his tablet and held them up.

"What kind of cryptic bullshit is that?" McBride demanded.

"The kind that means this was definitely a hit."

Declan nodded at Donahue. "Does anyone know if O'Brian had beef with somebody? If he'd changed his routine? Anything that gives us a place to start."

When no one spoke, Declan sighed. "People do not fuck with our people and get away with it. So take this back to your families, put them on alert, and if you hear something, I expect to be your first call."

He met each gaze in turn, waiting for their nod of understanding before dismissing them.

"I don't like that we're shooting into the dark here," Finn said once they all filed out.

"Neither do I. I want to call Maura's sister, Reagan, in to look at the scene. She works as a forensics tech for PPD, and she might be able to see something we didn't."

"Think that'll really work?" Aidan wondered.

"I don't know, but it's better than nothing."

Chapter Thirteen

By the time Declan picked her up early Friday morning, Evie was restless. With the revelation that her parents' murder might have been planned—or at least personal—she was anxious to figure out who and why. She'd tried to coax more information out of William over the phone, but he stubbornly refused to share anything unless it was in person.

Evie had considered making a run up to New York by herself instead of waiting for Declan but decided against it. She was probably going to need his help, though she hoped to avoid it. Still, there was no need to antagonize the man unnecessarily.

When she climbed into the passenger side of Declan's Range Rover, he handed her a large coffee and a brown paper bag.

"Good morning to you too."

"I figured you hadn't eaten. You always skip breakfast when you're nervous."

"I was going to eat on the train," she lied. It was

unnerving for him to know her so well even after all these years.

He grunted, pulling away from the curb. "You should eat."

She sipped her coffee instead. "I really can manage this by myself, you know. I'm just going up to—where are you going?" She demanded when he passed the turn for the train station.

"We're not taking the train."

She groaned. "Declan, the drive takes twice as long. Longer in traffic at this hour."

"I know that."

"Then what the hell are you doing?"

He didn't answer her as he took the exit for the airport and drove into the private craft section. Well, a jet wouldn't be half bad and a third of the time of taking the train. Except when he pulled to a stop and put the car in park, the only thing she could see was a helicopter.

"Where's the jet?"

He climbed out of the car and turned around to face her. "What jet?"

Pinching the bridge of her nose, she took a deep breath. God help her. "What are we doing at the airport if we're not taking a jet, Declan?"

He turned to stare at the helicopter that sat waiting about fifty yards away, and her eyes widened in horror. "Absolutely not."

His lips twitched, but he didn't smile. "It's not as fast as a jet, but faster than the train. And she's steadier than she looks."

He rounded the hood of the car and pulled open her door, lifting out the bag she'd set by her feet. When she still didn't move, he reached in and undid her seatbelt, chuckling when she slapped at him.

"I am not getting in that thing. It's an accident waiting to happen. We'll take the train. There's another one leaving in"—she checked her phone—"forty-five minutes. We can make it if we hurry."

"The Evie I knew was fearless."

Her head whipped around, and her eyes narrowed on his face. "That was a low blow, even for you."

"It's just a helicopter."

"Until you crash into the Delaware," she muttered.

Before he got the bright idea to bodily remove her from the car, she snatched her purse off the seat and hopped out, ignoring his amused chuckle as he followed her to the chopper. It was bigger than she expected, with a cockpit up front for the pilots separated from a passenger area by a pane of glass. The back looked more like a limo than a helicopter with black leather seats and cup holders and enough leg room not to feel cramped.

She hesitated when the ground crew opened the door for her. What in the hell was she thinking, agreeing to ride in this death trap? To buy herself some time, she tossed her purse onto an empty seat and quickly swept her hair up into a ponytail.

"Need some help?"

She jerked at the sound of his voice, shooting him a look over her shoulder. "No, of course not. I'm just…wondering what seat you're going to sit in."

He grinned as he climbed in, reaching back to offer her a hand up. She settled in the seat across from him, rubbing her hands on her thighs. She'd flown in private jets hundreds of times, but a helicopter felt thin and unsteady by comparison.

"You'll be fine," he assured her when the ground crew closed and locked the door, signaling to the pilots that everything was secure. "Put those on." He pointed to the headphones hanging on a hook next to her head.

She slipped them on and adjusted the microphone in front of her mouth. Even through the headphones, she could hear the low hum of the engines as they turned on, like the steady sound of a distant lawnmower.

"It's almost like taking a jet." The sound of his deep voice filled her ears. "The weather is clear, it's not very windy, and we'll be there before you know it."

"It is nothing like a jet," she mumbled as the blades began to rotate.

"You look a little green."

"Shut up," she gritted out, fingers gripping the armrest with white knuckles.

"All I'm saying is if this is going to be like the time you threw up cotton candy all over Sister Bernadette at the summer festival, please tell me now so I can get you a sick bag."

Her eyes snapped to his face. "I was nine! And it was potato salad."

"Was it?"

"Yes. Some idiot left it sitting out in the sun all day. My mother was furious."

"Oh, I remember that." He grinned. "You weren't at school for a week. But you're still alive."

"Yes. Although to this day I hate potato salad."

"No, I mean, you made it through take off."

He gestured out the window, and she realized they were hovering above the asphalt and slowly gaining altitude. It wasn't as steady as a plane, but it wasn't as shaky as she had been anticipating, either. She let her body relax as she watched the trees drop away, the houses shrinking to colored squares on a green patchwork.

"Where are we going to be landing?"

"On the Upper East Side." He pulled out his phone and

brought up the address to show her. "Is it far from your place?"

"No."

When she didn't offer up more, he shifted to stare out the window, and she took the opportunity to study him. Even today, he was wearing a suit. Navy this time, with a perfectly pressed white button-down. Didn't the man own a pair of jeans?

The stubble on his jaw was thicker, and she knew it would feel soft against her fingers if she trailed them across it. That was a dangerous and unproductive line of thinking.

If she was going to stay in Philadelphia, she had to figure out how to compartmentalize. She needed her past to stay in the past so she could focus.

Chapter Fourteen

They rode the rest of the way in silence, and Declan was less successful at distracting her during the landing. By the time the blades slowed and he pushed the door open, he had to pry her fingers off the armrests. Once she was out, she leaned back against the side of the chopper, hands on her knees.

"I just"—she waved him away—"need a minute."

Once she was steadier on her feet, he shouldered her go bag while she took her purse, and they rode the private elevator down to the lobby. They stepped out into the sunshine, and he followed her quick pace through the crowd. It was early yet, and they were surrounded mostly by professionals in suits and the occasional dog walker.

When they wound through the revolving door into the lobby of her building, the doorman greeted her by a name Declan didn't recognize. She ignored his curious stare as they took the elevator up to one of the upper floors.

She opened the door to an apartment that was bright and airy. It was one big room that offered a view of the city through a wall of windows. What had Cait called it when she convinced Finn to tear down the wall between the kitchen and living room? Open concept.

It was a beautiful place, but something about it felt... empty. Like she lived there, but it wasn't really her home. Modern art hung on the walls, and the furniture looked pristine in shades of earthy blues and greens.

A big flat-screen TV was mounted over the fireplace at the far end of the room, but the bookshelves that flanked it were styled with knickknacks rather than books. He found it odd that Evie, who'd always loved to read, wouldn't have bookcases filled with books.

He followed her down the hall past an office and into the master suite. More windows, another stunning view, and a balcony he hadn't noticed from the living room arranged with a table and chairs and some chaise lounges.

He handed her the duffle bag, stuffing his hands in his pockets as he wandered the room. Like the living room, she didn't have anything personal in here. No photos, no mementos, nothing strewn about that made it look lived in, and he wondered if she'd recently moved in or she refused to settle in.

She moved into the bathroom first, and he could hear her rummaging around as he moved to the window to admire the view. He much preferred the quiet of Glenmore House and its estate. Even the penthouse he kept in the city was out of habit more than necessity or enjoyment.

She emerged from the bathroom and set a large toiletries case on the edge of the bed before disappearing into the closet and coming back out with a large suitcase that she left sitting open on the floor.

"Are you moving to Philly after all?"

"Your talents are wasted in the syndicate, Declan. You should be doing standup."

He bit back a grin at her sarcasm. He'd missed that a little too much.

"I don't know how long I'll need to stay in Philly, and I'd rather pack more than I need than have to make another trip up here in that thing."

He watched her neatly fold and then roll an array of shirts, pants, and dresses, deftly stacking them in the suitcase. She filled in the empty spaces with underwear and shoes, and he forced himself not to dwell on the fact that she seemingly hadn't packed any pajamas.

When she finally zipped it shut and stepped back, he hefted it off the floor with a grunt, grateful the damn thing had wheels.

"Maybe you did come in handy after all." She grinned.

When she unexpectedly turned into the office, he stopped in the doorway and watched her cross to the desk and remove a small personal safe from the bottom drawer. She unlocked it with a code, and he moved closer out of curiosity. His eyebrows winged up when she removed a stack of passports and licenses, shuffling through until she found the ones she wanted. There was so much about her he was dying to know.

Next she pulled out a 9mm handgun and a holster that was a smaller version of the one he wore at the small of his back. He watched her expertly clip it to the waistband of her jeans and slide the gun in, tugging her shirt down to cover it. Well, that was fucking sexy.

She flipped through several bundles of foreign currency before finding US dollars and pulling them out. Closing the lid on the safe, she set it into her now empty duffel bag and hoisted it onto her shoulder.

"What?" she asked when she turned and saw the look on his face.

"Who are you?"

She cocked her head. "Wouldn't you like to know?"

She had no idea. After locking the apartment door behind them, they exited the building and quickly walked the three blocks back to the chopper now that the morning rush crowd had thinned out.

"Actually," she said as he climbed in. "There's someone I need to meet."

"I'll go with you."

"Declan, I don't need a babysitter."

He climbed out of the chopper. "Don't think of me as a babysitter. Think of me as a tourist, and you're my reluctant tour guide."

Her expression remained neutral, but he could sense the annoyance underneath. "But you're not a tourist. You've been here before."

"That was a lifetime ago. It was a great birthday though," he added, following her to the elevator. He cast her a sideways glance.

A smile ghosted her lips. "It was. Until you refused to ask for directions and we got stuck walking in the rain for six blocks." She punched the elevator button for the lobby.

"I made that up to you if I remember correctly." Her smile slowly fizzled out. "Why did you come here? After you left." The fact that he'd asked the question surprised him, but he still wanted an answer.

"Because it reminded me of you," she whispered.

He said nothing, and when they hit street level she took off out the door so fast he had to damn near jog to keep up. She went right, away from the direction of her apartment, and zig-zagged up two blocks, taking them down alleys and cutting through buildings. It took him a minute to realize she was avoiding surveillance cameras.

So she knew this route well and didn't want to be seen taking it. She took a sharp right turn down an alley lined with fire escapes and discarded shopping bags. She finally stopped in front of a whitewashed brownstone that had, according to the sign painted on the window, been converted into an antique shop.

The street was quiet, and the neighborhood itself seemed to be in transition from residential to upscale business. Exactly the kind of neighborhood he might like investing in at home. He jogged up the steps behind her and stepped into the shop with the tinkle of a bell.

It wasn't empty, as he expected it to be at this hour on a Friday, and Declan noticed an older man, maybe in his mid-fifties, recognize Evie and give her a quick nod before turning back to speak to a young couple who were admiring a table.

"In need of some trinkets before we head back?" Declan wondered, turning from his inspection of a glass unicorn.

She rolled her eyes, and when the couple finally left, the man crossed to the door and locked it, turning the sign from open to closed. Declan tensed. They were both strapped, but that didn't mean he liked the idea of being locked in an unfamiliar space with this guy.

"You're early," the man said, his voice tinted with a posh British accent. "And you brought a guest."

"William, this is Declan. Declan, William. Well?" Evie prompted when William merely eyed Declan with suspicion.

"Well, I wanted to do this without an audience, but…" William turned and motioned for Evie to follow him with a crook of his finger.

They wound through tables stacked with antique vases and cut glass bowls and into an office tucked in the back corner marked Staff. It was small, barely enough room for William to move around between the desk and the filing cabinets, let alone the three of them, so Declan leaned against the door frame instead.

"Interesting company you're keeping these days." William's eyes drifted over Declan.

Evie didn't even spare Declan a glance. "William, you insisted on meeting in person. What do you want?"

"You remember Peter?"

Evie shoved her hands in the back pockets of her jeans. Declan couldn't see her face, but her voice was tense when she asked, "What about Peter?"

"I heard from a contact that he's been asking around about you. He tried to burn someone else's identity in order to find you."

"Who?"

"Kiah."

Evie hissed out a breath. "What the fuck does he even want?"

"Who's Peter?" Declan asked.

"Now that I don't know," William said to Evie. "What I do know is that he isn't somebody you want to fuck with. He's got deep pockets, and he isn't happy with how things turned out in Morocco."

"Morocco?"

Declan gritted his teeth when they both continued to ignore him. Somebody was going to give him some fucking answers.

"Peter got what he wanted in Morocco. He doesn't need anything else from me."

William pinned her with a patronizing stare. "Apparently he didn't. Maybe you should lie low for a bit. Don't take any jobs where he could track you. Stick with Ken doll here until this all blows over."

Declan rolled his eyes at the insult. How the fuck did Evie know this guy, and why?

"Thanks, Will. That's very helpful. It's also not an option."

"Suit yourself. But don't say I didn't warn you."

When William stood, Declan straightened. He didn't trust this guy, even if Evie seemed to. William sent him a curious smile and turned to Evie.

"Definitely stay close to this one, darling. I imagine he'll help you out of a tight spot if you need it."

"I'll be in touch, William."

They left the shop, and Evie looped them back around to the chopper. He waited for an explanation while they locked the doors and readied for takeoff, waited as they rose above the buildings and set off for home, but still she said nothing.

"Stop looking at me like that," she snapped.

He clenched his jaw. "Like what?"

She leveled her gaze at him. "Like you expect answers to questions you haven't asked yet."

He held her gaze for a long moment until he finally asked, "How long have you known William?"

"About eight years."

"And?"

"And what?" Her expression was blank.

Christ Jesus, was she going to force him to extract it all detail by excruciating detail?

"And how do you know him?"

She shrugged. "He helped me get started in my career."

"What career would that be?" He was seriously losing his patience.

"I…acquire things for people."

"Uh huh. Legally?"

"Not generally speaking."

He collapsed into silence. A million questions swirled through his head and, for the life of him, he couldn't think of which one to ask first. She acquired things. So she was a thief. A well-paid one if her car and apartment were any measure. The thing that confused him the most was that somewhere under the shock was pride.

By the time they touched down in Philadelphia, Declan had made up his mind. He drove them out of the airport, and instead of taking the exit toward her hotel, he took the one for the Main Line.

It was just his good luck that she was so busy typing on her phone she didn't notice where they were until he pulled up to the gate. Her head jerked up when he stopped to wait for it to open.

"This is not my hotel."

"No, it isn't." He pulled into the driveway and cut the engine. "You're staying here from now on."

"The hell I am. Take me back to my hotel, Declan. Right now."

"Nope."

She reached for the door and bolted from the car, and he did the same, meeting her at the tailgate. If looks could kill, he'd be a pile of ash on the ground with the way her eyes spit fire at him right now.

"You cannot keep me here."

"You have some mysterious guy after you—and don't worry, I intend to find out just who the fuck that guy is—and your parents are dead. Murdered, in fact. Now it occurs to me that those two things might be related. Ah," he added when she crossed her arms over her chest. "It occurred to you too. Well, that's good. Now I know you haven't completely lost your mind."

He held up his hand when she opened her mouth to speak. "I'm not finished. Your father and mother were my responsibility, and I failed them. I won't be making the same mistake twice. So you can either walk your ass inside willingly, or I can carry you. Those are your options. But you aren't leaving until I can guarantee your safety."

He watched her brain work trying to decide on her best course of action and had to fight the overwhelming urge to haul her up against him and finally have a taste of her mouth. He imagined she could still give as good as she got.

She drilled her finger into his chest, snapping him back to the moment. "We're not finished talking about this," she gritted out before turning and storming up the front walk and into the house, slamming the door behind her with a crack that reverberated off the trees.

Maybe not, but at least he'd won this round.

Chapter Fifteen

"And then…and then!" Evie slapped the table with the palm of her hand. "He commanded me to stay there like…like…like some prisoner!"

Evie sat back in her chair with a huff. It had been nearly a week since Declan had all but kidnapped her. He hadn't exactly locked her in her room, but she had the sneaking suspicion that it wasn't his normal routine to work from his office at the house every single day. The fact that he was watching her to make sure she behaved pissed her off even more than his tyrannical decree over where she stayed.

"So why haven't you left?"

"What?"

Cait peered at Evie over the rim of her coffee mug. "He had your car brought over from the hotel a few days ago, and you're here, so you're obviously not a prisoner. So, why haven't you gotten in your car and left?"

Evie crossed her arms over her chest. "Because…" Damn it all to hell. "Because he would just track me down anyway. Being stalked and dragged back there like prey sounds even less appealing. Can't imagine why."

"Hmm."

"'Hmm.' What does that mean? 'Hmm'?" Evie snapped.

"It means I don't believe you. You need his help," Cait continued before Evie could interrupt. "You know it, I know it, and Declan knows it. But he also needs yours. Something he might be less willing to admit," she murmured.

"And believe me when I say the entire syndicate wants to find out who killed your parents. He'll throw the full weight of his men behind it if he has to."

Yet another reason to stay. "It suits him." Cait raised a brow. "The power, I mean. I always thought it would, but..." Evie shrugged. "It's different actually seeing him in action."

"You haven't seen anything yet. He gets this look in his eye," Cait gestured to her eyes with two fingers, "same as Finn."

"What look?"

Cait took a sip of coffee and considered. "Determined rage."

Reaching for one of the apple slices Cait set on the table, Evie tried to picture it. "I imagine it's not far off from the look his father used to get."

"Maybe not, but it feels different."

"How?"

"With Patrick, it scared me." Cait grinned. "And now it's just a little sexier than it should be when I see it on Finn."

Evie laughed. God, she missed this. She missed having friends. She missed this friend and the way Cait had always been able to make her laugh. When a twinge of guilt surfaced, she pushed it down. Guilt was a wasted emotion. Certainly not one that would help her find her parents' murderer.

Evie took another bite of apple, chewing it carefully while Cait got up to refill her mug from the pot. "How come he never got married?"

Cait did a slow turn, eyebrows raised. Evie would have

found the exaggerated gestures amusing if she wasn't so busy regretting that she'd even asked the question.

"That's an interesting thing for you to ask."

"Let's forget I did." What did she care if Declan was or wasn't married anyway? He was a grown man capable of making his own choices. One day, probably soon, he'd settle down with a nice syndicate woman and pop out a couple of kids. And if her chest burned at the thought, it was probably just the coffee.

The front door opened then, the chime of the alarm ringing out and saving Evie from any follow-up questions Cait might have been devising.

"Not expecting anyone?" Evie asked when she saw Cait's frown.

"No. Evan is at swim class with the nanny and won't be home for another thirty minutes or so. Finn would come in through the garage." She peeked over her shoulder.

Evie sat up straight in her chair, kicking herself for leaving the gun she'd brought back from New York in her bedroom at Glenmore House. She was fairly good at hand to hand, though, if the occasion called for it.

"Hello!" a familiar voice called from the hallway.

Evie shot an accusing glare at Cait, who held her hands up in defense.

"This is not a setup. I swear."

"Cait, I know Evan will be home soon, but I wanted to drop off that song list for the wed—" Maura stopped when she rounded the corner into the kitchen and saw Evie sitting at the table. "Oh. I didn't realize you had a guest." She said the last word like an insult. "I'll come back later."

"Stay," Cait replied, her voice hopeful. "Have some coffee."

Maura's gaze slid from Cait to Evie, and as much as Evie saw disdain there, she saw hurt too. That oily feeling of guilt coiled in her stomach again. Where Cait had always been soft and forgiving, Maura had been rigid and protective. It made her a great friend. And an even greater enemy.

"I don't have the time or the energy to deal with this." Maura flicked a dismissive hand at Evie. "I have too much going on with planning this wedding and then the honeymoon. I'll have to come back another time."

Except she didn't turn to leave. Instead she locked eyes with Evie, chin raised in defiance.

"Maura—"

"No," Evie said, laying a hand on Cait's arm and giving it a gentle squeeze. "I should get going. Thanks for the coffee."

Evie rose to leave, pausing next to Maura. She wanted to say something, anything, to erase the anger and pain that swirled in her friend's eyes. Only what was there to say? No explanation, no apology could make up for the way she'd left things, for disappearing for ten years.

So instead she said nothing, slipping quickly and quietly out of the house and jogging down the driveway and across the street to Declan's. Walking up the drive, she paused next to her car. She wasn't a prisoner. She was a grown-ass woman, and if she wanted to go out, she would damn well go out.

She looked up at the house and noticed Declan's car wasn't in the garage. Perfect. She let herself in, jogging up the stairs for her purse, and then out again. The growl of the engine made her smile, and she rolled the windows down before pulling around the circle drive and gunning it on the straight stretch of road.

She might need Declan's help, but that didn't mean he got to dictate her every move.

Chapter Sixteen

Declan pulled his phone out of his pocket when it signaled an incoming text. Helen had gotten her hands on the guest list for the mayor's fundraiser. He opened the document and scanned through it. Most of the names he recognized, but he was only looking for one in particular.

A grin crept across his lips. DiMarco was invited. Declan didn't know the man personally, but they ran in the same business circles. DiMarco owned a small chain of restaurants in Pennsylvania as a front for his dealings with the Italian mafia.

For the most part, Declan was fine to let him have his cake and eat it too. He didn't waste much time meddling in the affairs of other crime organizations in the city. Unless those affairs jeopardized the peace or his own business.

So far, DiMarco had managed to operate under the radar, which is why Declan left him alone, but there was something about him that rubbed Declan the wrong way. All he wanted to do at this point was collect dirt on DiMarco. A little insurance policy he could use when he needed it. Not before. The fundraiser would be a perfect way to do that.

Especially now that he had a thief living under his roof. Not that they were on speaking terms exactly. Other than the occasional grunt to acknowledge him when he spoke, Evie had done her best to say as few words as possible since he forced her to stay. Forced was a harsh word. He'd made a very persuasive argument.

An argument he'd won since she hadn't even left the house since Aidan had fetched her car from the hotel. Not that Declan gave her much of an opportunity, working from home most of the week to keep an eye on her. Satisfied that she'd behave herself and not do anything stupid, he'd left to meet his realtor today.

Business never slept, and he had his sights on a new property. He loved to breathe life into a new project. This time he wanted something with flexible zoning so the commercial and residential income would pay dividends for years.

Pulling to a stop in front of the building he'd arranged to see, he got out for a better look. Four stories of glass and steel gave it a modern feel compared to the older brick and stone buildings on the street. Foot traffic seemed good, steady for late morning on a weekday with people weaving in and out of other shops.

His realtor pulled up, parking behind him in a new Porsche she no doubt bought with the handsome commissions she earned from his very generous business. She got out, her blonde hair swinging to her shoulders. They'd hadn't slept together since he officially became a client—he didn't like to mix business and pleasure—but he could still appreciate a beautiful body when he saw one.

Rebecca stopped next to him, shooting him a flirtatious smile before turning to look up at the building. "Gorgeous, isn't it? Helen mentioned you were looking for something flexible."

"I'm thinking commercial on the bottom and apartments on the top."

She nodded, slipping comfortably into work mode as she led him across the sidewalk and unlocked the door. Rebecca was a shark, which is why he liked to work with her. And she hadn't been bad in bed either.

"You could definitely accomplish that in this space. It was previously a bank with the upper floors being used as offices, but those could easily be converted into apartments."

It smelled musty inside, but that was fixable, and he'd be willing to foot the bill on a rehab for the right tenant. He imagined something like a bookstore or a café would do well in this area of the city with its hipster vibes. There was a dog accessories boutique just up the block.

"The full building is about 13,000 square feet," she continued. "So you're looking at just under 3,300 per floor. Could do nice big three-bedroom apartments or even double up smaller units on each floor maybe."

"Three-bedroom apartments that big in this area would rent quick."

"And pay well," Rebecca agreed with a nod. "There's an elevator in the back, which is another nice feature for this part of town since most of the buildings are walk-ups. It could easily become a private elevator for residents."

They wandered into the back, and she used a key to activate the elevator, taking them up to the fourth floor. It was an open floor plan, which would make renovations easier, and the big floor-to-ceiling windows that gave the building its modern look let in a lot of natural light.

The views were great in this part of the city. From this vantage point, he could make out the green of a park a few blocks over. Even if he separated each floor into two or three apartments, they would rent at a great price with views like these.

"How much?"

"Four million, but it's been on the market almost two years, so I bet I could haggle it down."

He nodded. "If you can get it down to three point five, I'll take it."

"How much up front?"

He glanced around the floor, considering the cost and time for renovations. "Fifteen percent."

"Three point five should be a piece of cake," she said with a grin.

Declan left Rebecca to lock up and drove home. He'd have to text Helen and let her know he wasn't going to come back to the office after all. At least this time he wouldn't have to see her pinched frown. It was clear she disapproved of his working from home. Or of his working from home with Evie in the house.

They'd been rivals in high school. Silly kid stuff to Declan's mind, but not for Helen, apparently. He'd let her have her moods about it for now, but she'd have to get over it, or he was going to quickly lose his patience. The company he kept was no one's damn business, least of all his assistant and the daughter of one of his men.

Pulling into the bottom of the driveway, he punched in the code for the gate and waited. As he cleared the trees his mother had planted for privacy two decades before, the house filled his vision. He loved this house and everything it represented. Even if sometimes that legacy sat like a lead weight around his shoulders.

He parked in the garage and rounded the end of his car, moving to the door, pausing with his hand on the knob. Circling back to the open garage, he looked out at the driveway and realized what was missing. Evie's car was gone.

Frowning, he let himself in through the garage and took the stairs two at a time. At the top, he turned right to Evie's room instead of left toward his own. Her door was open, but the room was empty. He keyed up her phone number and sent her a text.

Where are you?

He waited for a reply. Nothing. Stalking across the room, he yanked open her closet door, and the irritation eased a bit when he saw all of her clothes still hanging. So she hadn't left; she'd just gone out. And not told him where she was going.

He clenched his teeth, jogging back downstairs and into his office, slamming the door. She was probably fine. The woman knew how to take care of herself. Besides, he wasn't her keeper. If she wanted to go out, she could. He'd have to impress upon her the...practicality of telling him where next time.

Peering out the window at his brother's house across the street, Declan crossed his arms over his chest. Cait would probably know where Evie was, but that didn't mean she'd tell him. His sister-in-law was fearless.

When his phone beeped, he leapt at it, snatching it from the edge of the desk. It was Helen, not Evie, with a link to his afternoon agenda and a note that she'd drop some paperwork by the house later. He could see her severe, disappointed face in his head, and he resisted the urge to throw his phone across the room. The hell with them both.

Pushing Evie out of his thoughts, he dropped into his desk chair and did what he did best. Lost himself in work.

Chapter Seventeen

Free from the house, Evie simply drove aimlessly, soaking up the familiar sights and sounds of home. Were you really in Philly if you didn't drive past a cheesesteak stand or get stuck behind two people fighting over a parking spot?

She'd lived all over the world and still nothing compared to Philadelphia and its unique blend of history and humanity. She parked in a cute neighborhood in Center City and wandered up and down the block, dropping money in an empty coffee can for a man playing Beethoven on a beat-up violin and buying a vintage necklace from a small boutique.

Which is how she found this restaurant. Something about it had tugged at her until she finally stepped inside and asked for a table by the window. This one gave her a great vantage point to watch the people that wandered past—families with small children and busy executives and college-aged girls laden with shopping bags.

The food was good, the wine selection even better. It reminded her of a restaurant she'd been to in Dublin a few years back with its dark wood and wrought iron fixtures. Breá. Irish for delicious. Well, it certainly fit.

Her phone announced yet another incoming message from Declan. She deeply regretted giving him her phone number at this point. This would all be so much neater, easier, faster if she could figure out what happened to her parents without his help.

Except she was at a bit of a loss with where to start. She knew from Cait that Declan had asked Maura's sister, Reagan, to sweep the house for clues that the cleaners might have left behind, but she didn't imagine it would yield many results.

The cleaners were supposed to make sure they didn't leave evidence that a PPD forensics tech could find. And they were very good at their jobs. Still, Reagan would probably have something for Declan in a few days. Even if it was nothing but apologies.

There was William's lead about Peter, but that was more a warning to watch her back than a smoking gun. Besides, the timing seemed off. Her parents had been dead for two days by the time William even reached out.

Even if Peter was out for revenge over whatever imagined slight from Morocco, what reason would he have for going after her parents instead of finding her directly? If he'd been able to find her parents in Philadelphia when she hadn't lived here in ten years, then her identity had already been burned, and she wouldn't have been much harder to find.

It didn't make any sense. But she couldn't shake that chilling message written in lipstick on her hotel mirror. YOU'RE NEXT. It hadn't escaped her how much the letters looked like blood.

It had been a long time since she'd had cause to kill a man —she'd only narrowly avoided it in Morocco—but she would not rest while her parents' murderer drew breath. Whatever she had to do, whatever lead she had to follow, however much blood she had to get on her hands, she would do it just for the satisfaction of revenge.

She paid the bill in cash and, after yet another text message from Declan demanding to know where she was and threatening her with a search party, she decided to head back. While imagining the muscle ticking in his jaw was entertaining, she'd have to get herself on speaking terms with him again eventually.

She waited for a small group to enter before reaching for the door, turning when she heard someone call her name. Helen Maguire. Still as thin and blonde as she ever was, with her severe features made even sharper by her forced smile.

"Evie, I heard you were back in town. Are you looking for Declan?"

Evie frowned. "No, I know where Declan is." Oh, Helen didn't seem to like that one bit.

Helen's overly polite smile vanished, and her eyes narrowed. "I'm sure we can both agree that after what happened ten years ago, you're better off staying as far away from Declan as possible. For however long you might be… gracing us with your presence."

"Oh, Hells, you'll never learn, will you?" Evie wondered, swallowing a grin at the way Helen bristled at the nickname.

"Learn what?" Helen said through gritted teeth.

"Just like in high school, my relationship with Declan is none of your business. Whether we're platonic friends or fucking like bunnies is no one's concern but ours and certainly not yours. Have a great day." Evie pushed out into the sunshine, leaving a sputtering Helen behind.

Beaming, Evie floated the two blocks back to her car and set off for the Main Line with the windows down and the radio up. As Beyoncé and her Single Ladies faded into a commercial, the car shimmied and pulled to the right.

Annoyed since she'd just bought the damn thing after moving back to New York, she pulled off onto the shoulder and got out.

She hoped it wasn't anything serious, otherwise she really would be trapped at Glenmore House, and that possibility was less than pleasant. Circling the car before popping the hood, she noticed the left rear tire was flat. Oh, well, that was an easy fix.

Turning her hazards on, she tied her hair back into a ponytail and opened the trunk, moving her refilled go bag and the bottle of wine she'd brought back from the restaurant into the backseat before lifting out the spare tire and the jack. It had been a while since she'd changed a tire on the side of the road, but it had to be like riding a bike, right?

She went over the steps in her head as she laid the donut on the ground next to the trunk and positioned the jack in the right spot. Loosen the nuts, jack the car, remove the tire. She could hear her father's voice in her head as she did it.

Despite her protestations, her father had insisted she learn how to change a tire and check her fluid levels. She'd groaned and complained through all the lessons and his little tests, but it was knowledge that had come in handy when she couldn't afford a mechanic in the early years after leavingPhiladelphia, and then one rainy night in Edinburgh when she'd been stranded without cell service.

The sun beat down on her back, and she swiped at the sweat that beaded on her forehead. Either she had gotten weaker, or these nuts were exceptionally tight. Finally loosening them all, she jacked the car so the tire was suspended just off the ground and removed it.

Replacing it with the donut, she tightened the nuts back into place and lowered the car before stowing everything in the trunk. She'd have to inspect the tire when she got back to the house and see if it could be repaired or needed to be replaced. Traffic had been slow, but that didn't mean she wanted to be exposed any longer than necessary.

She drove up the shoulder a bit to test the donut and, satisfied that it would at least get her back to Glenmore House, she eased back onto the road and drove the rest of the way in silence.

When she pulled into the driveway, Declan stalked out of the house, jaw clenched, and ate up the distance between them with long strides. She was too tired and too sweaty to listen to a lecture right now, but when she moved to push past him, his hands jerked her to a stop then wandered urgently over her arms, back, torso.

"What in the hell are you doing?" She swatted at his hands.

"Where have you been?" he demanded, ignoring her irritated slaps. "And why are you covered in dirt?"

"I don't see why either of those things are any of your business."

He slowly arched a single brow, and a shiver ran through her. Determined rage. Damn Cait for planting the seed in her head that that look was sexy. It definitely shouldn't be.

"Don't make me ask again."

She held his gaze defiantly but ultimately caved and replied, "I had a flat tire." She waved a hand at the spare.

His eyes followed her hand, then settled back on her face. He frowned. "Why didn't you call me?"

Evie rolled her eyes. "Because I know how to change a damn tire. I'm not your prisoner, Declan. And I'm not some helpless damsel in distress. Our hopefully very short time together will be much more pleasant if you stop treating me as such."

There was that muscle ticking in his jaw. When his eyes met hers again, she was suddenly acutely aware of how close he was standing, how his hands had settled at the small of her back, how the heat from those hands sent chills along her skin. If she pushed up onto her toes just the tiniest bit, their lips would be close enough that she could… Nope.

Tearing her eyes away from his mouth, she cleared her throat. "Can I go now, or are you going to strip search me for injuries?"

The gleam in his eye told her he was considering it, but he dropped his hands and stepped back. She took the opportunity to move to the trunk and lift out the damaged tire, setting it on the ground and running her fingers over it to look for a nail or a puncture.

When she crouched for a better look, Declan did the same, and their faces were inches apart again. She really needed to quit noticing shit like that.

"Where were you today?"

She bit back the irritation that rushed to the surface. "I went shopping and had some lunch."

"Alone?"

"Well, I don't exactly have many friends left in this city. Why does that matter?"

"Because this tire was sabotaged." He reached out and pried out a nail that had been jabbed into the sidewall of the tire, then looked up to meet her eyes.

"I probably ran over that."

"On the side of the tire?"

Evie pushed to her feet, pacing away from the car and back. "Okay, let's say that someone did that on purpose, and let's say that it wasn't some stupid kids. Why not just slash it? Or slash them all? I'd still be stranded."

Declan looked down at the nail in the palm of his hand and closed his fist around it. "Unless the goal was to get you alone by letting the tire slowly deflate instead."

Her head jerked up, and the thought sent a sobering chill through her. "But no one attacked me. It took me over thirty minutes to change that because I was rusty, and nothing happened. There wasn't even a lot of traffic."

God, she hadn't been paying attention to her surroundings other than watching for the occasional car. Someone could have easily overpowered her while she was on the ground, attention diverted. It wouldn't have taken more than thirty seconds. So why didn't they?

"Where did you stop to change it?"

She hugged herself tightly. "I'll show you."

They drove out to the spot not ten minutes away and got out. She walked the length of her tire tracks on the shoulder, spotting the displaced dirt and gravel from the rectangular base of the jack. There were houses around, and they sat pretty close to the street, but the neighborhood was quiet.

It wouldn't have been difficult for someone to make it look like they were offering help with no one the wiser. Declan walked the opposite shoulder until she saw him stop at a dirt patch under an overgrowth of trees and weeds. Checking for traffic, she jogged across the road to meet him.

He toed at what looked like tire tracks—not just from someone driving by, but from someone peeling out of the spot and taking off in the opposite direction. Evie stepped into the patch and looked back to where her car had been parked. She had a perfect view through the hanging branches.

"Whoever was parked here left in a hurry."

His voice was calm, but his clenched jaw and fisted hands betrayed him. He was furious. At her? At whoever had been in that car or sabotaged her tire? Maybe a little of both.

"I think you should consider utilizing the buddy system when you leave the house. Or not leave at all."

She studied him for a long moment, trying to get a read on him. She'd have known exactly what he was thinking once. "Buddy system sounds good."

Chapter Eighteen

By the time Declan was scheduled to meet with Reagan, Evie had all but convinced herself that he was completely overreacting about her flat tire. The guy at the auto shop who replaced it said it was entirely possible for a nail to puncture the sidewall without it being done on purpose.

Plus, she'd seen at least two cars make use of that little dirt patch to pull off and check for directions or wait for someone. The tire tracks were no doubt a weird coincidence. Besides, she would have noticed a car just sitting there watching her. Definitely. Noticing details was her best skill.

None of that convinced Declan, though. Not with the way he hovered, constantly breathing down her neck and watching her every move. She just needed some goddamn space.

Which is why she snuck across the street while Declan was out and Brogan—who she was convinced had been tasked with keeping an eye on her—was busy to commandeer a lounger by Cait's pool.

She hadn't brought a bathing suit or bothered to buy one

yet, so she settled for enjoying the weak stream of sunlight that shoved its way past the clouds. Even the weather was conspiring to keep her inside.

Eyes closed, she listened to the gentle lap of the water on the side of the pool and the breeze that rippled through the bushes that lined the patio, ignoring the chill it raised on her arms.

Everyone was out, so the house was quiet and she relished in the solitude. There was no tread of expensive Italian shoes across polished hardwood, no scent of spiced cologne to distract her every thought, no deep voice that floated every memory she'd so carefully buried up to the surface.

Only the whisper of the wind and the water. Until the shrill ring of her phone cut through the silence and she nearly fell face-first into the stone pavers in her mad grab for it.

"What?" she demanded without even checking to see who the caller was.

"It's lovely to speak to you as well." William's voice was cool and calm. If a raised eyebrow had a tone, that's what it would sound like.

"Hello, William, darling," she replied, her voice saccharine. "How can I help you today?"

"Sarcasm doesn't become you, Evelyn. I have an update for you. Would you like to hear it, or should I go?"

Evie sat up straight and shoved her hair out of her face, tucking the phone between her ear and shoulder to protect it from the wind.

"An update about Peter?"

"Well, I'm not sure why else I would call you directly."

Evie rolled her eyes. "I can't make it up to see you for a few days." She'd have to figure out a way to slip Declan's stranglehold so she could go by herself.

"That's fine. I don't want to see you again in person so soon."

"Oh, okay."

"Don't worry," he assured her. "I'll burn this phone as soon as I'm done. I think Peter might be more of a problem than I originally conveyed."

Evie tucked a leg up underneath her, frowning. "What do you mean?"

She heard him draw in a deep breath. "I was helping Kiah establish a new alias and burn all her old ones."

"Because Peter figured out her real identity."

It was rare to get burned if your docs were good quality and you were careful, but it happened. Evie didn't consider Kiah a close friend—they knew of each other more by name and reputation than anything else—but Evie had always known Kiah to be careful. Obsessively so.

"Kiah thinks he murdered her brother and sister-in-law."

"What?" Evie felt like all the air had been sucked out of her lungs. "Why would she think that?" She gripped the edge of the lounger so hard her fingers ached.

"She wanted to make sure they were okay before she disappeared for a bit. When she got there, she found the house roped off by police tape. A neighbor told her the police thought it was a murder-suicide."

"The wife was stabbed and the husband was shot?" She pushed to her feet to pace.

"How did you know that?" Will's voice was full of surprise.

"Lucky guess," Evie murmured. "How…" She cleared her throat. "Why does she think it was Peter and not what the cops think? Not a murder-suicide?"

"I asked her the same thing. She swears up and down her brother didn't own a gun. Evelyn."

"Yeah?"

"Be safe out there."

Without waiting for her to reply, he hung up, and Evie

tossed her phone on the lounger, raking her hands through her hair. Just because it was similar didn't mean it was the same. She could probably pull up a dozen murders with the same MO on the internet in less than five minutes. Would they all have a connection to Peter, though? Doubtful.

Releasing a thief's real name to their criminal circle could get ugly fast. Bounties, hitmen, kidnappers. As much as the rich liked to steal from each other for sport, they hated to be stolen from, and if they found out who had done the stealing, they didn't hesitate to strike back.

That's precisely why Kiah was on the run. If Evie had to put money on it, she'd bet Kiah had probably changed her appearance as well. She'd even heard stories of some people going so far as to have plastic surgery in a bid to start over.

So if Peter wanted to burn her identity, why hadn't he done it yet? Suppose he was here in Philadelphia after murdering her parents. Why put her in a vulnerable position on a relatively isolated stretch of road and then do nothing? What was his end game?

Snatching her phone up off the chair, she let herself out of Cait's house, re-arming the alarm with the code Cait had given her. She had to figure out exactly who Peter was. Whether he was responsible for her parents' deaths or not, he was a threat. One she wanted to eliminate so when this was over, she actually had a life to go back to.

The best place she knew to start was Morocco. Maybe if she sat down and wrote out every detail she could remember about that trip, the job, the oddities, something would jump out at her. It had to.

She let herself into Declan's house through the side door, stopping short when she noticed him standing in the living room, arms crossed over his broad chest. He wasn't wearing his suit jacket, and his sleeves were rolled up to his elbows, exposing a tattoo that swirled over his forearm and disappeared under the fabric. That was new.

"You're late." And just like that, her face flashed from worried to annoyed. He really had to get her to stop looking at him like that.

"Late for what?"

He sighed and rolled his sleeves down, buttoning the cuffs before slipping his arms into his jacket and adjusting it. The woman had never been on time for anything in her life and had clearly not gotten better at it with age.

"We're meeting Reagan at my office to go over what she found."

"We?" Her brow furrowed. "You are meeting Reagan at your office to go over what she found. I have something else to do."

"Something more important than avenging O'Brian and Mary Elizabeth?"

Now her eyes were angry, but she at least turned on her heel and slammed out the door. Seconds later, he heard the door on his Range Rover slam. Well, that was one way to get her into the car.

The drive was icy, and he let her stew in silence. Something was bothering her. He could tell by the way she was picking at the hole in the knee of her jeans. When she caught the direction of his glance, she clasped her hands in her lap to keep them still.

"You really think she's going to find something after the cleaners were there?"

"If she does, I'll need to hire new cleaners."

She snorted as he pulled into the parking lot of the restaurant. "I thought we were going to your office."

"We are. It's on the third floor. What?" he asked when he saw the look on her face.

"Your office is above this restaurant?"

He glanced out the windshield at the faded red brick. "Yes. I own the restaurant. The whole building, actually."

"Huh," she said as she climbed out of the car. He matched her stride across the parking lot to the employee entrance.

"What?" he asked again, holding the door open for her.

She waited until they were beyond the noise of the busy kitchen and in the elevator before replying. "This is where I had lunch the other day."

"And the food was terrible?"

She laughed, and the sound wrapped around him like a caress. "I should say yes, but no. It was fantastic, and your wine list is excellent. I bought an entire bottle. And on my way out I ran into Helen."

As if on cue, the doors opened on his assistant, who was waiting with a cup of coffee in one hand and a stack of files in the other. The smile she usually wore when he got off the elevator quickly faded when she noticed Evie standing beside him.

He motioned for Evie to step out ahead of him and had to bite back a smile at the way Helen scurried out of her way.

"Helen," Evie said, voice dripping with fake politeness. "Lovely to see you again so soon."

Helen turned back to face him as Evie wandered off to inspect the space, plastering a too-wide smile on her face. "Sorry, I didn't realize you were bringing someone with you to meet with Reagan. I would have made more coffee."

He very much doubted that.

"Reagan is already here, so I put her in the conference room. The bakery tenant got back to me, and I scheduled her into your calendar for two weeks from now. I'll make a review file for you next week."

He accepted the coffee from her and stopped at the glass door that led into the conference room. Evie had already found her way inside, and she was pacing, hands fidgeting nervously until she shoved them into her back pockets. Neither woman was speaking.

He hadn't considered how awkward this might be given that Reagan was Maura's sister and Maura's reception of Evie had been less than inviting. He thanked Helen and walked into the room. Both women turned to look at him, and he urged Reagan back into her seat as he took his at the head of the table.

He didn't like the grim look on her face. "Anything?"

She flipped open a thin manila folder as Evie took the seat to his left, directly across the table from Reagan, and shuffled some papers around.

"Nothing forensically when it comes to hair, tissue, finger-prints, anything like that." She glanced up at him. "But I suspect you knew that already. It looked like the cleaners came through the place."

He nodded.

"Guess you don't have to fire anyone after all," Evie said, and he chuckled.

"You said nothing forensically. Was there something else?"

"The front window looked like it had recently been replaced. You could smell fresh paint."

"That was me," Evie admitted. "I broke it to get in."

"Okay." Reagan moved a page to the bottom of the stack. "Other than the window, the only thing that really struck me as odd is that there was a knife missing from the butcher block."

"What's odd about that? We didn't find a gun either," Evie said.

Reagan looked at Declan, who nodded confirmation. "It's odd because if we're going with the theory that this was a planned attack, why would you need a weapon of opportunity?"

Evie sat back in her chair with a huff, rubbing at her temple with two fingers, and Declan could see her rolling it around in her brain.

"So you're saying whoever it was grabbed a knife out of the block because it was there and not because they intended to kill Mary Elizabeth?"

"That's my theory, but there isn't a lot to go on once the cleaners make a pass, so it's not exactly rock solid. It could be nothing. Maybe the knife has always been missing from the block."

Evie drummed her fingers on the tabletop. "No. That would drive Mom crazy. Reagan?" Evie's voice was quiet as Reagan got up to leave. "Which knife was it?"

"I don't think that—"

"Please," Evie interrupted, eyes sad as she met Reagan's gaze.

Reagan flicked a glance at Declan and waited for his nod before replying. "The butcher knife. If I can help with anything else, let me know. Evie, it's good to see you. I mean that," Reagan added before disappearing, the door closing behind her with a soft whoosh.

Evie said nothing, just slowly bent until her torso rested on the table, her head cradled in her arms. He reached over to brush her curls off her face and let his hand linger for a moment.

"What are you thinking?" he asked softly.

"I'm thinking," she began, voice muffled in the crook of her arm, "that nothing about this makes any fucking sense."

He couldn't disagree. None of his men had reported any murmurings about anything O'Brian might have been tangled up in. He'd had Brogan monitoring activity on other organizations in the city to see if anyone's patterns or behaviors had changed. So far, nothing.

They needed a lead soon, or he was going to start burning shit to the ground. Anything to get that haunted look out of Evie's eyes and punish the bastard who'd put it there.

He rose from the table and reached for her hand, pulling her to her feet. When her body brushed his and she didn't pull away, he lifted his hand to skim his knuckles along her jaw.

Her eyes dropped to his lips, and need surged through him. He hadn't been able to stop thinking about her since he'd first seen her standing, shaken, in her parents' living room. Her lips, her skin, her body under his.

He shouldn't. It was a terrible idea, all things considered. But he'd had terrible ideas before. This one couldn't be so bad.

When her lips parted, he slid his hand around to cup the back of her neck and tilt her face up. He'd thought about these lips, their taste, a million times in the last decade. He yearned for them like water in a desert.

Just as he bent down to taste her, the door opened, and Evie jumped back. He was going to kill Helen. Finding a new assistant would be a pain in the ass, but he'd muddle through.

"What?" he said through gritted teeth, turning to see Helen's look of shock.

She shrank back at the look on his face. "I, ah, you have a phone call from Councilman Rodriguez. About that solar project. I saw Reagan leave, so I thought you were…I thought that…" Helen cleared her throat, fought to keep her voice even. "I can tell him to call back."

"No," he snapped. "No," he said again, eyes drifting back to Evie standing almost a foot away now. "I'll be there in a minute."

Her face was unreadable. The only thing that gave her away was the way her fingers worried the frayed edges of the pocket of her jeans and the fact that she wouldn't meet his gaze.

He sighed. "Give me thirty minutes. Tops. Then I'll take you home."

When she only nodded, he slipped out of the room and down the hall to his office, lifting the receiver and pressing the blinking hold button.

"Councilman Rodriguez, sorry to keep you waiting. I hear you're finally ready to get that solar project off the ground."

He listened to the man drone on about his idea to get solar technology into tiny homes he wanted to build in underserved neighborhoods. Declan didn't need to be sold on it. The tech was a good investment, and the philanthropic donation was an even better way to maintain his image.

So while Rodriguez rattled off statistics and figures, Declan let his mind drift to Evie and every sinful thing he wanted to do to her. As soon as possible.

Chapter Nineteen

E vie expertly evaded Declan and any further discussion about their almost kiss for days by staying holed up in her room, writing down every single detail she could remember about her job in Morocco. She'd done her best to sort her notes into a chronological order of events and fanned them out around her on the bed in a semicircle. There had to be something in here, some tiny thread of information she could unravel.

Peter Waltzman wasn't his real name. At least she assumed it wasn't since her internet search had yielded zero results. It wasn't surprising. No one used their real names in her line of work, but then she'd never had reason to care if they did or didn't before now.

She pulled out a blank piece of paper and used her pen to sketch what she could remember of his face. She was rusty but had been fairly good at the occasional sketch in high school and figured it was worth a shot.

Peter had insisted on making his first payment face to face. Odd, but not entirely unusual. Sometimes people liked to look you in the eyes and make sure you weren't going to disappear and stiff them. Or intimidate you.

They'd agreed to meet at a café for a quick funds transfer. In and out in less than fifteen minutes. He'd made her uneasy. That was the first thing she thought when she saw him step out of the taxi from her vantage point across the street. She never arrived first when meeting a client.

She should have walked away then. Something told her to get up from the table where she watched, grab her bag, and leave Rome without a second thought. She'd been due to move on from her home base anyway, so disappearing would have been easy.

She was blinded by the payday, the price tag too good to turn down. It was what many in her field liked to call retirement money. Her cut would have set her up for life. In the end, she decided the rewards outweighed the risks. So instead of leaving, she crossed the street, sat down at the table, and shook his hand.

He held her hand a little too long, caressing the back of it with his long fingers. Even now, the memory made her shiver. It wasn't unusual for male clients to get handsy when they saw her. Most of them tried to get her into bed. All of them ended up disappointed.

He didn't talk much while he quickly transferred payment through a secure server, just watched her out of eyes so dark they were almost black. He continued to watch her when she got up from the table. She could feel his eyes boring into her back as she walked away, had to force herself not to glance behind her.

He made her so uneasy that she'd gone directly back to the hotel, packed up, and left instead of staying the full week like she intended. It was also the last time she ever agreed to meet a client in person. Now she only did hand-offs through trusted contacts and associates.

She looked down at the drawing in her lap. She was no pro, but she'd captured his sharp features and dead eyes perfectly, the severe angle of his jaw and high cheekbones, his thin lips and wide mouth. Even now, he gave her the creeps.

She reached for the first page of her notes as a knock sounded at the door. She glanced at the clock. Probably a maid wanting to come in and vacuum or clean the bathroom.

"Come in!"

When a shadow fell over the pages she was neatly stacking, she looked up into Declan's curious gaze. How did he make her mouth water just by standing there? He reached down and picked up her rough sketch of Peter's face, studying it.

"Peter?"

"How I remember him, anyway." He handed it back to her, and she added it to the bottom of the stack.

"I didn't know you still draw."

"I don't."

He stuffed his hands into his pockets, and for the first time since she'd been back, he looked at a loss for words.

"Declan, I—"

"I was wondering if you—"

They both spoke at once and then fell into silence. She liked it better when they were poking at each other instead of this awkward, stilted quiet that stretched between them now.

"You first," he offered.

"No, you." She had no idea what she'd been about to say. Odds are, it would have gotten her into trouble one way or another.

"I have something I'd like you to do on behalf of the syndicate. A job."

"What kind of job?"

"Someone has something I want, and I'd like for you to get it for me."

120

Her lips twitched into a grin. "My fees are very high."

His eyes raked down her body, and heat bloomed in her belly.

"I'm sure we can work something out."

Before she could respond, his phone rang, and he held it up to show her Nessa's name on the screen. Answering it, he put it on speaker.

"Hello?"

"Declan!" Nessa's voice was breathy. She sounded close to tears.

"What's wrong?"

"I just got home and…" She paused, and Evie could hear a series of noises in the background like someone was dragging something across the floor. "I think someone has been following me. I don't know what to do. I'm scared."

Evie could hear the tremble in Nessa's voice, and she met Declan's gaze with wide eyes. The threat, her tire, William's warning, and now Nessa was being followed?

"We're on our way."

Nessa let out a choked sob. "Thank you. Please, hurry."

Declan hung up and quickly moved to the door, and Evie rushed to keep up with him down the hall and the stairs he descended two at a time. She had no idea where Nessa even lived, but Declan seemed to.

They pulled up in front of a nice two-story, single-family home with dark blue siding and a red front door. It was new construction in one of those cookie-cutter neighborhoods that reminded you of every suburban housewife show on television.

The front lawn was neatly trimmed, and the only thing that really stuck out to her as they walked up the short drive was how there were no flowers. It seemed oddly out of place, considering every other house on the street seemed to have beds full of budding blooms.

Declan knocked on the door, and the curtain on the tall window beside the door fluttered before they heard what sounded like furniture being dragged away from the entrance. When Nessa opened the door, her eyes were wide and her smooth hair wild. Her eyes darted past them to the street, and she waved them inside, quickly closing the door behind her.

"You came," Nessa all but sobbed.

"Relax," Declan said, reaching out to grip Nessa's shoulders and giving them a quick rub. "Tell us what happened."

Nessa led them into the kitchen, where a bunch of forgotten grocery bags sat on the counter. Declan urged Nessa into a chair, and Evie kept her hands busy putting away the food while Nessa explained.

"For the past few days, I've been getting the sensation I'm being watched. You know that creepy feeling where the hair stands up on the back of your neck?" She rubbed her neck then dropped her hand into her lap. "I went to the store like I do every week and couldn't shake that feeling."

"Did you notice anyone who looked out of place?"

Nessa shook her head at Declan. "No. No one seemed to be following me, but…" She shuddered. "I rushed through the store. I wanted to get out of there as fast as I could. I'm sure I forgot something."

She watched Evie arrange vegetables in the crisper.

"Okay, so there was no one in the store. Was it someone in the parking lot?"

"I didn't see anyone specifically, but when I pulled out, a black car pulled out behind me. They took every turn I did all the way home. Once I noticed them, I made some wrong turns on purpose, but they stayed behind me. Always two or three lengths back."

Nessa crossed her arms in front of her, gripping her elbows. "I started to panic, so I ran a red light and finally lost them then. I came home and made sure all the doors and windows were locked. Then I called you."

Evie met Declan's gaze as Nessa dissolved into tears against his chest. She didn't like the idea of her sister being followed by God knows who and living in this house all by herself. They may not be close, but Nessa was the only family she had left.

"What if you came to stay at Glenmore House for a while?" The words tumbled out of Evie's mouth before she could stop them, and she shrugged at Declan's narrowed gaze. "Just until we find out who's doing this."

Nessa sniffled as she sat up and looked from Evie to Declan, who'd managed to slap a halfhearted smile onto his face. Nessa pushed back from the table and rummaged through a drawer, coming up with a packet of tissues. She pulled one out and dabbed at her eyes and nose.

"That's really a very sweet offer, but I don't know if I could. I wouldn't want to be in the way."

"You wouldn't be." Evie bit her lip when Declan's frown deepened.

Nessa smiled softly. "Even if that was true, I babysit for a neighbor a few times a week so she can work part-time while her husband is deployed. I couldn't leave her in the lurch like that."

Declan pushed back from the table and pulled his phone out of his pocket. "What about a protective detail? A guy or two who can sit outside the house, follow you when you run errands, stuff like that."

Nessa's hand settled on her throat. "That seems excessive."

"Nessa, you live here alone, and you think someone has been following you. Let us do something."

Lips pursed, Nessa nodded. "Maybe just at night to start? I really don't want to be a bother."

Declan nodded, giving Nessa's arm a reassuring pat. "We'll start there, and if things escalate we can add more shifts. Let me make some calls."

"Thank you. For coming over and for your help with…" She gestured at the groceries. "Everything."

"Of course. I only want you to be safe."

They fell into an awkward silence. For two people who started life sharing a womb, they had precious little to say to each other. Easy sisterly banter had never been a thing they shared. Evie had always come by that so much easier with Cait and Maura.

"I heard you're staying for a bit. Will you be going to Maura's wedding?"

Evie's smile was sad. "I don't think so. I haven't been invited."

"Owen Donahue will be here any minute." Declan breezed back in. "I know you said only at night, but it's getting late, so I'm having him come by a little early. He'll park at the curb and stay the night. You sure you're going to be ok?"

Nessa took a deep breath and plastered on a smile. "Of course. I appreciate you coming by and listening to my hysterics. I'm probably overreacting about the whole thing."

Evie and Declan shared a look behind Nessa's back while she led them to the door. She was definitely not overreacting. If anything, she was underreacting. Fear could make you brush red flags aside and minimize them. Hadn't she done the same thing with her tire?

She wanted to believe it was an accident because the truth was chilling. Someone might be after her. Someone determined enough to ruin her that he would kill two innocent people to get what he wanted.

They said their goodbyes and waited in Declan's SUV for Owen to arrive. When he pulled up in a plain gray sedan, he waved to Declan and parked but didn't get out. She watched her sister's house fade in the side mirror as they drove in silence back to Glenmore House.

"She'll be okay."

"Will she?" Evie turned in her seat to look at Declan as he pulled into the garage and put the car in park. "Or will he get her too?"

"Who? Peter?"

Evie dragged her tongue over her bottom lip. Was she ready to tell Declan about William's warning? Part of her wanted to do this on her own. Peter was her mess to clean up, but deep down she knew she needed Declan's help and his resources. Syndicate resources.

"I got a call from William the other day. He thinks Peter might be more dangerous than we realized."

Declan blew out a breath. "How much more?"

"Kill two innocent people and stalk a third dangerous," she replied, voice quiet.

She could hear his fingers drumming on the steering wheel. Something he used to do when he was thinking.

"Do you want my help, Evie?"

The question surprised her, and she turned to look at him. This man had been commanding her every move since she'd stepped foot in this city, and now he was asking her if she even wanted his help? Somehow, the fact that he'd asked before she could annoyed her.

"I need it."

He nodded slowly. "Then I think it's time to lay everything out on the table. About Peter, about Morocco, about whatever the hell that might have to do with your parents."

"Okay," she said after a long moment. "Okay, I can do that."

"I'll call a family meeting. I'm only going to tell them anyway," he added when she protested. "This cuts out the middleman and eliminates the chance of anything getting lost in translation."

She didn't relish the idea of exposing the parts of herself she'd kept hidden for so long to his entire family. Most of them didn't even like her. Except she knew he was right. If she needed syndicate resources to figure this out and get back to her life, she would need their help. All of them.

"Fine."

Chapter Twenty

There was a time when attending a Callahan family dinner wouldn't have made her so nervous. It had been fun getting together with the whole family then. Declan's father, Patrick, had always intimidated her, but the four brothers were close and loud and always laughing.

It had been even better when Finn and Brogan had started to date and she wasn't the only girl in the room. That was a lifetime ago, though, and she had no idea what to expect from any of them now.

Evie stared at herself in the mirror, tugging down the hem of her shirt. It didn't matter what she wore. She wasn't trying to impress anyone. She glanced at the time on her phone as she debated switching back to the green top she'd discarded on the pile on the bed. She was officially late.

Annoyed with herself, she deliberately turned from the mirror. Purple was a good color; she liked purple. She was not going to change her damn shirt again. Closing the bedroom door behind her to hide the mess, she descended the stairs to the sound of voices.

They preferred to gather in the family room that sat off the hall to the kitchen rather than the more formal living room in the front of the house. She wouldn't say it was cozier—none of the cavernous rooms in Glenmore House could really be considered cozy—but it was homey and comfortable with overstuffed furniture and a well-stocked minibar.

Pausing in the doorway, she leaned against the smooth, polished wood and watched. Declan was still dressed in a suit, but he'd discarded his jacket and rolled his sleeves up to his elbow. It was the most dressed down she'd ever seen him. A stark contrast to the boy who'd lived in jeans and too-tight t-shirts as a teenager.

He stood across the room, deep in conversation with his uncle Sean and cousin James, a glass of brandy in his hand. A small smile curved her lips. No, it was whiskey, definitely whiskey. His laugh carried across the room, and she sighed. It had been so long since she'd heard him laugh like that, and it still captivated her.

Brogan and Aidan sat on one of the sofas, locked in a heated debate about something, hands waving and fingers pointing. Every so often, they'd stop to take a swig of beer and then they were back at it. Not much had changed there.

They were, all of them, exactly as she remembered them, even though she'd tried so hard to forget.

"Looks different now, doesn't it?"

She turned at Finn's voice behind her, smiling warmly. She and Finn had been the same year in school, so she'd spent as much time with him as she had with Cait and Maura in their classes. Cait had hated Finn in school, and it amused her that sometime between then and now her friend had stopped hating the man she'd dubbed Declan's annoying little brother.

"When did you and Cait get together?"

His eyebrows lifted in surprise. "Okay, not what I expected you to say. Cait didn't tell you?"

Evie shrugged. "I haven't asked."

"She started spending a lot of time here after you left. I think she kept hoping Declan would be able to find you. He didn't tell you that," he said when her eyes widened. "Shit. He looked for you. For a while. When Dad finally forced him to stop looking, he…"

Finn rubbed the back of his neck and glanced at his brother. "And Cait was a mess. I'd like to think we'd have gotten together at some point without the push of her grief for you. But in a way, I'm kind of grateful. So, thanks."

Evie couldn't help but chuckle at his wide grin. "Well, at least some good came out of it."

"She's glad to have you back. But Evie," he went on, drawing her gaze. "If you hurt her again—"

"I know," she interrupted. "I'm going to do my best not to make the same mistakes twice. Speak of the devil." Evie spotted Cait making her way down the hall with a reluctant Maura in tow.

Maura breezed by her with an icy nod and crossed the room to James, rising onto her tiptoes to brush a kiss across his cheek. At least with James, Maura could smile. Evie could feel Maura's devotion to her fiancé from across the room. It warmed her, even if Maura wanted nothing to do with her.

When her gaze shifted to Declan, she found him staring back at her, blue eyes intense and searching. He'd looked for her. That thought stirred something unfamiliar in her chest. She'd wondered, in those first few months, if Declan had loved her enough to search for her and what she would have done if he actually found her, if he'd said all the right things and begged her to come home.

If he had, she'd probably be standing next to him across the room laughing along with him while their children slept upstairs, and Maura wouldn't be looking at her like she was a bug that needed crushing. If he had, she wouldn't be standing feet away from him feeling like they were miles apart.

"Am I interrupting?" Cait asked, looking from Evie to Declan and back again.

"No," Evie said, turning to wrap her friend in a tight hug. Pulling back, she cupped Cait's face in her hands, hazel eyes staring into Cait's blue ones. "I'm sorry, Caitlin."

Cait's smile was puzzled. "For what?"

"For…for all of it."

Cait's eyes misted as understanding dawned, and she wrapped Evie in another fierce hug. "I forgive you. You know that, right? You believe me when I say it?"

"I believe you," Evie whispered, voice hoarse through her own unshed tears.

"Come on," Cait said, releasing her then gripping Evie's hand. "Let's get a drink." She stopped in front of the minibar. "What'll it be?"

"The wine's good," Declan said in her ear.

His voice melted through her like liquid gold, and she turned to look up at him. He was so close she could smell the spicy notes of his aftershave, and she had to stop herself from taking another step closer and breathing him in.

"I bet you drink red," he added, moving to lift a bottle from the rest.

It was the same brand she'd brought back from the restaurant. "That's an easy guess."

He grinned and opened it for her, pouring her a glass. When he handed it to her, she took a step back. It was hard to think standing that close to him. She took a slow sip while he watched her. Still just as good as the first taste she'd had at the restaurant.

"You'll have to tell me where I can buy this once I go back to New York."

He cocked his head, expression neutral. "We'll see."

He turned when his uncle called his name, and she frowned, unsure if he'd been referring to the wine or her leaving. They settled into pockets of conversation, and she perched on the arm of the sofa, not knowing enough to participate and not entirely sure she'd be welcome if she tried with the looks Aidan and Maura were giving her.

"Evie," Cait called from her spot on the couch, drawing her attention. "The nun who taught chemistry, with the glasses and the freckles, what was her name?"

Evie scrunched her nose, trying to bring the woman's face into view. "Sister Mary Francis?"

"That's it!" Cait snapped her fingers and pointed at Evie before returning to her story. "Sister Mary Francis was caught in the coat closet with the janitor. And they weren't hanging up coats."

Maura groaned, head in her hands. "Mom was telling me all about that last week! Sister Mary Francis is the last person I ever want to picture doing anything like that."

"Wonder if she likes to use the ruler still."

Evie hadn't realized she'd said that loud enough for anyone to hear until Declan barked out a laugh. She felt her cheeks heat while Cait giggled and Maura groaned again.

"An even worse visual!" Maura complained

"Mary Francis was nothing compared to Sister Eugenie," Cait added.

"Oh, Christ," Finn said, rubbing his knuckles at the memory. "She hit entirely too hard for a woman her age."

"Evie knows all about that. I was the good one."

"The good one." Evie snorted. "Whose weed did I get in trouble for senior year?"

Cait sipped at her wine to hide her blush. "I said I was sorry! And it's not like you got kicked out of school."

"No, my parents just had to make a huge donation, and I walked around with bruised knuckles for a week."

She noted the way Declan's gaze darkened as he sipped his whiskey. He hadn't liked seeing marks on her then, and it appeared he didn't like being reminded of them now.

"Can we get to the real reason we're here tonight? The walk down memory lane is a snooze fest."

The room fell silent, and Brogan reached over to punch Aidan on the arm. "You're such a buzzkill, little brother."

In the tension that hung, a maid stepped up to the door and announced that dinner was ready. They crossed silently into the dining room, and when a knot twisted in her stomach, Evie smoothed it away with her hand. Lowering herself into the chair Declan held out for her, she took a sip of wine.

"Right," Declan said into the expectant silence. "Most of you know some of it, but I want everyone at this table to have all the details."

"Details about what?" Aidan wondered.

"About what happened to O'Brian and Mary Elizabeth and everything that's happened since." Declan glanced at Evie, who twirled her finger in the air to indicate he should take it from the top.

"We all know McGee originally thought murder-suicide."

"I thought he changed his mind after the autopsy?" Finn replied.

"He did." Declan nodded. "Said the cuts were shallow and then deep, like there was hesitation at first. Not unheard of, but unusual with something like that."

"Reagan's theory agrees with McGee's," Evie continued.

"You met with my sister?" Maura's tone was cold.

"We did," Declan replied, and Maura shifted in her seat. "There wasn't a lot of evidence left by the cleaners, but the one thing that stuck out to her was that a knife was missing from the block. Probably the murder weapon."

"That would have driven your mother crazy," Cait said. "She'd never have kept a mismatched set."

"That's what I said," Evie agreed. "Which means the killer used it as a weapon of opportunity and then took it with them. If it was my dad"—she swallowed around the lump in her throat—"we would've found the knife."

"Weapon of opportunity could still be a random burglary. We were floating that idea around at first, weren't we?"

"We were. But I think the notes on Evie's mirror, and Nessa's, plus the flat tire and Nessa being followed mean we have to consider it was targeted."

"Wait," Brogan said. "Back up."

"Nessa said she feels like someone has been watching her, and someone tailed her on the way home from the grocery store yesterday." Evie pushed a glazed carrot across her plate.

"She called, frantic, and we went over there. She was pretty shaken up."

"And that's why Owen is sitting on her place at night," Sean replied.

"Yes. She didn't want someone 24/7, so we compromised." Declan sipped his whiskey.

"And the flat tire?" Cait wondered.

"Evie got a flat tire on her way back from Center City the other week, and we don't think that was an accident."

"How do you know?"

"We don't. Not really," Evie said to Declan when he started to argue. "It could have been an accident, but considering everything else, it might not have been."

"I'll play along," Aidan replied, leaning back in his chair. "Why would someone target the O'Brians? To what end? Especially when Evie hasn't even lived here in ten years."

"You already have someone in mind for this," Finn said when Evie and Declan shared a look.

Declan circled his finger in the air when Evie paused, and her lips twitched.

"His name is Peter," she began, "and I did a job for him in Morocco last year."

Aidan's eyes narrowed. "What kind of job?"

"He wanted something and I got it for him."

"You stole it?" Cait's voice was surprised.

Evie met her friend's gaze across the table. "I did."

"Been doing that a while?" Aidan wondered, tone sarcastic as he took a pull of his beer.

"Careful, Aidan," Declan warned.

"I'm only asking a question."

Evie sat up straighter in her chair. She needed their help if she didn't want to have to burn her whole life to the ground and start over again. So she'd take Aidan's snarky comments in stride if it meant getting out of this in one piece.

"About eight years or so."

"So this Peter guy," Brogan said, "he's dangerous?"

"Very likely. I got a call from a contact the other day that someone who runs in my circles—"

"Another thief," Aidan sneered.

"Is on the run and thinks Peter killed her brother and sister-in-law. The only family she has left."

"So why is he after you?"

"I have no idea. The only one who almost got screwed over in Morocco was me. If it is him and he isn't stopped, he could expose every identity I've ever used."

"And then what?" Finn asked.

"And then it's a race to see who catches and kills me first."

Cait covered her mouth with her hand, and even Maura looked pale. Evie hadn't meant to be so blunt about it, but it was the truth. Peter wasn't playing games; he was playing God. And he didn't strike her as the type of man who walked away until he got what he wanted.

"If Peter is the one who killed your parents, then he

already knows your identity. Couldn't he have exposed you already?"

Evie shook her head at Brogan. "I've never worked under my real name. Only aliases. So knowing my real name is a start, but it doesn't give him the kind of leverage that leaks all my identities. I imagine that's what he's trying to find out."

"Fascinating. How does someone even get into that line of work?"

Evie pinned Aidan with a hard stare. "I don't know, Aidan. How does someone become a mobster?"

Aidan's eyes narrowed when Brogan chuckled. "What I'm hearing is you want to put this family into harm's way to clean up your mess. Why should we take a bullet for you?"

"I'm not asking you to."

"Aren't you? What's the point of this little meeting?" He sneered the word. "If not to make your case and beg for our help?"

"No one's begging," Finn said.

Evie clenched her fists in her lap, struggling to keep her voice even. "I'm not here to beg. I didn't bring my parents into this. Their killer did. If that's Peter, I can own my choices here, but I won't apologize to anyone for something I didn't do. Least of all you."

"I would expect nothing less from you. You've made your bed. Maybe you should lie in it instead of expecting us to pick up the pieces of the mess you've made."

"Fuck you, Aidan." Evie shot out of her chair so fast it nearly toppled to the floor. She leaned forward, bracing her hands on the edge of the table. "God forbid you ever make a rash decision that takes you so far from where you want to be you don't know how to get back again. Although maybe you're already there considering how far up your own ass your head is."

Throwing her napkin down on the table, Evie stalked out

of the dining room, slamming the door to the back patio behind her. She wanted to scream, kick something, throw things. Fuck Aidan and his insinuation that this was somehow her fault. She'd stolen for dozens of people over the years, and not one of them had ever tried to murder her family.

She picked up a small planter that sat on the low stone wall that edged the patio and heaved it into the yard. That, at least, made her feel marginally better.

"What did that plant ever do to you?"

Evie whirled at the sound of Declan's voice. How long had he been standing there?

"Aidan is an asshole. And he does not speak for this family." He crossed the patio to stand next to her. "Peter became my problem when he targeted my people."

He reached up to cup her face, pulling her closer. "And, however long you've been gone, wherever you go, you are my people too, Evie. Mine to protect."

She blinked at the tears that burned her eyes and leaned into his hand. In that moment, she realized how easy it would be to get lost in him again, to be consumed by him. She couldn't afford that kind of distraction, but she wasn't sure how much longer she'd be able to resist the constant pull of him.

She stepped out of his arms, hugging herself tightly when he frowned. "I need your help. To bring my parents' killer to justice so I can go back to my life. But that's all this can be, Declan. Nothing else."

When he said nothing, she turned and let herself back into the house, skirting the dining room full of arguing voices. She made it all the way upstairs to her room before the tears fell. Pushing her clothes onto the floor, she crawled into bed and curled into a ball under the covers.

Chapter Twenty-One

Sleep eluded him. After Evie left him standing on the patio, he'd eventually gone back inside, disbanded the group, and sent Aidan off to do scut work if for no other reason than it gave him immense pleasure to do so.

That finished, Declan attempted some work in his office, but it was impossible to concentrate. Every time it seemed like Evie was opening up, she slammed the door and shut him out. He'd meant what he said about protecting her. He'd do whatever it took to make sure she was safe.

Giving up on work, he'd put in a punishing two hours at the home gym he kept in the basement, working out his frustration. Not even that was enough to send him into sleep.

So now here he was, wide awake at almost one in the morning and annoyed with it. Throwing back the covers, he padded barefoot down the stairs and back toward the family room. A shot of whiskey should do the trick.

When he neared the family room, he noticed a light from the kitchen. Brows knitted together, he changed course. He heard the staff head to bed hours ago, and no one else usually roamed the house this late at night.

When he walked into the kitchen, her back was facing him. Steam rose from the mug on the counter while she scooped tea leaves out of a small bag and into a strainer, dropping it into the water.

She fit there, better than he'd ever imagined, and he liked the look of her in his space, among his things. She knew her way around the kitchen better than he did, pulling spoons out of drawers and replacing the bag of tea in exactly the right spot. It made him wonder how many late nights she'd had down here, making tea when she couldn't sleep.

When she turned and spotted him she jolted, quickly swiping at her cheeks with her fingertips, then tugging down the sleeve of her robe to wipe her eyes. She'd been crying. He thought the overwhelming urge to protect her from anything or anyone who would hurt her would have faded after all this time. It hadn't.

He wanted to comfort her like he would have when they were younger. Hold her while she cried and kiss away her tears. Knowing she didn't want that, at least not from him, he did the next best thing and offered her a distraction instead.

"Good, you're up. I wanted to talk to you about that job."

She cleared her throat, glancing over her shoulder at the clock on the stove. "Now?"

"No time like the present. We'll talk in my office."

He turned on his heel and led her back the way he'd come and into his office, flicking on the light so the lamps in the corner and on his desk lit up the space. She stood in the doorway while he moved to his desk, watching him over the rim of her mug.

"What?"

"I didn't know you owned any other clothes besides tailored Italian suits."

His lips twitched into a grin as he glanced down at the sweatpants he pulled on before coming downstairs, noting the way her gaze traveled up over his bare chest and the tattoo that covered much of his left pec and shoulder before curling over his bicep and down to his elbow.

"So," she said, eyes snapping back to his face as she cleared her throat, "what job?"

He motioned to one of the chairs that sat across from his desk and waited for her to sit before flipping open a folder and pulling a picture out.

"This is Andrea DiMarco." Across the desk, he slid the picture of a man in his late fifties with dark hair graying at the temples. "He moves big money in the city."

"For the Italians?" She set her mug on the edge of the desk to study the photo.

"He started with the Italians, but now he seems to be playing house with the Russians too."

Evie's brows drew together. "That's not good."

Lust for her arrowed through him. She'd always understood their business as well as he did. It was one of many reasons they'd made the perfect match.

"No. He carries this thumb drive around with him everywhere. I'm not ready to make a move on him yet, mostly because I don't know what he's up to, and until I do, I don't care to stir up trouble."

"But you want to know what's on that drive."

He nodded. "Exactly."

He handed her another photo, and she squinted at the blown-up pixelated image of what looked like an engraved lighter. "What can you tell me about him? I have to know about him, his habits, his likes, so I can figure out how to get that for you," she added when Declan raised a single brow.

"I happen to know that he'll be at a fundraiser for the mayor's re-election campaign this weekend, and I have an invitation for myself and a guest," Declan said. "We can go together, and you can do whatever it is you do to get it from him."

"No," Evie replied, lifting her mug to her lips and studying the picture of DiMarco again.

"No?"

Setting the mug down, she glanced up at Declan. "Does he know who you are?"

"I've never met him, but I would have to assume so, yes."

"Would he know who I am?"

He could see where she was going with this, but he wasn't sure he liked it. "He's only been in the city for about five years, so probably not."

"If you want me to get close enough to him to steal a flash drive he most likely keeps in his breast pocket after only knowing him a few hours without getting caught, then we can't be seen together. We can't even appear to know each other."

"And if he makes you?"

"He won't. I've been doing this a long time, Declan. Have a little faith."

He studied her carefully. He didn't like the idea of her being alone with this guy. "How would you get into the fundraiser if you don't have an invitation?"

"Who can resist a damsel in distress?" Evie rose, grinning. "Give me a couple days to think it over, and then we can talk details." She moved to the door, pausing with her hand on the knob. "This'll be fun."

"What about your fees?"

Her eyes trailed down his tattoo again. "We can work it out later."

As the door clicked closed behind her, his hands clenched into fists, and it took every ounce of his willpower not to go after her and fuck her against every available surface between here and his bedroom. It was killing him being this close and not being able to have her. And he didn't know how much longer he'd be able to keep his hands to himself.

It took him another hour to relax enough to head upstairs to bed. He'd listened to Aidan come in from his assignment at the warehouse and then left his office, shutting off all the lights, locking up the house, and activating the alarm.

He'd have to spend some time thinking up more scut work for his brother to do. The kid needed to be brought into line. Declan was getting tired of his childish outbursts.

Halfway up the stairs, a frantic, piercing scream jarred his thoughts. Evie. He sprinted the rest of the way up and down the hall to her room, shoving the door open, eyes scanning the room for the threat.

When she let out another scream, then a gasping sob, he realized she was having a nightmare, her body thrashing, her face wet with tears.

He ate up the distance to the bed in quick strides, sinking down next to her to grip her shoulders. "Evie, wake up." His voice was firm, but even he could hear the fear laced in it. "It's just a dream. Come on, love."

He gave her shoulders a rough shake, and she startled awake, shoving herself up, her breath coming in terrified, raspy gasps. It took a minute for her to recognize him, but when she did, she flung her arms around his neck, pressing her face against his throat.

"Oh God, Declan. The blood. So much blood."

"It's okay. You're okay." He rubbed her back in gentle circles while her tears fell hot and wet against his skin. "It's just a dream."

She gripped his shoulders, turning her head to press her cheek against his collarbone. "Just a dream." She inhaled slow, deep breaths.

When he ran his hand over her curls, smoothing them, she leaned back, and her eyes fell to his lips. He wasn't sure who initiated the kiss, but when their lips met, he lifted her onto his lap, groaning when she wrapped her legs around his waist.

He dragged his tongue over her bottom lip so they parted, and she moaned softly when he slid his tongue against hers. Fisting his hands in her hair as her hands roamed over his shoulders and down his back, her fingernails scoring across his skin as he devoured her.

He wanted to feel her under him, surrounding him. He wanted, desperately, to be inside her, to hear his name on her lips while she came around him.

Then someone cleared their throat from the doorway, and Evie yelped as she broke their kiss.

"Go away," Declan growled, arm tightening around Evie's waist when she tried to scoot off his lap.

"What. The fuck."

"Go to bed, Brogan," Declan said with a glance at his brother's hulking frame in the doorway. "Everything is fine."

"It didn't sound fine a minute ago. It sounded like someone was being murdered, and now…" Brogan waved his hand at the two of them wrapped around each other on the bed. "This is consensual, right?"

Declan shot a warning look at the door, ignoring Evie's snicker, and waited until Brogan retreated, mumbling under his breath.

"I'm sorry," Evie said once Brogan was gone, leaving the door open to the hallway.

"Don't be," Declan replied, pressing a kiss to her temple. "It's not the first time he's caught us."

She laughed then, and for a moment, everything felt normal and uncomplicated.

"We were good together once, weren't we?"

He brushed her hair off her face, rubbing the pad of his thumb over her cheek. "Yeah, we were."

She cupped his face in her hands, pressing a soft kiss against his lips, and when she moved to slide off his lap again, he didn't stop her. Unsure of what to say, or if there was even really anything to say, he crossed to the door.

"Goodnight, Evie," he murmured before closing the door with a soft click.

Chapter Twenty-Two

They spent the better part of three days going back and forth over the plan to get the drive from DiMarco. Evie wasn't used to working with a partner, let alone one as...opinionated as Declan. That was the only nice way she could think of to put it.

Declan had originally argued that she get in, get the drive, and get out, presumably for her safety, but if Declan didn't want DiMarco to know the drive was missing—and he didn't—then the plan was going to be more complicated than that.

She would need to get the drive away from DiMarco, hand it off to Brogan to download the files, and slip it back into DiMarco's possession without him being any the wiser. Entirely doable if Declan didn't freak out and blow her cover.

At least the planning of this job had kept her mind off Declan's lips and free of any thoughts about how much she wanted to kiss him again. Mostly. In any case, for the next few hours she needed to focus on the task at hand.

When headlights slashed across the trees, she straightened, pushing thoughts of Declan to the back of her mind. Aidan insisted that DiMarco, a creature of habit, would drive through this quiet neighborhood of McMansions to get to the fundraiser the mayor held every year for his biggest donors. Which is why she'd parked her Maserati on the gravel shoulder, popped the hood, and waited.

Hitting the remote to cut the engine, she dumped a bottle of water on the hot metal so it hissed and steamed just as a black town car crested the hill. She stepped out from behind the car so the headlights illuminated her in the dark.

The royal blue dress she'd bought fit like a dream, clinging to every curve with a slit up to her thigh and a plunging neckline that showed off the swell of her breasts.

Cocking her hip to expose the pale length of her leg as the car slowed, Evie pasted on a relieved smile when the rear window rolled down.

"Oh, thank goodness you came by," she called without crossing the road, "I've been out here for I don't even know how long."

"Have you called someone?" DiMarco's voice was a rich baritone with a lyrical Italian accent.

"I would, but my battery is dead. Do you have one I can borrow?" She bent slightly at the waist to expose more of her cleavage and bit back a smile when his eyes dipped down to her breasts and back up to her face. Christ, men were so simple.

He reached into his coat pocket and held a phone out the window, waiting for her to jog across the street. "Where are you headed in such a beautiful dress?"

"Oh." She feigned shyness at the flattery and dialed the number for the burner phone Declan had given her. "Some event in Center City." She offered him a smile and took two steps away to pretend at privacy.

"Hello?"

She smiled at Declan's voice in her ear. "Hey, I'm broken

down on Fremont just past the turn off for…" She twirled her finger in the air as if she couldn't think of the word.

"Bishop's Corner," DiMarco offered.

"Bishop's Corner!" Evie shot him a winning smile. "And I need you to come get me."

"It's a little unnerving how good you are at this."

"Two hours?!" She turned slightly away from the car and hissed loudly, "What are you even doing that it would take you two hours to drive out here? You know what?" she snapped. "I don't want to know who you're with."

She ended the call on Declan's amused chuckle and stalked back across the road to hand the phone back to DiMarco.

"Everything all right?"

"I…" she blew out a frustrated breath, pressing her fingers to her temples. "I'm not sure. You wouldn't happen to know the number for a tow truck service, would you?"

He made a show of checking his watch, glancing back at her, eyes traveling up and down her body again. "You said you were going to an event in Center City?"

"Yeah. A fundraiser for the mayor?"

"Well, then." For the first time, he flashed her a disarming smile. "I think we might be going to the same place. I can give you a ride if you like."

Evie reached out to squeeze his forearm. "Oh, really? You are a lifesaver. Let me grab my bag and just…" She waved a hand at her car.

He nodded. "Of course."

After she retrieved her bag from her car and lowered the hood, she slid into the back of DiMarco's black Lincoln, letting the slit from her dress ride high on her thigh before closing the door and plunging them into darkness.

"I really appreciate you helping me out like this," Evie

said, angling her body toward his as the car rolled away from the shoulder. "I'm Victoria, by the way."

He took the hand she held out and leaned down to press his lips against the backs of her fingers. "Andrea. I'm glad I could be of assistance, Victoria. You know the mayor?"

"Well, my father does. He's forever worried I'm not rubbing elbows with the right people, so he asked me to come tonight in his place. You?"

"I make sure to always rub elbows with the right people."

She giggled. "Lucky I met you then."

When they pulled up in front of the two-story Gothic building, she waited for him to help her out of the car and let him lead her up the front steps. On his arm, no one at the door even asked her for the invitation she didn't have. They just waved them both through into a ballroom decorated in white and gray with standing tables set up throughout so people could mingle.

White-jacketed waiters carried around trays of canapés and champagne, and an open bar nestled into the back corner was serving cocktails. She caught Declan's eye where he chatted with a couple of men in tuxes, lifting a shoulder when his jaw tightened at the sight of her arm tucked into DiMarco's.

"Let me buy you a drink." She gestured to the bar with her clutch, smiling sweetly when he turned to look at her.

"I think the bar is free," he replied, eyes amused.

"I have to do something to repay your kindness."

"A drink then," he agreed, nodding at people as they crossed the room, "and maybe a dance later."

"But there's no music."

"Much later and in private, perhaps?"

She bit her lip and sent him a flirtatious smile. A bold invitation for a man old enough to be her father. When they stepped up to the bar, he ordered a bourbon for himself, smiling at her indulgently when she asked for a cosmo.

He guided her around the room with his hand on the small of her back, making mundane conversation with other guests. He introduced her as Victoria but didn't seem all that interested in knowing who her mysterious father was. She was beautiful, she was young, and she was at the party, so she must be in someone's elite circle. No one seemed to care which one.

She was getting impatient when Declan finally signaled from across the room that Brogan was in position. Her eyes scanned the room and landed on a couple moving in their direction.

She moved, ever so slightly, so the man bumped into her shoulder, and she made a big show of lurching forward and pouring her drink down DiMarco's arm.

"Oh my God," she gasped, quickly setting her empty glass on the nearest table and grabbing a napkin, dabbing at the liquid that had soaked through the jacket. "I'm so sorry."

He jerked toward her, annoyance in his eyes, and Evie forced a tremble into her voice. "Please, let me take it into the bathroom and try and get some of that out."

He actually looked pleased with her distress and reached up to cup her cheek. "Don't fret, my dear. It's only a jacket. But you may try if you wish," he added when her eyes continued to plead.

He slipped the jacket off and handed it to her, and Evie rose up to brush a quick kiss across his cheek. "Thank you," she said, relieved, and hurried off to the bathroom.

As soon as he was out of sight, she quickly searched his coat pockets for the flash drive, sighing with relief when her fingers closed around the cool metal in his left breast pocket. She slipped into the bathroom, locking herself in the first stall, and plugged the drive into the device Brogan had given her.

She knew he had the signal when the device blinked to life, and she watched the bars jump up and down to indicate the file transfer had been initiated. It took five long, excruciating minutes until the device beeped, and then the text came through from Brogan that it was done.

She unplugged the drive, slipping it back into the pocket and dropping Brogan's device into her bag. She held the jacket under the dryer for a quick minute until she was satisfied it looked like she had tried and then made her way back out to the ballroom.

She flashed a tentative smile when he caught sight of her, and he met her across the room, turning so she could help him into his jacket. She brushed at the shoulders and then the lapels when he turned.

"It's not dry cleaning, but it'll do for the night. I really am very sorry."

He waved a hand. "Don't be. It was an accident. It's lucky you didn't get anything on that beautiful dress of yours." His eyes wandered up and down her body again. "Come. I must show my face for thirty minutes more, and then we can go."

"Actually, my father called while I was in the bathroom. He's sending a car for me." She leaned in to press a kiss to his cheek and whispered in his ear, "Maybe we can have that dance another time."

When she turned to go, he grabbed her arm, just hard enough to have worry settle into her stomach.

"I thought you said your phone was dead."

Shit. She forced a smile, trying to remember if there were plugs in the bathroom where she could have charged her phone to support her lie. No doubt he'd check. Christ, she hoped there were.

"I found a plug by the couch that gave me enough of a charge to check messages."

He stared at her for a long moment. "Who did you say your father was again?"

Evie fought to keep her face serene, but her mind frantically scanned a list of names. Did she toss one out or try and play coy to distract him? He was too smart for an outright lie like that. Coy would have to do.

She sent him a teasing grin. "I don't think I did say." She stroked a hand down his arm, sending Declan a signal to relax behind DiMarco's back. "I could tell you all about him another time, in private. But he generally kills the mood."

When a grin slowly spread across his face she relaxed, giving his arm a playful squeeze. "Well, we wouldn't want to ruin the mood. It's a shame you have to go, but let me give you my card."

She returned his grin, stomach doing flip flops while she watched him pat his pockets and pull out a silver embossed business card holder. He slipped one out and handed it to her.

"I hope to see you again very soon, Andrea," she purred, leaning up to brush a kiss across his cheek.

Without another word, she turned on her heel and forced herself to slowly skirt the ballroom, turning to reward DiMarco with one last flirtatious smile and catching Declan's eye instead.

The way he looked at her made every thought she'd tried to push out of her head over the last few days come flooding back. She slipped out the front door and into the black sedan that waited for her, smiling at Brogan as he drove around the corner and waited for Declan.

"That was perfectly executed. I'm very impressed. Imagine what we could do with your skill set. The possibilities are endless."

Declan waited the agreed-upon fifteen minutes and then climbed into the back of the car.

"What was that about?" Declan asked as Brogan pulled away from the curb and drove back toward Evie's car.

"He got suspicious there at the end. I had to practically promise to sleep with him to get him to relax."

Declan's eyes flashed. "He gave you something before you left."

She held out the business card to him, barely hiding a grin when he snatched it, turning it over in his fingers. "I promise not to call him, unless sex is the next part of your plan."

He held her gaze while he slowly ripped up the card into tiny pieces and released the bits of paper out the window. "You get what you needed?" he asked Brogan.

"Every single kilobyte. And there was a lot of it. I'm going to enjoy going through all of that."

"Good." Declan's gaze shifted to Evie. She could feel the desire rolling off him, and it sent a wave of need through her. "How long until you can get me something?"

"Couple days. I started digging into Peter too. Haven't found anything yet, but I'll keep looking. I have a few more angles I want to try."

When Brogan pulled up alongside Evie's car, she got out and Declan followed suit, waiting for Brogan's tail lights to fade before gripping Evie's hand and yanking her up against him.

"I haven't been able to stop thinking about doing this all night."

The kiss he gave her was deep and demanding, and his lips never left hers as he urged her backward until she was pressed against the door of her car, the Maserati shielding them from the road. He fisted his hand in her hair, tilting her head back and scraping his teeth along the line of her jaw.

She should stop him. Sex with Declan could go nowhere good. But ever since that kiss the other night, it was all she could think about. His hands, his lips, his teeth on her skin.

Being with Declan would have consequences, but to hell with them. She'd deal with them later. She wanted this, wanted him more than she'd let herself want anything in a long time. And she meant to take it.

"Someone is going to see us," she said, pulse racing and voice breathy with it.

His grin was quick and wicked. "You didn't use to mind getting caught."

His hands slid down her back and cupped her ass, squeezing before lifting her up. When she wrapped her legs around his waist, he groaned, grinding against her as his lips traveled the column of her throat, kissing, biting, sucking.

"Declan," she panted, reaching down between them to fumble with his zipper, fingers brushing against the hard length of his cock.

On a hiss, he sank his teeth into her shoulder while she stroked him through the fabric of his pants. He moved his hand on top of hers, helping her free his cock and shuddering when she wrapped her fingers around his length.

He thrust against her palm while he shoved her dress higher, dropping his head to kiss the rounded tops of her breasts while she stroked him. He whispered her name in her ear as he drove himself inside her, and she bucked her hips against his.

She could feel his fingers digging into her ass as he pumped in and out of her, and she pulled his mouth to hers for another searing kiss, dragging her teeth over his bottom lip.

Grinding her hips against him, her body tingled, begging for release, and she dragged her teeth across his upper lip, shivering when he growled, hips thrusting faster.

"Yes. Declan," she panted, digging her fingernails into the base of his neck just to feel his skin hot under her hands.

She cried out with her own orgasm just as he emptied

himself inside her, his thrusts slowing to a torturing rhythm that made her shudder in his arms.

"Turns out," she said, trying to catch her breath, "I still don't mind getting caught."

He laughed against the crook of her neck, pressing his lips against it. "Somehow that's better than I remember it."

"Without a fucking doubt."

When he pulled back to look at her, his eyes were dark with desire, and that rush of need skittered along her skin again. When a car topped the hill, he lowered her to her feet, adjusting himself while she tugged her dress down.

They waved away the driver's offer of assistance, and Declan pulled her in for another kiss, sinking into it in a way that had her heart doing somersaults into her stomach.

"I'm not finished with you yet," he whispered against her lips, reaching around her and opening the car door.

She climbed in and watched him race around the front and catapult himself into the driver's seat. Yes, there would be consequences for sleeping with Declan Callahan again, but for even one night with him, she'd gladly pay them all.

Chapter Twenty-Three

Declan almost rammed the gate tearing into the driveway. Had the goddamned thing always been so slow? He had barely thrown the car in park and cut the engine before he was sprinting around the hood to yank her door open and pull her to her feet.

Without a second thought, he hauled her up against him, one hand sliding around to her neck to tilt her head back for his lips. Heat pumped through him as her fingers tugged his shirt from his waistband, her teeth grazing over his lower lip.

"I'm not fucking you in the driveway," she said, voice husky.

He would have taken her there, anywhere, but he was in a mood to oblige her, so he lifted her off her feet and carried her inside, setting her on the carpeted floor in the foyer, shutting and locking the door behind him.

"Better?"

She laughed, and he relished the sound. He hadn't realized how much he'd missed it until just then.

"Brogan is home, and you want to strip me naked in the hallway?"

His gaze flicked to the stairs and back to her face, eyes traveling down the length of her body. She made his mouth water. He had to be inside her again.

"In the hallway, on the stairs, in every fucking room in this house. But you make a good point."

He took her mouth again, fast and greedy, his tongue sweeping against hers as she slid her hands under the lapels of his jacket, pushing it off his shoulders and onto the floor before kicking off her shoes and taking a step away from him.

He followed her to the stairs, pulling her back against him when she turned to go up and pressing a kiss to her exposed shoulder. He slid his fingers down her arm to capture her hand and led her up to his bedroom, kicking the door shut behind him.

They'd snuck into his room to have sex more times than he could count when they were younger. But he never thought he'd get to have her in this room. Where he was king and she was his queen, and he wanted that, if only for tonight.

She wandered away from him, turning to face him in the middle of the room, eyes locked on his as she reached behind her to tug down the zipper of her dress, slipping the fabric off her shoulders and letting it pool with a whisper at her feet.

Stepping out of it, she teased her fingertips up her thighs, over the thin lace straps of her panties and the sheer cups of her matching bra. He watched her cup her breasts as he toed off his shoes and socks, barely able to catch his breath.

When she reached for him, he rushed to her, his fingertips digging into the skin of her shoulders as he dragged down her bra straps, freeing the clasp so her breasts filled his palms. He cupped them, squeezing, and she let out a ragged breath when his thumbs scraped against her nipples. Christ, he loved that sound.

When she dropped her head back, his lips found her throat, and he kissed and nibbled across it. His fingers twisted her nipple, and when she groaned, his lips curved into a smile against her skin.

"Declan, wait."

He groaned into the crook of her neck, his hands stilling on her breasts. "Please, God, don't ask me to stop."

"I don't want you to stop. But—" A shuddering groan escaped her when his fingers tightened on her nipple again.

"You don't have to say it," he murmured, trailing his lips over her jaw to her earlobe, giving it a gentle tug with his teeth. "Just let me touch you."

When she sighed in response, he bent to capture her nipple between his lips, swirling his tongue around it and dragging his teeth across it so she gasped. Everything about her felt both familiar and foreign.

The sounds she made, the way her body arched against him in one fluid motion when he teased her nipples, the way her hands roamed over his skin. No woman had ever invaded every single one of his senses like Evie O'Brian.

He wanted to take his time with her in a way he couldn't earlier, to remind himself why no one else had ever mattered, to make her sob his name and beg for release.

Her hands gripped his head as he teased first one nipple and then the other one before kissing between her breasts and down over her stomach. He nibbled and licked his way up her thigh and across her hip as he hooked his thumbs into the waistband of her panties, helping her step out of them.

When he slicked the flat of his tongue against her slit, her knees wobbled, but he wrapped his arms around her, cupping her ass in his hands as he flicked his tongue against her clit, once, twice, a third time, retreating each time.

He grazed his teeth against it, making her shudder as he slid his hand down to slide a finger inside her, pumping it in and out as he wrapped his lips around her clit, sucking so she bucked against him, her voice hoarse when she said his name.

He could feel her orgasm building in the way her muscles quivered and her hips jerked, and he worked his tongue and finger against her, inside her, driving her closer and closer to the edge until finally she cried out, her nails raking over the exposed skin of his neck.

When she went limp, he stood and scooped her up, carrying her to the edge of the bed, grinning as she collapsed back against the covers. He watched her for a minute, the rosy flush of her skin, the quick rise and fall of her chest as she got her breath back, the satisfied smile she gave him. He'd never in his life seen anyone more beautiful.

"You've certainly gotten better at that. And instead of jealous, I'll just be grateful." She sat up to make quick work of his belt and zipper while he undid the buttons on his shirt, flinging it across the room.

"You're the only one that ever really mattered," he murmured, covering her body with his, pressing kisses against her shoulder, scoring it with his teeth.

"That was exactly the right thing to say."

Sliding his hand over her breast, he grinned, enjoying the way she arched up against him when he pinched her nipple and twisted it roughly. He moved his fingers down her belly to cup her, wet in his hand. He slid another finger inside her, watching her eyes go smoky as she bucked up against his hand.

He slid in another finger, making her gasp as his thumb circled her clit, dragging her toward another orgasm as his head dipped to draw her nipple into his mouth, grazing it with his tongue while her fingernails dug into the skin of his back.

He pushed her harder and faster toward the edge until

she all but sobbed his name, and as she was coming down, he slid inside her—slow, deep, deliberate. He gripped the sheets in his fists as she clenched and pulsed around his cock, wrapping her long legs around his waist and pulling him in deeper.

He wanted to go slow, to savor every minute he was inside her in case it never happened again, but the way she was writhing underneath him, grinding her hips against his, he wasn't sure he had enough control to take it slow. He pressed a kiss to her lips, dragging his teeth over her lower lip and nibbling his way across her jaw as he slid slowly in and out.

Her breath hitched as she leaned up to nibble his earlobe and whisper, "Declan. Fuck me."

He groaned and slid his hand down to cup her ass, digging his fingers in as he held her tight against him. When she arched up against him, her hard nipples dragging against his chest, he pulled back and drove into her. Her nails bit into his skin, raking down his back as he thrust again.

No, she wouldn't get slow and gentle tonight. And she didn't seem to want it, meeting him thrust for thrust as her legs tightened around his waist and her body slid against his. When he felt her body go taut, he thrust harder, faster, and when she clenched around him with her own release, he emptied himself inside her.

Her fingertips made lazy circles across his back, and he knew he should move so he didn't crush her. When he rolled onto his back, he reached for her, tucking her up against his side, smiling when she curled around him again.

"I should probably invest in a box of condoms if we're going to do that again. I wasn't thinking."

"No," she said, voice dreamy.

"No?"

"I'm protected, and I haven't been with anyone else since I last got tested." Her fingers stilled on his chest. "Have you?"

He covered her hand with his. "No, I haven't either."

She stifled a yawn, snuggling in closer. "Good. Then nothing between us."

He smiled, and when he felt her body relax, her breathing deep and even, he couldn't imagine anywhere else he'd rather be.

Chapter Twenty-Four

When Evie woke, the sunlight fell in bright slashes across the bed and floor. She sighed at the feel of Declan's chest against her back, the way his arm wrapped protectively around her waist, holding her tight against him. She could feel his breath warm against her shoulder.

Last night had been…so much more than she ever imagined was possible to feel with him again. Really, Declan was the only man who had ever made her feel anything at all. It was why last night had been so dangerous.

He was all-consuming, and she had been sucked into his orbit a second time. She could get up, leave, and resolve never to do that again, but she was older now. She wasn't a girl anymore, lovesick and head over heels. It was possible to have her fun with Declan, to feel alive and electrified in his arms, and not be consumed by him.

There was no point in regretting something she wanted to do again anyway—as many times as possible. She was sore in places she didn't even remember existed, and that was its own delicious aftermath. Regret was pointless. She was going to focus on enjoying herself instead.

She contemplated staying in bed just a bit longer, reveling in his warmth or waking him up with her mouth on his cock. By the feel of him, he wouldn't have protested, but her stomach growled indignantly. Her mouth watered at the thought of pancakes. Maybe some bacon. Definitely some coffee.

Carefully she lifted his arm off her middle and wiggled out from underneath it, scooting slowly toward the edge of the bed so as not to wake him. Just before she put her feet on the floor, his arm snaked out and grabbed her by the waist, pulling her back against him so she could feel the length of his cock against her backside.

"Where are you going?" he murmured against her shoulder.

"To make breakfast."

"Ring Marta. She'll make breakfast, and you can stay in bed with me." He rocked his hips against her, and she grinned. "And do other things."

"That's very tempting, but it's Sunday. Marta doesn't work on Sundays. So we must forage our own breakfasts like the commoners do. And this commoner wants pancakes."

She tried to wiggle free, but his arm held tight. "Declan, you kept me up half the night. Don't deny me pancakes."

"I kept you up?"

She sat up and leaned down to press a kiss against his lips, lingering for a moment before pulling away. "That's my story and I'm sticking to it."

Chuckling, he sat up, frowning as he watched her search around in their pile of clothes. "What are you looking for?"

"Something I can wear to run back to my room and get dressed."

She slipped her arms into his button-down and squeaked

when he reached out and caught her arm, tugging her against him. He slid his hands up the backs of her thighs to cup her ass.

"You look very good in my shirt."

She grinned, leaning in to tease his bottom lip with her teeth. "I'll file that away for future use. But now it's pancakes." She danced out of his reach and laughed as his groan followed her down the hall.

When she met him at the top of the stairs, she was wearing a pair of leggings and a loose tank top, her hair swept up into a messy bun. She smiled when he pulled her up onto her tiptoes to brush a kiss lightly against her lips.

"I don't know if anyone's ever told you, but you look very sexy in leggings."

The house was quiet even in the early afternoon, and they had the kitchen to themselves while Evie set bacon to frying and measured out all the ingredients for pancakes. She wasn't a fantastic cook, but she could make a handful of things, mostly breakfast or pasta.

Declan put a pot of coffee on while she flipped the bacon in the pan and tried not to think about how comfortable it felt to be in his kitchen making breakfast like she belonged there. Easier said than done when he kept looking at her like that.

She moved bacon to drain and added more as a shirtless Brogan wandered in, likely enticed by the smells. "Home-made breakfast on a Sunday. Excellent." He snagged a piece off the plate Declan set in the middle of the island. "What's the occasion?"

"We burned a lot of calories last night," Evie replied with a cheeky grin, making Declan laugh.

"That's disgusting."

Evie snorted out a laugh, ladling another batch of pancakes onto the skillet. "It's a very natural thing. You see, when two people like each other very much—"

Declan nearly choked on his coffee, sputtering with laughter while Brogan threw up his hand to stop her.

"You're going to make me sick, and it would be a shame to throw up perfectly cooked bacon."

"Okay, okay, fine. Declan can give you the talk," she added with a wink, flipping the last pancake onto the platter and setting it on the island.

"I think I liked you better when you were sullen and moody," Brogan mumbled, piling his plate with pancakes.

"I'm not moody. I'm mysterious."

Brogan snorted. "Keep telling yourself that, kid. I can't stay here with you two or I'll never keep my breakfast down."

"You're welcome!" Evie called to Brogan's retreating back.

When they were alone again, Declan tilted Evie's chin up with his finger, leaning down for a kiss that was soft and sweet.

"What was that for?"

He kissed her forehead. "Just because."

They moved to sit at the bar stools lining the island counter, and she took a sip of coffee before nibbling a piece of bacon. "Brogan's right. This is perfectly cooked. So what are you up to today?"

"Paperwork. My life is an endless parade of boring paperwork."

"Tell Helen I said hi. I'm sure she misses me."

"She mentions it all the time. What are you up to today?"

Evie peered out the windows at the rain clouds that gathered beyond the trees. "If the weather holds, I'm going to go for a run later. I haven't been in weeks."

"You like to run?"

"Why do you sound so surprised?"

He shrugged. "I figured you for yoga or pilates or something," he said around a mouthful of pancake.

"Do you even know what pilates is?"

"It's like yoga, but with more stuff."

She laughed and sipped her coffee. "An eloquent summation. Sadly, I'm not patient enough for pilates or flexible enough for yoga—"

"Oh, I wouldn't say that."

"And running is something I can do anywhere," she finished, giving him a light elbow when he leaned down to kiss her exposed shoulder.

"Fine, but be careful. Don't give me that look," he added when she pinned him with a bland stare, "or I'll make Brogan go with you."

"God forbid," she muttered as she got up to clear the dishes and clean up.

It was raining by the time Evie strapped on her running shoes and headed out the front door. She considered it her penance for being unable to resist Declan in the shower. The man had learned some things in the last ten years.

She set off down the driveway at an easy pace and kept tight to the edge of the road. This neighborhood was usually quiet, not a lot of traffic even on its busiest days, but she kept her earbuds out and ran in the silence anyway, just in case. With everything going on right now, it was better to be safe than sorry.

She'd done some digging on Kiah's brother and sister-in-law after prying more details out of William. She couldn't make the timeline match up in her head until she found news articles about the deaths.

They'd been dead nearly a week before someone found them, plenty of time for Peter to kill them in Nebraska and find his way to Philly to murder her parents. But why?

It had to be Peter because nothing else made sense, but

she didn't understand why he would want to expose her, to punish her. William refused to give up details about Kiah, claiming the less Evie knew, the better. Which was probably true.

But it left her flapping in the wind trying to understand not just why Peter had done this but what he might do next. She felt better knowing that Nessa had some protection, that Cait and Maura went home to Finn and James every night, and that if push really came to shove, Declan wouldn't leave her side.

Although that was its own complication. One night with Declan had stirred up everything she hadn't let herself feel in a decade. The worst part was that she didn't mind nearly as much as she should have.

They were different now. Older, wiser, more mature. They could handle this like adults, enjoying each other's company until it was time to move on. She would go wherever was next after this, and he would go back to his life, and they'd part ways as friends. Simple as that.

When she reached the cross street, she paused, jogging in place. The rain had slowed to a gentle mist, and the sun filtered weakly through the thinning clouds. Soaked, she made the turn for home. A quick run was better than nothing.

Something seemed off as she jogged up the slight rise, and her eyes scanned the trees that lined the side of the road. There were no cars, no signs of anyone else out on the road, no birds chirping. It was quiet. Eerily so.

The road curved to the left and she followed it, moving out of the shade from the trees. A chill swept over her skin, and she stopped, turning a slow circle to scan her surroundings again. No one. There was no one there, but she couldn't shake that sensation.

Her breath quickened as she took off at a sprint toward the driveway, as much from exertion as anxiety. Someone was watching her. They had to be. Otherwise why did she suddenly feel so exposed, so vulnerable?

When the bottom of the driveway came into view, she pushed herself hard, feet slapping the pavement, and quickly punched in the code on the gate, skirting around it when it opened enough for her to slip through.

She didn't stop running until she reached the door, flinging herself against it in a bid to shove it open. She slammed it behind her and leaned her forehead against the wood, gasping for air while her heartbeat slowed.

Minutes ticked by, agonizingly slow, while she watched the patch of road she could see through the window. Nothing. No one drove or even walked by. Huffing out a relieved breath, she rubbed a hand over her chest. Christ, she was getting paranoid.

Chapter Twenty-Five

Declan waited impatiently for days for Brogan to find something useful on DiMarco's drive. The waiting was starting to piss him off. He'd even been working almost exclusively from home unless he had a meeting that pulled him into the city. He wanted to be close if Brogan did find something. Mostly.

It didn't hurt that working from home meant he could wander the house whenever he felt like it and find Evie somewhere. She was usually pecking away at her laptop, combing through the notes she'd made about Morocco, convinced Peter's silver bullet was somewhere in those pages.

Declan was as eager to get rid of Peter as Evie was, if not for entirely different reasons. She couldn't stop talking about getting back to her real life once Peter had been dealt with. It didn't matter how many nights she spent in his bed or how many glimpses he caught of the girl he'd loved; she seemed as eager to get away as he was to keep her.

And keep her was exactly what he wanted to do. She'd slipped through his grasp once, and he'd be damned if he'd let it happen again.

They still hadn't discussed whatever made her leave in the first place, something they'd eventually have to drag out into the light of day and deal with. They could focus on that later, though, once Peter was gone and they didn't have any more obstacles standing between them.

Unable to concentrate on the final project proposal from Rodriguez, Declan rose from behind the desk and went in search of the very thing he couldn't stop thinking about. Opening the door to his office, he nearly ran into Brogan, fist poised to knock.

"Good, you're not busy."

"You've got something?"

"It's something," Brogan agreed.

In his lair, Brogan had all of his screens up, an array of open files spread across each one. Each document was nothing but a series of random numbers and letters, listed in rows in three columns on every single page. At least a dozen pages.

Brogan dropped into his chair and swiveled toward the desk, dragging one image onto the biggest screen to enlarge it. Declan frowned. What the fuck was that?

"This," Brogan began, as if in response to Declan's unasked question, "is what every single document on this goddamn drive looks like."

Declan moved closer to study the combinations of numbers and letters. They seemed to be separated into groups of about ten, but other than that, he could see no rhyme or reason to any of it.

"Please tell me you know what the hell this means and your silence is for dramatic effect." When Brogan said nothing, Declan bit off a curse and turned to his brother. "Seriously? Nothing?"

Brogan highlighted the first column. "Best guess is that these are dates based on the number of characters and the dashes. I think these," he added, highlighting the second and third columns, "are locations."

"Why?"

"They look like coordinates. Longitude and latitude."

Declan looked closer and could make out the breakdown of each line. "Can't you run these through some program and unscramble them?"

"Despite what people with only a basic understanding of a smartphone and a search engine might believe, technology isn't magic."

Declan shot Brogan a warning glare. "I'm not interested in your mouth today. Can you figure it out or not?"

"Not. It's a cipher and not a common one. I tried those already. Without the specific key DiMarco uses to create this code, I can't tell you what it says."

"So we're exactly where we started."

Brogan arched a brow. "I wouldn't call dozens of hours of work nothing, but we don't have as much as I'd hoped we would. If I had to guess, these are lists of product he's moving from one location to another on certain days and times. What that product is, when it's being moved, or where? I couldn't tell you."

Declan's fingers curled into a fist. He allowed men to operate in his city, to run their drugs and their illegal fight rings and their stolen cars. They existed only by his good graces, and these bastards were pissing on his authority and rule with this cloak and dagger bullshit. That wouldn't last long for them.

"Brogan?"

"Yeah?"

"Find me another angle to work. If these pricks are up to something, I want to know what it is."

"On it."

The clacking of Brogan's keyboard followed Declan to the door, where he paused. "Anything on this Peter guy?"

"Ask your girlfriend," Brogan replied without looking up from his screen.

"What?"

"Evie was in here earlier, giving me some more info to look up. Not that I found much. Peter Waltzman is locked down tight."

"Hmm."

Declan jogged down the stairs to see Evie slipping her purse over her shoulder, keys in hand. "Where are you going?"

She turned slowly, a single eyebrow raised to let him know she didn't appreciate his tone.

He tried again. "I didn't know you had plans today."

"Cait called and invited me to lunch. I didn't know I had to clear it with the warden first."

"I only want you to be careful."

She patted his chest. "I'm always careful. And I'm packing."

He chuckled as she walked away. Christ, that woman drove him crazy. He scrubbed a hand over his face as he heard her car growl out of the driveway. Maybe getting out of the house would do him some good too. Go for a drive or grab a drink.

Except for Helen's constant reminders that she had plenty of things for him to sign at the office. Then there was that buyer Finn was trying to line up for their next shipment that he should check in on.

He sighed. There was always work to be done and a roof to keep over everyone's heads. At least he could ride into the office with the windows down.

Chapter Twenty-Six

"Oh my God, you're sleeping together."

Several heads at nearby tables turned at Cait's declaration.

"Jesus Christ, Caitlin," Evie hissed, dropping into her chair and smacking her friend's arm. "I don't think that was information the entire restaurant needed."

Cait leaned her elbows on the table, eyes glittering with excitement. "You are, though, aren't you?"

Evie sighed and cast her eyes to the ceiling. "We are."

"I knew it!" Cait squealed. "How could you not tell me?" she added, dropping her voice when heads swiveled in their direction again.

Snatching her glass as soon as the waiter filled it with water, Evie took a deep drink. "I haven't really seen you much."

Cait's eyes narrowed. "I live across the street."

"I don't know." Evie waved her hands in the air. "I'm out of practice at the whole friend thing."

"Well." Cait dropped her chin into her hand and wiggled her brows. "There's no time like the present."

Evie blinked.

"Oh, come on!" Cait protested. "I want details. Is it as good as you remember?"

Evie couldn't help but grin. "Better."

Picking up her menu to browse it, Cait chuckled. "I had no doubt. You don't exactly look well-rested."

"Thank you. That's so nice. In any case, I wouldn't think you'd need me to update you on Declan's sexual prowess. I'm sure his girlfriends have given you plenty of dirt over the years."

Evie hated the way the words twisted in her gut as she spoke them, but she plastered on a grin anyway.

"What?" she asked in response to Cait's amused smirk.

"Declan doesn't do girlfriends. I'm sure he's had lovers, but he does not bring them home. Ever. As far as I know, you're the only woman he's ever slept with at Glenmore House."

That couldn't be true. And so what if he had brought women home? It's not like she'd been wondering how many others had slept in the bed she now shared with him every night. Much.

"So what does he…"

Cait's voice trailed off, and Evie followed her gaze across the restaurant in time to see Maura weaving her way through the tables. She looked about as happy as Evie felt at the idea of a public exchange.

Maura stopped short next to the table, ignoring Evie to glare at Cait. "If you had told me she was going to be here, I wouldn't have come."

"Exactly," Cait replied. "This time it really is a setup. Now sit down. I said sit down," Cait snapped when Maura protested. "So help me God, Maura Elizabeth, if you don't sit, I will not hesitate to make you. If I can buckle a screaming toddler into a car seat, I can body check you into that chair."

Maura's gaze shifted to the chair Cait was pointing at, and she sank into it with a reluctant huff, muttering to herself as the waiter brought more water and a basket of warm bread.

"Now," Cait said when the waiter left with their order, "we're going to sit here until we sort this out or we die. Whichever one comes first. It's up to you two."

"There isn't anything to sort out. I'm done with her."

"This isn't going to work."

"I don't accept that." Cait shook her head. "Our whole lives we were sisters in everything but name. And sisters are supposed to love each other no matter what, forgive each other no matter what."

"It's irritating how nice you are sometimes."

"Yeah, for once can't you just be an asshole like the rest of us?" Maura agreed.

"Well, at least you two see eye to eye on something," Cait said brightly.

"It's a nice sentiment, Cait, but I can't forgive someone for abandoning me for ten years over something so stupid."

"Excuse me?"

For the first time, Maura met Evie's gaze with a hard stare. "I know you left because you didn't want to get married. And that's a shitty fucking reason to abandon everyone who loves you."

Well, that wasn't exactly the reason.

"It's not that simple. Christ, Maura," Evie added when Maura scoffed. "What do you want me to say? That I fucked up? Because I did. Everyone at this table knows that."

Evie hooked her thumb at Cait. "Even the nice one. My reasons for leaving made sense to me at the time, and you don't know how many times I've wished I could take it back, how many times I've wished I could undo it all. But I can't.

"So I've learned to live with it instead. To create a new life and a new normal and pretend I was happy because at some point it was easier to stay gone than to come back and try to fix it."

"Would you even be here if not for what happened to your parents?" Maura asked.

"Probably not. I hurt you," Evie admitted. "Both of you. All of you. And I'm sorry for that. I don't know if you believe that or not, but you didn't deserve what I did to you. Just like my parents didn't deserve to suffer for my bad choices."

"Evie," Cait whispered, reaching out to cover Evie's hand with hers.

Evie jerked her hand away and cleared her throat against the lump that had gathered. "The more I think about it, the more I realize if I had never left, I would never have gotten tangled up with Peter, and they would still be alive."

"That is not your fault."

"She's right," Maura said softly. "I'm still mad at you, but I could never tell you what happened to them is your fault because it isn't. It's Peter's and Peter's alone. You can't blame yourself."

A sad smile tugged at her lips, and Evie blinked back tears. "That's much easier said than done."

"Well," Cait began, giving Evie's hand a reassuring squeeze. "I'll be here to remind you as often as it takes."

"We will," Maura replied. "We'll remind you. Are you sleeping with Declan yet?"

The change in subject caught Evie off guard, and she nearly choked on her water while Cait laughed. "Is there a sign on my forehead or something?"

Maura grinned. "You look terrible, like you haven't been getting much sleep."

"She thinks Declan's had girlfriends," Cait added around a mouthful of bread.

"Oh, yeah, definitely not. The only thing Declan devoted himself to once you left was work."

It was amazing how easy it was to slip back into friendship with these two women who had always meant so much to her. There was still tension there, a lull of silence after an inside joke or a teasing remark before conversation resumed, but something had thawed in Maura and for that Evie was grateful.

At least now she could leave Philadelphia on good terms. Maybe she could even come back and visit every once in a while. She hadn't thought this would ever be possible and now, knowing it was, she didn't want to waste the opportunity to keep these people in her life for as long as they would have her.

Eventually the conversation drifted to the wedding, and Maura indulged Evie's questions about the ceremony and the flowers and the cake.

"It sounds like you took your childhood dream and made it a reality."

Maura's smile was dreamy. "I kind of did."

"God, you should see the dress," Cait breathed. "It's absolutely stunning. Miles of tulle and lace with the most beautiful beading on the bodice."

"Sounds exquisite."

"You should see it, actually," Maura agreed. "Ah," she shifted nervously in her seat. "My final dress fitting is in a few days. You should come. If you don't have any plans."

"I...um...no. I mean, no, I don't have plans," Evie added in a rush, satisfied when Maura's face relaxed from embarrassed to relieved. "I'd love to be there."

"Good." Maura smiled. "I've got to run, but Cait can give you my number, and I'll see you at the fitting."

"Yeah. Oh no," Evie added when Maura pulled out her wallet. "My treat."

"If I'd known you were going to buy lunch, I'd have made you apologize a lot sooner."

Evie chuckled as Maura left and turned to Cait, who had tears in her eyes. "If you start, I'm going to start."

Cait blinked rapidly. "Start what? I'm not starting anything. I've got to run, too, though. The nanny needs to go home early today. Evie," Cait added as she rose, "for however long you stay, I'm glad you're back."

"Me too," Evie murmured once she was alone.

Chapter Twenty-Seven

E vie sat in her car in the parking lot of the bridal boutique Maura had directed her to. The building may have undergone a makeover from red to white-washed brick, wooden railings and accents swapped out for wrought iron ones, but that hadn't erased the history.

The last time she'd been here was for her own final dress fitting what seemed like a lifetime ago now. She'd thought about chiding Cait for not warning her, but she knew as well as Cait likely did that if Evie had known ahead of time, she very well might not have come. Which meant the only thing she could do was get her ass out of the car and into the shop.

She fidgeted with the zipper pull on her purse. All this was so much easier to deal with when it was buried. Steeling herself, she climbed out of the car and crossed the parking lot, pushing into the shop with the tinkle of a bell.

It was bigger than she remembered, the walls lined with gowns in various cuts and shapes. Yards of satin and lace and tulle spilled from velvet hangers. They ranged in shades from blush pink to white, and Evie moved over to finger the lace sleeve of an ivory gown.

It wasn't that she hadn't wanted to get married, as Maura assumed. It was infinitely more complicated than that, because the truth was, she had wanted to marry Declan. At that time in her life, she'd never wanted anything more.

She'd known him since diapers and loved him since she was fifteen, but sometimes love wasn't enough. Sometimes you needed more. And when she found out that he couldn't give her more, she left. Not well, not in the right way, but that was a decision she couldn't change.

Now she was back—in his bed, in his arms, in his life. Everything she had carefully packed into boxes and shoved into the recesses of her mind was strewn across the floor now. There was nowhere to hide from it.

When she woke wrapped around him, when he made love to her, when he remembered exactly how she took her coffee or the way she liked her eggs, it unpacked a little more. Each moment was excruciatingly beautiful, knowing it was only temporary, that she still couldn't have it.

He had his life and she had hers, and eventually they'd have to get back to them. They were different now, going in different directions. Like everything else in her life, this was a fleeting stop before she moved on to something else. Except the thought of moving on had never bothered her before.

She caught the approach of one of the bridal consultants out of the corner of her eye and turned just as the woman stopped beside her.

"Can't go wrong with Lazaro. When is the happy day?"

Evie smiled. It's come and gone. "I'm actually here for the Kelly bridal party? For her final fitting?"

"Oh, of course. The bride isn't here yet, but her sister is." She led Evie to the back of the shop and into a separate seating area set up in front of a huge tri-fold mirror. "Can I get you something to drink? Sparkling water? Coffee? Champagne?"

"Ah, no, thank you."

"Oh, come on," Reagan said from behind them. "If you can't day drink champagne at a bridal shop, when can you?"

"I should have known you'd be the one with champagne in her hand. You always were the troublemaker."

Evie joined Reagan on the couch, studying Maura's little sister. She'd been a wild child in school, and it had surprised Evie to learn that the Reagan who'd always bucked authority ended up working for PPD.

"No crimes to solve today?"

"It's my day off. Which means when I'm done with this, I'll be solving crimes for the family instead."

Evie cocked her head at Reagan's tone. "You enjoy it. Working for both sides."

"Is that a question?" Reagan sipped her champagne, studying Evie over the rim. "No, I don't suppose it is. Yes, I enjoy it."

"Doesn't it get…confusing…working on both sides of the law?"

Reagan shrugged. "I like to think of it more like keeping my conscience clear. The more guys I help the city put in jail, the fewer Hail Marys I need to say for keeping some guys out. It's called balance."

Evie chuckled.

"Maura's glad you're back, you know. She doesn't know how to show it. I think a part of her doesn't want to be because of how you hurt her, but she's glad. Deep down inside, she's glad to see you again."

Evie didn't get a chance to answer before the curtain separating the seating area from the rest of the shop parted, and Maura entered, followed by her mother, Cait, and two women Evie didn't recognize.

"Evie," Alice Kelly said, moving to wrap Evie in a tight

hug. "You're a sight for sore eyes and as beautiful as ever. I'm so happy you're here."

Alice cupped Evie's face in her hands and pressed a kiss to her forehead the way she had when they were children, releasing her with a smile.

"Reagan Anne Kelly, why are you drinking champagne at two in the afternoon?"

Reagan downed the rest of the flute before her mother could take it away from her and grinned. "Because I'm not working today. Not officially anyway. I'm indulging a little, mother. So sue me. Besides, if the shop didn't want people to drink champagne at this hour, they shouldn't offer you champagne."

"Evie," Maura said, drawing her amused grin away from Alice and Reagan's exchange. "This is Becca and Trish. We work together at the hospital."

"Are you ER nurses too?" Evie asked, noting Maura's surprise at Evie's mention of her job.

"I am," Rebecca replied with a kind smile.

"I work in L&D. Labor and delivery," Trish said. "How do you know Maura?"

"Evie is a childhood friend."

Evie's heart squeezed at Maura's use of the word is and not was. That seemed like progress.

"Ok, you guys sit there, and I'm going to go try on this dress. If it doesn't fit, we revolt."

"If that thing doesn't fit after the way she's been complaining about her calorie intake for the last two months, I'll scream," Reagan muttered, earning a light smack from her mother.

When Maura emerged from the fitting room and stepped up on the dais, Evie's mouth fell open, tears gathering in her eyes.

"Holy shit," she breathed, making Reagan laugh.

Fluffing out the skirts, Maura grinned. "That's exactly the kind of reaction I'm going for from James." Maura lifted the white tulle overlay to reveal the blush pink satin skirt. "I wanted pink, but mom wanted white, so we compromised. I think the results are perfect."

"It's beautiful. You're beautiful," Evie added.

Maura turned to the mirror, and the consultant fluffed out the generous train while the seamstress checked the fit, adding a few pins and markers. Lace sleeves hung loosely across her upper arms, and the lace bodice was studded with white and blush beads that caught the light when Maura moved.

You could just make out the blush of the skirt under the tulle, which gave the dress an ethereal glow, like something straight out of a fairy tale. Lace appliqués on the overskirt added to the fantasy feel for a look that was completely and utterly Maura.

"I told you it was stunning," Cait whispered, nudging Evie with her elbow. "I'm glad you're here. I was worried you wouldn't come once you knew."

"I almost didn't. But I wouldn't miss this. Not after…after everything."

"Is it hard being here?" Cait wondered while Alice and Maura argued over what length veil was appropriate for a Catholic wedding.

The lie would have rolled neatly off her tongue, but she surprised herself with honesty instead. "Yes. It's not that I didn't want to marry him."

"I know. I never believed that, even when Declan and Maura clung to it."

"I get why they think that. It was complicated."

Cait nodded. "And being back doesn't make it any less complicated, does it?"

Evie smiled, amazed her friend knew her so well even

after all this time. "No, it doesn't. If anything, it makes it harder."

"Maybe it can be different this time." Cait's voice was full of hope. "Maybe you can work out whatever happened between you before, and it can be different, better than it was."

As quickly as the tiny spark of hope ignited in her chest, it extinguished. She couldn't afford wishful thinking. It would only make the inevitable harder. But she'd let Cait have it a bit longer.

"Maybe."

Evie hadn't known so many different headpieces existed until she watched Maura try on every single one of them with the veil she and her mother finally agreed on. In the end, she settled on a tiara that made her look every bit the princess she'd always dreamed of being on her wedding day.

Once Maura changed and rushed off to meet her wedding planner, they said their goodbyes and Evie walked to her car alone in the side parking lot. She waved to Cait, who honked as she pulled out.

As she drew closer to her car, she noticed something tucked under the windshield wiper. Probably a flyer for some charity. Lifting the wiper, she plucked it out before the wind took it and unfolded it, brows knitting together at the red letters that slashed across the page.

HE CAN'T PROTECT YOU FOREVER.

Evie's head jerked up, eyes scanning the parking lot. A group of women giggled and chatted as they entered the bridal shop, a couple of runners jogged by on the sidewalk that lined the street-facing side of the building, but no one looked out of place.

It had been nearly a week since anything happened. No movement, nothing threatening toward her or Nessa. Every potential lead she'd taken to Brogan had resulted in a dead-end. Peter was in the wind, and William was no help because he still refused to tell her anything about Kiah that might unlock something useful for them.

She was used to being able to put her hands on information any time she needed it. She thrived on details, anticipating what was coming, and planning for every eventuality. This felt more like she was stumbling around blind in the dark.

Folding the note carefully, she tucked it into her pocket, eyes alert as she slid behind the wheel and locked the doors. It wasn't a smoking gun on where to find Peter, but it was more than she'd had yesterday, and Declan was undoubtedly going to be interested in the fact that Peter had made contact again.

Chapter Twenty-Eight

Declan didn't notice it had gone dark until Helen buzzed him on the intercom asking if he wanted dinner sent up. He hadn't worked this late in weeks, and it felt good to lose himself in the drudgery of decision-making and contract signing.

Rebecca had come through on an even better deal than he'd anticipated for the new building, and he'd already called his architect to have him start drafting plans for the remodel. He'd finally inked a deal and cut a check with the councilman for the solar project.

The meeting with the tenant hoping for an expansion had gone well, and he'd agreed to foot the bill if she signed a five-year lease. Not the offer she'd been expecting, but one she happily accepted. He'd sent the details to the lawyer to draft a new contract.

Then there was DiMarco. Brogan still hadn't found him an angle to work, a button to press, a weakness to exploit. Andrea DiMarco kept his life as buttoned up as Declan did.

He'd shifted his patterns too. It had been gradual but

deliberate. They'd watched him long enough to notice the subtle change in routine. Declan wanted to know what the fuck this guy was up to. He didn't like being in the dark about what was going on in his own city.

He looked up at the knock on the door, motioning Helen forward when she poked her head in. She set a covered tray down on his desk and moved to the decanter on the cart by the window to pour him a glass of whiskey, setting it next to the tray.

"I haven't seen you working this late in a while. It's nice to have you back in the office."

Declan paused with the glass halfway to his mouth and set it back on the desk with a thunk, amber liquid sloshing up to the rim. He'd heard enough grumbling from Aidan about his seemingly declining work ethic, enough reminding from Sean not to let himself get distracted. He wasn't about to take shit from his assistant about it too.

"We're not behind on any deadlines that I'm aware of."

She caught the iciness in his tone, and her fingers jerked on the mail she was arranging into stacks on the edge of his desk.

"No. Everything is in order. I only meant that you don't normally work from home. I imagine it must be hard to concentrate there."

"Why would it be hard to concentrate?"

He could tell that she debated whether she should answer him or not. In the end, she decided not to evade a direct question.

"With your house guest."

"Helen, you're aware that who does and doesn't stay in my house is none of your business, correct?"

She carefully straightened the last stack of mail before placing her hands in her lap. "I'm aware."

"Presumably you're also aware that where I work is none of your business." He waited for her curt nod. "Good. Now that we've established that, I want to be very clear. If you no longer enjoy your job or the way I do mine, then I am no longer in need of your services. And I'd be happy to help you find a job elsewhere."

He watched her head dip, fingers clenched in her lap. "Well?"

"That won't be necessary."

"Wonderful." He pushed to his feet and reached for his jacket, sliding it on. "We've worked together for a long time, Helen, known each other for even longer. Don't confuse history with familiarity."

"You're not going to eat?" she asked when he crossed to the door.

"Suddenly I'm not hungry."

He slammed his office door behind him because it made him feel better and took the two flights of stairs down to the kitchen instead of the elevator. He wanted to go home and distract himself with Evie underneath him, naked and begging, so he drove to the club instead.

It was busy for a weeknight, but then it never mattered what day of the week it was. Reign was always busy. Even with the crowd, the bartender had a glass of whiskey waiting for him at the end of the bar as soon as she spotted him.

Climbing the stairs to the VIP lounge, he let himself get lost in the thumping bass and the neon lights. Nodding at the bouncer who let him in without hesitating, he wound his way around to the booth he always kept reserved for himself in the back corner.

The dance floor below teemed with scantily clad women and men who reeked of booze and too much cologne, hoping to get lucky. In the past, when he'd needed to work out his frustrations, he'd choose someone—maybe the blonde in the too-tight sequined dress that showed off the rounded curve of her breasts or the voluptuous brunette with her siren-red lips—and take them back to the apartment he kept in the city.

Not to the house, never to the house as Aidan often did. His father had taught him that mistresses and one-night stands never crossed the threshold of Glenmore House. So he'd take them to his penthouse apartment, fuck them until they were both sated, and send them on their way.

But that was before Evie O'Brian reappeared in this life with her gold-flecked eyes and wild curls. Before he was reminded of everything he'd been missing all these years.

Since he was sixteen, it had only ever been Evie for him. No one had ever come close to matching her, not that he'd let anyone try. The longer Evie stayed, the more he let himself believe in a future he'd closed the door on a long time ago.

He knew it was probably smarter to let her go, to leave the door closed and let whatever they had between them now be enough. But he wanted more with her. He'd always wanted more with Evie.

Annoyed with himself, Declan tossed the rest of his whiskey back and set the empty glass on a nearby table. Turning from the balcony, he saw Aidan sitting in one of the circular booths, two women draped all over him in dresses so low cut they were one deep breath from being topless.

Declan cast his eyes to the ceiling. There was the asshole who'd been lecturing him about work ethic, drunk at—he checked the time on his watch—ten o'clock and dry humping two women whose names Declan would bet money he didn't even know.

"Declan!" Aidan shouted over the music when he spotted his brother, a stupid half-drunk grin plastered on his face. "Come join us!"

The blonde on Aidan's right uncurled herself from his

side and crossed to Declan with a sultry smile, taking his hand and tugging him toward their booth.

"Ladies, you know my brother, Declan." Aidan circled his finger in the air for the waitress to signal he wanted another round.

"It's barely ten and you're already hammered."

"Half hammered," Aidan insisted, waving his brother's scowl away. "You're too uptight, man. Why not have a drink and a woman"—he chuckled as the redhead still curled around him leaned in to nibble his earlobe—"and relax."

"He's cut off," Declan said, motioning to Aidan when the waitress returned with a tray of drinks. "And them too." He pointed to the two women while Aidan protested.

Aidan shoved to his feet, swaying a little at the sudden movement and weaving behind Declan to the top of the stairs. "What the fuck is your problem? You never have any fun, so now no one gets to have any?"

"My problem is that it's ten o'clock on a Wednesday and you're hammered and dry humping two bimbos in my club! Try making yourself useful for a change."

"Christ, Evie's got you so pussy whipped it's embarrassing."

Declan spun around and grabbed Aidan by the shirt, shoving him back against the wall and up onto his tiptoes to the sound of gasps from nearby patrons.

"At some point, little brother, you're going to have to grow the fuck up. You will not speak about Evie that way again, or we'll have bigger problems than you pouting about being cut off. And if you value your life, don't step foot in my fucking house tonight."

Releasing his brother to readjust his shirt and his pride, Declan jogged down the stairs and out into the cool night air. Slamming into his Range Rover, he took the winding, tree-lined roads toward home.

He heard Evie before he saw her. Music blaring from the back of the house led him through the living room, down the hall, and into the solarium. When he stepped into the doorway, she was singing at the top of her lungs as she danced around the room.

She caught his reflection in the windows and whirled to face him, all smiles as she pointed her finger at him and sang the chorus to a song he didn't know. When it ended, she pressed a button on the speaker, and a slow song came on. All his tension melted away when she crooked a finger at him and he joined her in the middle of the room.

They didn't speak as he wrapped his arms around her waist, drawing her close, and she laid her head on his shoulder. He buried his face in her hair, breathing in the soft, sweet scent of her. He remembered her smelling of peaches when they were younger, but now it was more a heady mix of vanilla and some spice he couldn't name.

The song faded into another one, and she slid her hand up to cup the back of his neck, pulling back to look up at him.

"What's wrong?"

"What makes you think something's wrong?"

"Because," she began, brushing her thumb across the curve of his jaw, "when you're upset, this muscle ticks in your jaw, and it was ticking when I first saw you standing there."

He leaned down and pressed his forehead against hers. "Is it ticking now?"

She smiled. "No."

"Then nothing's wrong. How was your day?"

"It was good. Maura invited me to her final dress fitting. It's absolutely gorgeous, and she looks gorgeous in it. And then I…oh! I almost completely forgot. Wait here."

She darted out of his arms, and he was left alone with the woman singing about an ordinary world from the speaker. When Evie returned, she was holding a slip of folded-up paper. She handed it to him, reaching down to silence the music.

He unfolded it, eyes narrowing on the message. *He can't protect you forever.*

"What is this?"

"It's the note I found on my car."

His head jerked up and he studied her face. "When did you find this?"

"This afternoon. When I left the boutique after the fitting."

"Why didn't you tell me?"

He could tell his tone was sharp by the way she lifted a brow then frowned. "I am telling you. This is me telling you."

He crumpled the note in his fist then smoothed it out again. "I mean, why didn't you tell me sooner?"

Her jaw tightened. "What were you going to do? Rush down there and run a handwriting analysis?"

Declan scowled, reading the note again. She had all day to text him about this, and he hadn't heard a word from her. "If this had happened ten years ago, you would have told me immediately. I don't know why you still don't trust me."

"I think the better question is why don't you trust me?" She held her arms out to the side. "I don't know if you've noticed, but I'm not the same girl I was ten years ago, Declan. I don't come running to you with every problem anymore because I don't need to."

She dropped her arms with an exasperated snort. "You keep trying to force me into this perfect image you have of me. Do you want to get to know the person I am now? Or do you keep hoping the girl I used to be will magically appear? Because if that's what you're waiting for, you're going to be disappointed. She's gone, and she isn't coming back."

Without another word, she turned on her heel and left the room. Declan squeezed the note in his fist and tossed it across the room. Fuck. Had he been putting her into a box? Probably.

Memories were all he had of her, all he saw when he looked at her. If he didn't want to fuck this up, he was going to have to stop seeing the past and start seeing what was right in front of him.

Chapter Twenty-Nine

S he heard him step into her room, catching his reflection in the mirror over her shoulder when he stopped in the doorway to the bathroom. The fact that he looked at least a little chastised made her feel slightly less pissed off.

"I want to show you something," he murmured.

"Is it an apology?" She made eye contact in the mirror while she rubbed moisturizer into her skin. "That's about the only thing you need to say right now."

"Please?"

She sighed, turning to face him and placing her hand in his outstretched one. He guided her up the stairs to the third floor, but instead of turning toward Brogan's lair, he led her down the hall to where the old library used to be.

He turned the knob and led her inside. When he flipped on the lights, her breath caught in the back of her throat.

She'd discovered this room one rainy summer day when Declan had been called away by his father to do something for the syndicate and she'd been left to her own devices. It had been covered in a layer of dust, what little furniture it had draped with white sheets. The few books that remained on the shelves had been in terrible condition.

She'd brought a few old journals downstairs and asked Marta about them. Inside the journals were pages and pages of short stories written by Faith Callahan, Declan's great-grandmother.

She'd shown the journals to Declan when he got home, and all she'd been able to talk about for months after was the library and how she wanted to restore it to its former glory, maybe even expand it into the empty room next to it.

There'd be a place for reading in front of the fireplace, a cozy window seat, a drawing desk where she could sketch, and floor-to-ceiling bookshelves lined with books in every genre. He'd taken her dream and made it real.

The library, exactly as she'd pictured it in her head, stretched before her. He'd even knocked down the wall between the adjoining room to make one big space. The window seat was stacked with pillows in her favorite colors, the rug under the seating area swirled with greens and golds.

When she turned to face him, he was staring at her. "You did this from memory?" He nodded. "When?"

"A couple years ago."

"A couple…"

She did a slow turn, taking in the room again, and noticed a glass case tucked into the corner. When she approached it, she recognized Faith's journals inside. One of them lay flipped open to the story that had always been her favorite, about a woman who fled west seeking escape and adventure and the man who'd followed her because he loved her.

"I have kept you in a box," Declan said, drawing her attention. "I didn't know where else to keep you."

She moved to stand in front of him while he weighed his words carefully.

"When my father died, Aidan wanted to turn this room

into a home theater. Take out the windows, tear down the bookcases. But I couldn't let this room go. It felt like the last tangible thing I had to remind me of you."

He reached up to cup her face, brushing the pad of his thumb across her cheek. "I couldn't tear down the last thing I had of you. So I rebuilt it instead. I made it into something new, something uniquely you, for you. Even if you never saw it."

When a tear slipped down her cheek, he leaned in to kiss it away. "I see the girl you were sometimes, the one who was quick to laugh or tease. She's there under the razor-sharp wit and calculating gaze. But you're so much more than the girl you were, Evie. And I want to know you."

She pushed onto her toes, pulling his lips down to meet hers in a kiss that was soft and sweet. Her body tingled when his hands moved to her waist, his fingertips playing over the skin at the small of her back.

She didn't know why the library meant so much to her, but it did. Not just the fact that he had taken something she was passionate about and brought it to life, but that he had remembered all the little details.

Sliding her hands down his neck, she pushed at the lapels of his jacket, easing it off his shoulders and arms and onto the floor. He deepened the kiss then, his hands gliding up her back as his tongue swept against hers. She broke it momentarily so he could lift her shirt off, then pulled him in again, hungry for him.

When his hands palmed her breasts, squeezing them through the fabric of her bra, she groaned against his lips. Her fingers trembled as she tugged his shirt free, undoing the long line of buttons until she revealed the smooth, hard plane of his chest.

She ran her fingernails across him lightly, catching his nipple and eliciting a groan that made her smile. He ducked his head, sucking her nipple between his lips through her bra, and she dropped her head back with a needy sigh.

When he backed her toward one of the overstuffed chairs that flanked the fireplace, she turned, pushing him into it instead and dropping to her knees between his legs. She watched his light blue eyes go sapphire as she slid her hands up his thighs, brushing her fingertips over the hard length of his cock, making his hips jerk.

She watched him while she undid his belt and the button of his pants, tugging down the zipper. When her fingers wrapped around his shaft, he groaned, and when she swirled her tongue around his tip, his hands gripped the armrests of the chair so hard she thought he might break them.

She worked him with her mouth, using her tongue and fingers to lick and squeeze. When she pulled back to nibble his tip, he rocked his hips, pushing his shaft into her mouth with a groan.

"Evie," he panted, reaching out to fist his hand in her hair as he slowly pumped in and out of her mouth.

When he could resist her no longer, he pulled her up, kissing her roughly, his teeth scraping across her lower lip. Evie helped him work her leggings down over her hips and off, straddling him while he unhooked her bra and captured her nipple between his teeth.

She hissed, raking her nails across his shoulders. Reaching down between them to grip his shaft, she stroked him before guiding him inside her and sinking down onto his length with a groan.

The slow pace was torture, but the sensations that rippled through her with each deliberate thrust were addictive. When he moved his hands to her hips in an effort to quicken their pace, she held them trapped against her thighs and rode him slow and deep, grinding her hips against his.

She guided his hand to her clit, gasping when he circled

his finger around it. She moved faster, urgently, desperate for her own release as his fingers pressed, pinched, teased her clit.

When he leaned forward to suck her nipple into his mouth again, his hand gripping her thigh, she came undone in his arms, body shuddering against his as he followed her over the edge. Collapsing against him, she pressed a kiss to the side of his neck, breath ragged.

"You just keep getting better and better," he murmured against her ear, making her laugh. He twirled a curl around his finger while his hand lazily stroked up and down her back. "Tell me how many places you've lived and which one was your favorite."

His words wrapped around her heart and squeezed at the wall she'd built there, exposing a crack. When she answered, the tiniest bit of hope slithered through and took root. Maybe Cait was right after all, and things could be different this time.

Chapter Thirty

"And he wants to renegotiate his rate."

Declan turned from the window to look at Finn, who was stretched out in one of the chairs that faced his desk.

"Renegotiate it to what?"

"Three fifty each."

Declan laughed, tossing the stress ball he held from one hand to the other. "He's insane. I could call up two guys right now and get a better deal than that. And a faster turnaround time too."

"That's what I told him," Finn replied. "He didn't back down, though. Seemed to think he had the upper hand and could sell to someone else in the city if he wanted to."

"He'll find out the hard way that isn't true."

"And when he does?"

"I guess he'll be up shit's creek trying to offload his weapons to someone else. I'm not interested in being black-mailed. Contact Erickson. See what kind of product he's moving these days."

"Last I heard, he'd moved on to heavy machinery and preferred to work in the Middle East. What about Michaels?"

"Yeah. And Gregor. Cover all our bases."

"You hear that Aisling Donahue is being promoted to detective?"

Declan grinned, dropping into the chair next to Finn's. "I did. Be nice to have another detective in the family. I'm sure her mother will throw some kind of party. I'd send Aidan, but he's likely to put his dick somewhere it doesn't belong. Maybe I'll make an appearance."

"You should take Evie."

Declan eyed his brother. "Not you too."

"Me too, what?"

"If I have to listen to another lecture about my relationship with Evie, someone is going to get shot."

"I'm not lecturing." Finn chuckled. "I'm not! People like Evie, they always have. She makes you look like a real person instead of a tyrant. So if you're going to go, take her so you don't make people nervous."

"Maybe I want people to look at me like I'm a tyrant. A little fear never hurt anyone."

Finn snorted. "How's that going, by the way?"

"Are we going to braid each other's hair and talk about girls now?"

"Oh, so it's serious," Finn replied to Declan's sarcasm. "That's interesting."

"It's also none of your business," Declan snapped.

"I wouldn't say that. My son can't hold the future of the Callahan syndicate up by himself forever. You're going to have to get busy making little Declans sometime."

"So everyone keeps reminding me," he mumbled.

Finn slapped Declan on the shoulder. "I like her. Cait's been devising ways to get her to stay since she first ran into her. I'm sure you two could come up with something."

"Mmm."

Declan was saved from answering when Helen knocked then poked her head in. "I'm sorry to interrupt, but someone left a note for you with the hostess. They said it was urgent."

Helen placed the note into Declan's outstretched hand and then left, closing the door quietly behind her. He quickly ran his finger under the sealed flap of the envelope and slid out a piece of stationery with the initials EG at the top.

Evie O'Brian is in danger, the looping script read. *She's got a fifty thousand dollar bounty on her head the Italians are eager to collect. Watch your back.*

Declan shot to his feet and crossed the office in two quick strides, yanking open the door. "When did they leave this note?"

Startled, Helen jerked around to face him. "Amy said she sent it right up. So less than five minutes ago."

Declan slammed the door and stalked back to his desk, throwing the note at Finn as he reached for his phone and punched in Brogan's number. Finn bit off a curse.

"It's not signed. You think this is legit?"

"We're about to find out. Brogan," Declan said when his brother answered, "I need you to pull up the security cameras in the lobby of Breá from about five minutes ago."

His tone brooked no argument, and he could hear Brogan sprinting up the stairs seconds before the clacking of keys.

"Someone dropped a note off to the hostess." Declan paced in the silence, rage twining with fear in his chest.

"Got her. A woman, blonde, curvy. I can only see her profile, but she hands a sealed envelope to the hostess and leans in to whisper something. Hang on." More clicking. "She's Italian."

Stopping short, he demanded, "How do you know?"

"She's got a Giordano tattoo on her forearm."

Declan disconnected the call, shoving his phone into his

pocket. "It's legit," he said to Finn as he crossed to the door. "I've got to find Evie."

"Shit. Fuck." Finn followed him out the door. "She's at the park right now. The one closest to our house."

"How do you know that?" Declan asked, slamming into the stairwell and taking the stairs two at a time.

"Because she's there with my wife and kid."

Evie hefted the bag Cait pointed to from the trunk of her Escalade with a grunt. "Jesus, woman. Do you have bricks in here?"

"Jesus, woman!" Evan shouted as he ran down the grassy hill from the car to the playground.

Evie's eyes widened, glancing at Cait. "Oh my God. I'm so sorry."

Waving a hand in the air, Cait laughed as she hit the button to close the automatic door. "I promise you he hears much worse from Finn."

They followed Evan down the gentle slope to one of the picnic tables that ringed the play area, and Evie dropped the bag on the table with a dull thud, huffing out a breath.

"I'm going to have to do more pushups or something," she said, massaging her biceps. "Running isn't going to cut it if I'm going to be hauling your crap around all the time."

"I greatly appreciate your assistance," Cait said as she pulled containers of food out and set them on the table, one eye watching Evan climb the stairs to the slide. "Maura should be on her way. I didn't think you'd mind," Cait added, looking away from Evan.

"No, of course not. I thought the fitting went well."

"Very well. Great job, Evan!" she yelled as Evan jumped

off the end of the slide, arms raised in triumph before racing up the stairs again. "Speak of the devil."

Evie looked up to see Maura making her way through the grass in a pretty purple sundress that complemented her red hair.

"You look like a mermaid," Evie said with a grin.

Maura did a little turn before sliding onto the seat next to Cait. "I bought one of these in white for the honeymoon. Thought I'd give it a test run."

"Where are you two going?" Evie picked up a piece of pineapple from one of the containers and popped it into her mouth.

"Paris," Maura sighed. "For two whole weeks."

"Oh, you'll love it there. Do you still like Napoleon pastries?"

"Oh God," Maura groaned. "More than anything."

"Visit Amelie in Bastille. Best one in Paris. But don't call it a Napoleon or they'll laugh you out of the patisserie. Ask for a *mille-feuille*."

"I'm writing that down," Maura said, quickly typing on her phone. "What else?"

"The opera house. It's not a huge draw for tourists, so it shouldn't be too busy. You can wander, but the guided tours are great. Definitely do a boat café or restaurant. The food is always fabulous."

Evie tilted her head, considering. "James might like the catacombs. Very creepy down there, and the guides tell good ghost stories. Really though just eat all the food. If you haven't come back twenty pounds heavier, it's like you didn't even try."

Maura laughed and dropped her phone into her bag. "Duly noted. Before I lose my nerve, I wanted to give you this." She pulled an embossed envelope out of her bag and pushed it across the table to Evie.

Evie flipped it over and pried out the unsealed flap, pulling out a wedding invitation, the swirling font inviting her and a guest to attend. She looked up at Maura in shock.

"Declan would have brought you as his plus one to the wedding with or without this, but I wanted you to know, without a doubt, that I want you there."

Evie knuckled away a tear, reaching across the table to grip Maura's outstretched hand. "I wouldn't miss it for the world. Thank you."

"I didn't realize it was the one thing that was missing until I heard you were back in town. Frankly, it pissed me off that I still missed you," she added with a chuckle.

"I get that. I think missing you guys, home, all of this was what brought me back to New York. I didn't really think about it until now, but I had this restlessness living in Europe I couldn't shake. So I came back as close as I dared."

"And re-established communication with your mom."

"Yeah. I wish I had done that a long time ago."

Cait reached out and covered Evie and Maura's joined hands with her own, giving them both a squeeze.

"Aunt Evie!" Evan exclaimed, breathless as he raced over with something clenched in his fist. "I found this for you." He held out his hand, palm up, opening his fingers to reveal a flat gray pebble that sparkled when he wiggled his fingers. "It's pretty like you!"

"Oh wow! Thank you!" Evie took the pebble and set it on the table, rolling it around with her finger so the sun caught the flecks of quartz. "It's my most favorite pebble."

Evan beamed. "You're welcome! Bye, Aunt Evie!"

"Well, that's adorable." Evie rubbed her thumb across the pebble before slipping it into her pocket. "You make cute kids, Cait."

"James and I want to start trying as soon as we get married. I already technically went off the pill."

"You didn't tell me that!" Cait nudged Maura with her shoulder. "Finn and I are trying again too. It took so long to get pregnant with Evan, so we figured we'd get a jump on it."

"Speaking of marriage and babies," Maura said, and Evie's eyebrows shot up. "How are things with you and Declan?"

"That's quite a leap."

Maura cocked her head. "Is it, though?"

Evie looked to Cait to intervene, but her traitorous friend only grinned. "Things are fine. Though definitely not marriage and baby level fine."

"Do you want them to be?"

Did she? "No."

"You hesitated." Maura extended a finger to point at Evie, lips twitching in a barely contained grin.

"What? No, I didn't."

"You totally did," Cait agreed.

"He just…did you know about the library?"

Cait's smile was dreamy. "Yeah. I thought it was so romantic. Why? You didn't like it?"

"No, I liked it. I liked it so much I had sex with him in there. Three times."

"That's impressive."

Evie rolled her eyes at Maura. "The problem is, though, it doesn't change what happened ten years ago."

"What do you mean?"

"I mean, ten years ago he had a chance to be the person I needed him to be, and he blew it."

"People change. Careful, Evan!" Maura yelled when Evan came a little too close to falling off the balance beam.

"I don't want to hope for that. It's easier not to."

"Why?"

"Because," Evie replied, "if you don't hope, you can't be disappointed."

"Do you love him?"

Evie refused to meet Cait's gaze. She couldn't, because she already knew the answer. She'd known it since the moment the door had swung in on the library. "Yes," she replied softly. "I'm not sure I ever really stopped."

"Maybe that's enough for now. The feeling is there, so you might as well let it be. Focus on Peter until he's dealt with, and you can figure everything else out later."

"How's everything going with that, by the way? With the whole Peter situation?" Maura wondered.

Evie blew out a breath. "Seems like he's escalating. After I found that note, Nessa called to say she thought someone had been in her house when she was out. She would come home and find things moved around. At first she thought she was being forgetful, but…Declan upped her security to round the clock. She's not happy about it, but I'd rather err on the side of caution."

"That's smart. Better to have nothing happen at all than something happen and no one is there to protect her."

"Yeah," Evie agreed, nodding to Maura. "I just…feel so helpless. I don't know what I'm missing. Peter's hidden his identity as well as I've hidden mine. How do you find a ghost?"

"Have y—"

When a child started wailing, they all turned their heads in unison to see Evan flat on his back next to the balance beam that was a few inches off the ground. When Cait rose, Maura put a hand on her arm.

"I'll get him."

Cait kept her eyes on Evan as Maura scooped him up. "She's right, you know. Love can be enough for now. Don't think about the past, don't worry about the future, just enjoy whatever the moment has to offer. Besides," she added, smiling when Maura tickled a laugh out of Evan, "with everything going on with Peter, now is a terrible time to make life choices."

"You're probably right."

Evie tilted her head, studying a car on its fifth loop around the parking lot despite there being plenty of open spaces. It was a dark-colored, late model sedan with tinted windows too dark to make out the driver. They could be circling, waiting for someone, but it struck her as odd.

She waited for it to slow again as it completed the loop. Reaching for her phone to take down the plate number, she was distracted by the black SUV that screeched into the parking lot. When she looked back again, the sedan was gone.

She tensed when she recognized Declan's Range Rover seconds before he got out, Finn following from the passenger side. Something was wrong.

"Cait, get Evan and Maura."

"We're here," Maura said, breathless as she bounced a giggling Evan on her hip.

"You're okay," Finn said, reaching for his son and pulling Cait close, pressing a kiss to the top of her head. "Thank Christ."

The look on Declan's face made Evie nervous. "What's going on?"

Declan cupped her face in his hands, pressing a soft kiss to her lips. "We need to get out of the open."

"Why?" Maura wondered, voice shaky.

"Because someone put a hit out on Evie."

Evie jerked in Declan's arms. "They what?"

"Come on," Declan said, looping his arm around Evie's waist as Cait and Maura stuffed everything back into the bag. "I'll tell you what I know back at the house. Is your car here?"

Evie shook her head, fighting to keep her voice even. "No. No, I rode with Cait."

"Mine is," Maura replied. "I can follow you back to the house."

"I'd prefer if you rode with us," Evie said, looking up at Declan, who nodded.

"I'll send someone to get your car," Declan promised, ushering them all toward the parking lot, eyes scanning their surroundings.

The drive back to the house was fast, and they rode it in silence. Finn left a hungry Evan in the kitchen with Marta before joining the rest of them in Declan's office.

"This is Peter," Evie said once the door was closed. "It has to be."

"Why?" Brogan wondered. "I thought his goal was to burn all your aliases."

"His goal," Evie replied, pacing in front of the window, "is to kill me. I very much doubt he cares about the means. God, what if it was him in that car?"

Declan came around his desk to stand in front of Evie, gripping her shoulders to keep her still. "What car?"

"There was this car, navy blue or black maybe. It looped the parking lot five or six times. There were plenty of spaces, so it seemed weird. I was going to take down the plate just before you showed up. When I tried to find it again, it was gone."

Declan looked at Brogan.

"Yeah, I might be able to get a plate from security cameras if there are any."

"You're going to hate this," Declan said, giving Evie's shoulders a squeeze. "But I don't want you going anywhere alone until we've got this guy."

"I think I can live with that," Evie said, hating the shakiness in her own voice.

"Finn, I want to put a security detail at the restaurant and extra bouncers at the club. The house should be secure,"

Declan added, waiting for Brogan's nod. "But it wouldn't hurt to make sure security is tight here too."

James burst through the door, followed quickly by Aidan and Sean.

"What the hell is going on?" James demanded, wrapping Maura up in a hug.

"Someone put a hit out on Evie with the Italians."

"That's bold," Sean said.

"And very stupid," Declan agreed. "We've got plans for extra security. You can get the details from Finn."

"Let me get Cait and Evan settled at home first, then we can meet at the club. Aidan?"

"I'll make the calls."

"My car is still at the park," Maura said as everyone filed out.

"I'll drop you and James off on my way," Sean replied.

When they were alone again, Evie collapsed against Declan's chest, suddenly exhausted, and wrapped her arms around his waist.

"What if we don't get him?" she whispered, voice hoarse.

"We will," Declan assured her, pressing his cheek against the top of her head and holding on tight. "I swear it."

Chapter Thirty-One

When she jolted awake, it was dark, and her eyes took a minute to adjust. Declan slept on his side, curled away from her, and she was glad her nightmare hadn't woken him.

Peter had been quiet for two days. No more notes, no more threats. Brogan had been monitoring communications between the Italians as much as he could. He had some theories on who they might task with the hit, but so far no one had made a move.

Not that Declan had given them much opportunity. He'd kept her close, working from home though he hadn't done much work. The sense of urgency in the house was palpable, and Evie hated knowing people she loved were in the crosshairs because of her.

She turned to study Declan in the dim light, the lean muscles of his back and the Celtic tree of life tattoo that spread across his shoulder and wrapped around his bicep. Resisting the urge to trace it with her finger, she rolled out of bed, hand searching in the dark for her shirt. When she pulled Declan's button-down from the floor, she slipped her arms through it, holding it closed as she stepped out onto the balcony.

It was warm for early May, and she could smell the rain in the forecast, but the stone was cool under her feet, and she let the sensation clear out the rest of her nightmare. She hated this helpless feeling, this not knowing. It clawed at her throat until she felt like she couldn't breathe.

She sensed more than heard Declan join her on the balcony, leaning back against him when he wrapped his arms around her and pressed a kiss to the top of her head.

"He isn't going to win this."

She kept her eyes fixed on the trees as the sky slowly lightened, casting the world in somber gray. "You don't know that."

"I do." He turned her slowly in his arms, lifting her chin so their eyes met. "Because I know you and how strong you are. And I know I will do whatever it takes to make sure you're safe. No lengths are too great, no body count is too high, no amount of money is too much. This isn't over until his blood is on my hands."

The thought was oddly comforting. "I made my bed. Maybe I should lie in it."

Declan scowled. "Don't parrot Aidan. He's young and stupid and selfish. And he has no idea what he's talking about. You are not in this alone, Evie."

For the first time in a long time, she didn't feel alone. The crack in the wall around her heart widened as hope swelled a bit more. But…

"Why should you have to clean up my mess?"

His hand gripped the back of her neck, tilting her head up, eyes searching hers. "You know why," he said before bringing his lips down against hers in a kiss that stole her breath and sent heat racing along her skin.

He backed her against the railing, one hand fisted in her

hair while the other slid under his shirt and cupped her breast, squeezing as his thumb circled her nipple.

He lifted her up, setting her on the cool stone, but she could feel only him and the fire he ignited inside her. Wrapping her legs around his waist, she drew him in tight against her. He was already hard, wanting, as his mouth swept over hers and she tilted her head back and let him take.

He pushed the shirt off her shoulders, exposing her breasts to the cool air so her nipples hardened. When he brushed his fingertips against them, she gasped, arching her hips against his and eliciting a growl from low in his throat that made her feel heady, powerful.

As the sun peeked through the trees, he slipped inside her, coaxing a groan from her lips. She let the thoughts that plagued her drain from her head and gave in to the sensations that filled her. The slow, steady thrust of his hips, the feel of his teeth grazing across the column of her throat, the way his palm cupped her breast, the shivers he sent through her as he circled her nipple with his thumb.

And when he took them both over the edge, she knew she didn't want to be anywhere but here in his arms, whatever the future held.

Still inside her, he trailed his lips lazily up the side of her neck and across her jaw to her lips, kissing her softly.

"Let's get out of the house for a bit and go to the club tonight."

"Really? What about the—"

"Italians, I know. There's plenty of security there, and I'll get some men to follow us there and back if it'll make you feel better." He tucked a strand of hair behind her ear. "You'll go insane if you stay cooped up in this house much longer."

She chuckled softly. "It wasn't that long ago that you were all but threatening to keep me prisoner."

He kissed the tip of her nose. "Times change."

She wrapped her arms around his neck. "Yes, they do."

"Now come back to bed."

"I'm not really that tired anymore."

He grinned, lifting her off the railing and turning back toward the bedroom. "Sleep wasn't exactly what I had in mind."

That evening Evie stood in front of the mirror and tugged on the hem of the dress Cait had let her borrow. The deep burgundy brought out the green in her eyes as Cait said it would, but the skintight dress left absolutely nothing to the imagination.

The knee-length dress hit Evie high on the thigh since she was so much taller than her friend, and the criss-cross halter top stretched across her breasts, leaving a small keyhole cutout that revealed smooth, pale skin. She hadn't even been able to wear any underwear with the damn thing.

Twisting, she checked that the pins she'd shoved into her messy braided bun were holding, deciding that a few loose tendrils only added to the look. The purple and gray shadow she'd smudged onto her lids enhanced her eyes even more than the dress, and she'd opted for a nude lip to keep the focus where she wanted it.

She had to admit that she killed in this dress, but Cait's advice to tell Declan she loved him was making her nervous. She pressed a hand to her belly as she stepped out of the bathroom, shutting off the light. It was a big step, and they were words she couldn't take back.

However Declan responded, those three words would alter her future. It was no small thing to say them. She fixed silver chandelier earrings into her ears and slipped on a pair of black stilettos.

The smoldering look he gave her when he saw her walking down the stairs, eyes raking up and down her body, quieted the butterflies. It was all white-hot heat and desperate need, and it made her mouth water. Surely a man who looked at her like that could handle the three simplest words in the English language.

"I changed my mind," he growled when she stopped in front of him. "We should stay home so I can tell you every-thing I'm going to do to you while I remove that dress and then show you."

"That is a deliciously tempting offer, Mr. Callahan, but," she braced a hand on his chest when he moved to kiss her, "it took me an embarrassingly long time to shimmy into this thing, and I am not taking it off again until someone besides you sees me in it."

As if on cue, Brogan strolled into the foyer holding a very large sandwich in one hand and a can of soda in the other. He whistled in appreciation, grinning when Declan shot him a look.

"Someone you're not related to," she added before Declan could point out that Brogan met her terms.

"Fine. It'll give me more time to make a longer list," Declan murmured, grabbing his keys and following her out the door.

The line for Reign snaked around the side of the building while broad, towering bouncers manned velvet ropes and fended off flirting women begging to get inside. At the sight of Declan, they unhooked the rope and let them pass, nodding at them both.

Inside, people thronged the dance floor, writhing bodies grinding to the beat from the DJ that was cast in neon lights on a small stage. More neon lights bounced around, reflecting off the chrome and glass, their colors changing in a mesmer-izing kaleidoscope. The music hummed through her like electricity as Declan shouldered his way to the stairs that led up to the VIP lounge on the second floor.

The lounge ringed the first floor on three sides, offering a great vantage point of the dance floor and the DJ. Large half-circle booths lined the space, each with a set of sheer curtains that could be pulled for at least an illusion of privacy. A thin illusion, she thought as Declan led her past two women making out while a third woman watched.

They stopped at a booth that had a reserved sign, and she scooted around the table, sinking into the soft leather. The music seemed muted in the protection of the booth, and she was impressed at the thought that had been put into the design.

"So Breá and Reign. How much of the city do you own, exactly?" she asked once the waitress took their drink order.

"Enough."

She laughed. "This is what you always wanted. The empire. Is it everything you thought it would be?"

His stare was intense, and she shivered. "Almost. Even until his death, my father didn't really understand the vision I had for the syndicate. I think he always assumed these businesses were an excuse to get out of my duties to the family."

"But they're so much more than that. They're a gateway into levels of society you can't reach underground."

He smiled as their waitress set their drinks on the table and left. "You were the only one who ever really understood what I was trying to do."

"How did he die? Your father."

"A freak accident. He ran off the road during an ice storm and wrapped his car around a tree. I imagine going out like that probably pissed him off." He chuckled. "It felt weird to realize I was an orphan."

"Do you miss her?"

"My mom? I don't know. Aidan is still big on celebrating

her birthday every year, so I guess it comes up from time to time. But I wouldn't say it was a constant ache. It won't be like that for you forever."

"I know." She sighed. "Tell me something about you I don't know."

He lifted a brow at her over the rim of his whiskey glass. "How could there possibly be anything about me you don't know?"

"Ten years is a long time for things to happen to you that I don't know about."

He twirled his glass on the table, thinking. "I hate sharks."

She threw her head back with a laugh. "How can you hate sharks? Have you ever met a shark?"

"Why do I have to meet a shark to decide I don't like them? What, I'm going to have a conversation with one and suddenly change my mind?"

She chuckled again. "Okay, fine. You can hate sharks. Although I think they get a bad rap. I went cage diving with sharks in New Zealand once. It was amazing."

"Were you there for work?"

"No." She shook her head. "Just for fun. I was living in Dublin at the time and desperately wanted to get away from the winter. So I fled to New Zealand for a few weeks, got a nice tan, met some sharks."

He reached up to wrap one of her curls that had fallen loose from her bun around his finger. "You are fascinating. What are you thinking right now?"

"That I'm not wearing anything under this dress."

His eyes darkened and he slid closer to her, thigh brushing against hers as he leaned down to skim his teeth across her bare shoulder. "What else are you thinking?"

"All the sinful things I want to do to you."

He slid his hand up her leg, fingernails scratching lightly against her inner thigh. When his fingers found her bare, as promised, and wet, she had to swallow a groan. He pressed against her, his fingertip stroking her clit in slow, deliberate motions.

She tried to wriggle her skirt up so she could spread her legs wider, but he held her in place, slipping a finger inside her and capturing her moan with his lips. He pumped his finger in and out, thumb circling her clit in painfully slow circles that sent shock waves through her.

Her fingernails dug into his thigh as his lips brushed her earlobe, tugging it between his teeth before whispering, "I want to feel you come for me."

Her breath hitched, and her hips jerked against his hand as he fingered her faster, his tongue and teeth working the sensitive skin behind her earlobe. He pressed and circled and rubbed her clit, his lips trailing across her jaw to her lips as she shuddered.

And when she came apart in his hand, he stroked her to another orgasm until she dropped her forehead to his shoulder with ragged breaths. He slipped his hand out from between her thighs, eyes locked on hers as he slid his finger into his mouth, licking it clean.

"You could have told me that," she said as her breathing returned to normal.

"Told you what?"

"That you know how to drive me crazy like that. When I asked about something I didn't know about you."

He chuckled, gripping her chin in his hand and pressing a kiss to her lips. "If you don't know that by now, you aren't paying attention."

She shivered as much from his words as the electricity that still hummed through her from his touch.

"Dance with me."

"What?"

He scooted around the edge of the booth and stood, holding out his hand to her. "Dance with me."

"I prefer to dance in the privacy of four walls and no one watching."

"We can dance in private later too."

She caught her lip between her teeth, sliding out the other side of the booth and taking his hand.

"I hope that's a promise."

He laughed, leading her back down the stairs and onto the dance floor and the throng of bodies, wrapping his arms around her waist and pulling her tight against him.

She let herself get lost in the pulse of the bass and the neon lights. For a few glorious moments, she let all the stress and the guilt and the anxiety about Peter and her parents and her growing feelings for Declan melt away.

All that mattered was this exact moment and the feel of his hands on her hips, the heat of his chest against her back, and the energy of the crowd that ebbed and flowed around them to the music.

When the song changed, she spun in his arms, linking her hands around his neck. It was rare for her to catch a glimpse of the boy she'd known, but she saw him then in his indulgent smile, the way one side of his mouth quirked up higher than the other and the edge of his eyebrow lifted ever so slightly.

Her heart swelled, and she leaned up to press her lips against his ear. "Declan, I l—"

She froze at the face she saw in the crowd of people lining the dance floor. Peter. But just as quickly as he was there, he was gone, and she tried to convince herself she'd imagined it. It wasn't real. He couldn't really be there, watching them.

Declan sensed her stillness and his hands tightened on her waist. When he stepped back and caught sight of her face, his confusion turned to concern.

"What's wrong?" he shouted over the music.

"Peter!" she yelled, and his whole body went taut as he spun to scan the crowd.

He gripped her hand, flagging down two bouncers to walk them to the car. They waited while he helped her in and buckled her seatbelt for her when her fingers trembled. Declan waited for the lead car to pull out before following, and once they were on the road, he pulled out his phone.

"Finn. Call Brogan and Aidan and have them meet us at your house. We need to talk. Evie saw Peter at the club tonight." He glanced over at her when she rubbed at her arms to warm them. "I know. We're twenty minutes out."

He disconnected the call and tossed his phone onto the console, reaching for her hand and twining his fingers with hers. "You're okay, Evie. I've got you."

Chapter Thirty-Two

As soon as they walked in, Declan could sense the worry in the house, confirmed by the way Cait threw her arms around Evie and wouldn't let go.

"I'm fine," Evie promised, running her hand down Cait's back.

"You're freezing. Come on. I'll make some tea."

He followed Evie and Cait down the hall to the kitchen where his brothers waited. Their murmured conversation stopped when they walked in, and Finn straightened.

"He didn't try to make contact?"

Evie shook her head while Cait fluttered around, setting the kettle on and pulling mugs down from the cabinet. When Evie rubbed her arms, he slipped his jacket off and set it around her shoulders.

"No. I just…he…we were…"

"Breathe," Declan instructed, squeezing her arms and rubbing warmth into them.

"I didn't expect to just…see him there. It felt…"

"Exposed?" Brogan offered.

"Yeah." Evie nodded, taking the mug Cait handed her and

wrapping her fingers around it. "Exposed. We were dancing, the music was loud, there were people everywhere. And then he was just…there. It's like his face appeared for the barest of seconds and then it was gone. Like he melted back into the crowd."

"It's the closest he's come that we know of," Declan said.

"So why didn't he make contact?"

Finn shrugged. "It's Friday night. The place was packed. He can't afford that many witnesses."

"What's he even doing here, though?" Aidan wondered.

"I think we all know the answer to that." Declan's stare was unamused.

"No, what I mean is, why would he put a bounty on her head and then show up to do the job himself?"

"Maybe he's too impatient to wait."

"Maybe." Aidan shrugged. "But people willing to drop fifty grand on a hit generally have a bit more patience."

"I don't think the why he's here matters nearly as much as the what the fuck we're going to do about it."

Declan nodded, happy to see some color coming back into Evie's cheeks. "I agree. I don't want to sit around and wait for this asshole to take his shot. If he's here, he's staying somewhere."

"Under an alias, obviously." Finn looked to Brogan.

"Definitely not using Peter Walztman. I've had that name flagged at airports, bus terminals, train stations, car rentals, you name it, in case he decided to show. Nothing so far."

"Okay, we need to back this up. You did a job for him in Morocco, right? And something went south?" Evie nodded. "If that's your only connection with him, then there's got to be something in there, some detail we're missing to figure out who he is or why he's after you."

Evie shook her head. "I feel like I've been through it a million times. I don't know what I'm not seeing."

"Take us through it again," Finn insisted. "As many details as you can remember."

Declan reached for her hand when she hesitated, giving it a soft squeeze.

"I got a call from William about a job, a lucrative one. He's not my only contact who funnels clients my way, but he does usually manage to find the highest-paying ones.

"I was living in Europe then, in Vienna, and a quick jump to Africa sounded fun, so I took it. I met him in person in Rome to collect payment and get the file about a month before."

"You met him?"

Evie shot a look at Declan. "Yeah. It's not unusual for some people to want to meet. Some clients want the plausible deniability of never seeing you face to face, and some clients want to look you in the eyes and make sure you're not going to screw them. I thought Peter was the latter. I left that meeting never wanting to meet another client in person, though."

"Why?" Cait wondered.

"He creeped me the fuck out. From the moment he arrived he gave me a bad feeling. I should have walked away right then and turned down the job."

"But you didn't."

"No, the payout was too good. I'm talking millions of dollars for stealing a suitcase's worth of vases from a museum collection."

"You stole from a museum?"

Declan pressed a kiss to the top of her head. "No one is judging you here."

"I'm kind of impressed," Finn replied, coaxing a wan smile out of her.

"I flew private because it's easier security, and I stayed in a suite at the Royal Mansour in Marrakech. The file made it sound like I'd be in and out in a matter of days, but the schedule was wrong."

"What schedule?" Brogan asked.

"The file Peter gave me had a delivery schedule of when the pieces I needed were going to be coming into the museum, but it wasn't even close to accurate. I had to wait weeks for the shipments to start arriving, and even then, they didn't arrive in the right order."

"Is that normal? To get so much information about a job?" Cait wondered.

Evie shook her head. "No. But I thought the guy was really thorough or something, and with everything that happened after, I just wanted to be done with it, so I didn't dig into it any further. I told Will I wouldn't take any other jobs from him and left it at that."

"So the schedule was probably a setup. What else? That's a lot of time to kill when you only expected to be there for a few days."

Evie's fingers stilled on her forehead, and she jerked her head up to meet Declan's gaze.

"What?"

"Well"—she shifted in her seat—"there was one way I found to pass the time. A waiter."

Declan tensed, his hand tightening on hers, but he forced himself to relax. Every detail was important. Even if he'd rather gouge his eye out with a rusty spoon than listen to her talk about one of her lovers.

"Go ahead." He gave her hand a reassuring squeeze, lips curving when she squeezed back.

"I'd been there for nearly a week, and I was getting bored. Bored and pissed off that it was taking so damn long. I called Will that day and told him if the shipments didn't start arriving soon, I was gone, and I was keeping the deposit."

"Where did you call him from?"

Evie frowned. "My hotel room, I think? No." She shook her head. "From a restaurant. I was sitting at an outside table when I called him. I told him I was wasting time and bleeding money, and if a shipment didn't arrive by the next day, I was done. Almost as soon as I hung up with William, he came over to take my order."

Declan shared a knowing look with Brogan.

"God, I feel so stupid that I never put it together before."

"What next? How'd you go from waiter and patron to lovers?"

"Is that really necessary?" Evie wondered.

"Yes," Declan replied softly.

Evie sighed. "I don't know. He was hot. I was bored. His English was better than my Arabic, and he flirted with me. We left together at the end of his shift and went back to my hotel room. The next day a shipment came in."

"But you were there for another two weeks after that."

"Yeah." Evie shook her head. "They came sporadically every few days. I thought it was weird, but the file said it was a rare collection of artifacts, so I figured maybe the museum was being overly cautious by staggering the shipments."

"It's possible. Not likely," Brogan added, "but possible."

"Whenever there was a lull in shipments, I'd spend my free time with Ahmet." She frowned, rubbing her forehead again.

"What is it?" Finn prompted when she didn't continue.

"One night, toward the end of the trip, we were walking back from this street fair he took me to. Someone recognized him and stopped us, but they didn't call him Ahmet. They called him Demir."

"What did he do?"

Evie glanced at Finn. "He played the whole thing off like the guy was mistaken. They were talking in Arabic, so it's not like I could understand them anyway. Ahmet walked me back to my hotel and dropped me off. I didn't really have much time to think about it because the final shipment was scheduled to arrive two days later. So I spent the next thirty-six hours going over my plans and my escape route."

She snorted. "I'm such an idiot. The whole thing was a setup from start to fucking finish. He was probably sending that shit into the museum from a private collection. Everything about it was a parade of red flags that I ignored. Even the police response was suspicious."

"Suspicious how?"

"It was too fast." She shoved her hands through her hair. "Moroccan cops do not respond to anything quickly, but they were there within minutes, sirens blaring."

"Like someone called in a tip?"

Evie nodded at Declan. "Exactly like that. But I looked like any other tourist lugging a suitcase into an airport taxi, and they didn't even give me a second glance."

"If he wanted you dead," Brogan said, "why not just kill you? Why go to all the trouble of setting you up?"

"Because I don't think he wanted me dead. At least not then. I think he wanted to toy with me."

"Or to get a feel for how you worked. Watch you in action, maybe?"

"Maybe. So what now? How does that help us?"

Brogan rose from his seat at the kitchen table. "The name of this waiter is another thread to pull we haven't tried before. Do you remember the name of the restaurant?"

"Salama. Which is ironic."

"Why?" Cait asked, setting dishes into the sink.

"Because it means peace."

Declan let Cait fuss over Evie for a few minutes more before pulling her away. He could see the exhaustion in Evie's eyes. Seeing Peter had shaken her tonight, and he wanted nothing more than to tuck her into bed and hold her while she slept.

Alone in his bedroom, he helped her out of her dress, tossing it over a nearby chair while she stepped into the bathroom to get ready for bed. He hadn't commented on the fact that she'd gradually moved some of her things into his bathroom over the last few weeks, her bottles of lotions and creams lined up on the other side of the sink that had always been meant for her. The maids had even started hanging her clothes up in his closet, though she still had a few things in her room.

He was already in bed when she flicked off the light in the bathroom and crossed to the bed. She slid under the covers with a sigh, and he reached over to turn off the light, plunging the room into darkness. Turning onto his side, he pulled her back against him, pressing a kiss to her shoulder.

He lay awake, his arm cradling her head and breathing in the scent of her until he felt her slip into sleep, her body fully relaxing. He would do whatever it took to keep her safe. Even if it meant sacrificing himself.

Chapter Thirty-Three

He found Evie on the balcony the following evening, tucked into the corner of the sofa, one leg stretched out and one propped up, a glass of wine dangling from her hand. Her eyes were closed, but she smiled.

"Hi."

Her eyes fluttered open, and the look she gave him arrowed straight to his heart. "Hi."

She wore a sweater against the chill, and when he sat down next to her, she laid her legs across his lap.

"Anything?"

"Nothing yet."

She sighed, taking a sip of her wine before offering him the glass. "I don't think I should go to the wedding tomorrow."

He nodded. He'd been waiting all day for her to bring this up. He wanted to tell her she was being ridiculous, that nothing was going to happen, but he knew her concern wasn't for herself. It was for Maura and her wedding day.

"I'll stay home with you."

She looked at him, surprised. "You can't do that."

He raised a brow as he took a sip. "Why not?"

"Because it's a syndicate wedding, a family wedding. We both know that's important."

"You're important."

She reached for the glass, setting it on the table before sliding onto his lap and pressing her cheek against his. "This is more important. I'll be fine here, and Maura will understand. Besides, I'd hate for anything to upstage her on her wedding day."

She ran her fingers through his hair. "Just make sure you bring me a piece of cake."

He laughed, wrapping his arms around her and pressing a kiss to her temple. "Just the cake?"

"Mmm, maybe a flower arrangement from one of the tables. They sound lovely."

"Deal. I don't like the idea of you being here by yourself all day."

"What's the worst that could happen?"

He took a deep breath and released it slowly. He was trying not to think about it. Brogan had been diligently working on tugging those leads, holed up in his lair since last night. It was best not to disturb him when he was in the zone.

Declan knew when Brogan had something he would let them know, but the waiting was killing him. He wanted all of this to be over so he could get on with the next phase of his plan. He didn't want anything hanging over their heads when he asked her to marry him.

"Richard Feinman." Brogan hurried onto the balcony, eyes bright with excitement.

"What?" Evie said.

"Peter. His real name is Richard Feinman."

Evie shoved off Declan's lap, snatching the paper Brogan held out. "How can you be sure?"

"Your buddy Ahmet. Turns out his real name is Demir

226

Yavuz." He handed over a photo of a man with bright green eyes and a stubbly beard. "He received a series of payments a little over a year ago from a Richard Feinman, an American expat living in Naples."

"Naples," Evie murmured, glancing at Declan when he stepped closer to peer at the photo.

"Yeah. A week before you arrived in Morocco, the payments switched to coming from our buddy Peter, so Richard got wise to his paper trail, I'm guessing."

"And where is Demir now?" Declan wondered.

"Dead. He died in a tragic bike accident two days after you left Marrakech."

"Tying up loose ends."

"My thoughts. This"—Brogan pulled another photo out of the stack and passed it to Evie—"is Richard Feinman."

Evie sucked in a sharp breath. "That's him. I've only ever known him as a brunette, but that's him."

The man that stared back at them from the photo had sharp features and a tight-lipped smile, but he resembled Evie's drawing perfectly. "He looks just like your sketch. Who's the woman?"

"His wife," Brogan replied.

As if noticing her for the first time, Evie studied the petite blonde with straight hair swinging to her shoulders. She looked the opposite of Feinman in every way, including her wide, genuine smile.

"I know her," Evie murmured.

"How?"

She looked up at Brogan. "You said they lived in Naples?"

"For about five years. No kids, but she was an interior designer, and he owned a bunch of real estate."

"I did a job for her. About ten or so months before Morocco."

She sank down onto the edge of the sofa, and Declan

joined her, taking the picture from her hands to study it. "What job?"

"She wanted a little marble statue of Venus that belonged to a billionaire with a summer villa in Capri. She met me for the hand-off herself and said something about giving it to her husband for their anniversary."

Brogan frowned, taking the picture back from Evie and shuffling it into the stack. "Why pay someone to steal something like that when you could just have one commissioned?"

"I have no idea why the super-rich like to have what isn't theirs. I only care about getting paid and not getting caught."

"Where is he now?" Declan asked.

"I can't find any other known associated aliases with Feinman's name, so if I had to guess, I'd say he's probably operating under his real name in the States. He has no reason to suspect we'd be able to connect the dots, and he could fly completely under the radar in the US that way. He's got a secure bank account I'm trying to get into to see where he's spending his money."

"What if he's using cash?"

Brogan crossed to the door. "Hopefully he's dumber than that."

When they were alone again, Evie got up to pace in the shaft of light that streamed from the bedroom.

"We're close, Evie. The closest we've been. We need one last piece of the puzzle, and we've got him."

"I know that." She turned to face him, and he was surprised at the wide grin on her face. "This might actually be over soon." She laughed, and the sound floated around him. "I was starting to mentally prepare myself to go on the run like Kiah did."

"You what?" The thought made his heart stutter in his chest.

"I wasn't going to sit here and wait around for him to

strike. To kill someone else I loved. I've lived life as a ghost for a long time, but…"

He cupped her face in his hands. "But?"

"But I didn't want to. The thought made me sick to my stomach. I would have, no doubt about it. If that's what it would have taken, I'd have done it. But I'd have hated every minute of it. Every minute…" her voice caught. "Every minute away from you."

"I'd never have let you go."

She grinned, eyebrows raised. "Who says you could have stopped me?"

He chuckled, sliding his hand down to her lower back and pulling her closer. "I guess we'll never have to find out."

She rose on her tiptoes and pressed a soft kiss against his lips. "I guess not."

Declan lifted her into his arms and carried her into the bedroom, kicking the door to the balcony shut, closing out the crisp night air and the man who watched from the trees.

Chapter Thirty-Four

E vie was jolted awake by the ear-shattering shriek of the alarm. She sat up, covering her ears with her hands as Declan reached for the light.

"What the fuck makes the alarm go off?" she yelled over the shrill warning tone.

"Someone forcing a door, motion, shattering glass. I'll go check the house."

"I'll go with you."

"No," he pressed a quick kiss to her lips. "Stay where I know you're safe."

She watched him roll out of bed and pull on a pair of sweats, reaching into the nightstand to pull out a handgun and flick off the safety. He raced out, and she reached over to turn on the light on her side of the bed.

When the alarm finally stopped shrieking, she shook her head to clear it and slid off the mattress, quickly dressing. The silence was just as deafening as the alarm had been. It was probably nothing. An animal or Aidan coming in drunk.

She moved to the door to peer out into the night, leaping back on a strangled scream when a face peered back at her.

She turned on her heel to run, tripping over the leg of a chair when the glass of the balcony door shattered behind her.

She rolled to face the door, not wanting to leave her back exposed, eyes darting for anything close enough she could use as a weapon.

"Hello, Evelyn. I've been looking for you."

Evie looked up to see him standing just inside the door, dressed all in black, a sinister grin on his face. She scrambled to her feet and took small, slow steps backward to put distance between them.

"You've gone back to blonde, I see," she said, flicking a glance at the door. If she could scramble across the bed fast enough, she might be able to make a run for it.

"The brown was a nice touch, though, wasn't it?" He ran a hand through his hair, taking a step forward as if reading her thoughts.

"It wasn't my favorite, but then I can't say I care one way or the other, Peter. Or do you prefer Richard?"

Heart pounding, knowing she'd thrown him off by using his real name, she launched herself toward the bed, but he was faster, leaping toward her and yanking her back by her hair, chuckling when she cried out.

"Now, now," he tsked. "I only want to talk. We have a lot to discuss, you and I," he whispered in her ear.

"I have nothing to say to you," she spat, struggling against his hold on her.

He held a gun up, tracing a line down her cheek with the muzzle, and she stilled. "I thought that might change your mind. You took something very precious from me, and I have some things to…get off my chest." He traced the shape of her breast with the gun, and she swallowed against the nausea that threatened to choke her.

"Evelyn? Do you remember your last trip to Italy?"

"You mean meeting you for that farce of a Morocco job?"

231

"No, the one before that," he replied, grinning against her cheek.

She hissed when he gripped her hair tighter. "That was a long time ago."

"Nineteen months and twenty-six days, to be exact. That's how long it's been since you stole the kindest, most giving person the world has ever known."

"Debatable," Evie gritted out, "considering she was paying me to steal something."

"Such a mouth on you," Peter said, pressing the gun into her cheek.

"She was perfectly fine when she left with her statue and I left with my money."

"Except she didn't make it home perfectly fine, did she?" Peter demanded, yanking her hair. Evie stumbled back a step. "She never made it home at all. And if not for you and your fucking statue, she would've never been on that road, never been in the path of that driver who fell asleep at the wheel, never been ejected from the car and pinned underneath it."

Evie tilted her head away when he pressed the gun painfully into her cheek, but he moved his hand to her throat, holding her in place. That's what this whole thing was about? A vendetta over his wife's accidental death? How was she supposed to convince a madman who'd spent years hunting her that she hadn't killed his dead wife?

Declan swept each room of the first floor while Brogan took the basement. Everything from the kitchen to the solarium was in pristine condition. Not a throw pillow or photo out of place. Confused and pissed off about being jerked out of sleep for nothing, he met a shirtless and alert Brogan on the stairs.

"Anything?" Declan asked.

"Yeah, someone threw a rock through the patio door."

Brogan passed the rock to Declan, who turned it over in his hands. When he saw the words scrawled across it in red, he froze. *She's mine.*

"Fuck." Fear squeezed Declan's heart like a vice when the realization hit him. "Brogan, call Aidan and go get Finn. Now!"

Without waiting for his brother to respond, Declan sprinted for the stairs. If that bastard laid a hand on Evie, he would pay a thousand times over.

They both heard Declan's footsteps at the same time, and Peter grinned. "Looks like lover boy is about to join us."

When Declan stepped into the doorway, Evie saw the murder flash through his eyes, the fear, but she didn't see the gun. When he saw her gaze dip down to his hands and back up to his face, he nodded ever so slightly.

"You should let go of her," Declan warned.

"Or what?" Peter leaned close to Evie, inhaling the scent of her hair. "This doesn't concern you, but I suppose you can stay. Hands where I can see them. That's it," he added when Declan held his hands up, palms out. "Now where were we?"

"We were talking about how you're delusional."

Peter tightened his grip on her throat, squeezing until she sputtered. "I said stay back!" he screamed, pressing the gun to Evie's temple when Declan took another step into the room. "You move again, and she fucking dies. Which would really disappoint me because I want to take my time with her."

"Declan." Evie coughed, her fingers clawing at Peter's hand. "I'm okay."

"See?" Peter's laugh was tinged with madness. "She's fine!" He loosened his grip on her throat but didn't remove his hand.

"I would have found you a lot faster if Kiah hadn't stiffed me."

"Kiah?"

"I paid her to find you, and she took my money and ran."

"So you punished her."

"Of course. I couldn't let her get away with that. She was much easier to find than you have been, though. She couldn't stay away from that hick brother of hers and his horse-faced wife."

"So you killed them too? As punishment?"

He shrugged. "Enough about them. Let's talk about us."

"There is no us."

He leaned down to trace his tongue over her earlobe, and she shuddered. "Of course there is, my dear. We have a history. I've spent so much money looking for you. Not that it matters," he continued. "My Anna was worth everything to me. There's no amount of money I wouldn't have spent to make you pay."

"I didn't kill your wife," Evie rasped. "The other driver did."

"Well, he's dead, now isn't he? Can't kill a dead guy. But you, you're right here. Living, breathing." Peter's gaze slid to Declan. "Fucking. Maybe killing you isn't enough. Maybe you should watch your lover die first." He raised his arm, leveling the gun at Declan's chest.

"No! No, you don't have to do this."

"I mean, I know I don't *have* to." Peter chuckled. "But it might be fun for me! Tell me, do you love him?"

"What?"

"It's a simple question. Do you love him?" He punctuated each word with a wave of the gun.

She held Declan's gaze, heart pounding. "Yes. Yes, I love him."

"Good."

He took aim at Declan again, and she shoved her hand up into his elbow. The bullet missed its target, instead firing into the ceiling above Declan's head. When Peter swung at her, she ducked, driving her elbow into his stomach and knocking him back a few steps.

She could hear Declan scrambling behind her, lunging forward and shoving her behind his back. When Peter raised his gun again, Declan brought his arm down hard against Peter's elbow, and she heard a sickening crack that had Peter screaming, the gun clattering onto the floor.

Evie dove for it at the same time Peter did, and they both scrambled for the weapon. Evie hissed at the pain in her side from the glass as she skidded across the floor, kicking out at Peter when he gripped her foot and tried to yank her away.

Before he could put his hands on her again, Declan gripped Peter by the back of his shirt and hauled him to his feet, punching him in the face. Peter's head snapped back, and he reached up with his good arm to cradle his bloody, broken nose.

Evie pushed to her feet, gun in hand, as Peter fell to his knees and Declan took aim. Peter looked past Declan to Evie, the blood from his nose coating his teeth when he grinned at her, eyes wild.

Heart pounding in her ears, she watched Declan shoot him once, twice, a third time in the center of his chest, Declan shoving her back when he lurched forward. Rolling onto his back, Peter pulled his hand away from his chest, staring in awe at the blood that covered his fingers.

"Anna," he breathed as the life left his eyes.

On a choked sob, Evie stumbled forward, and Declan turned in time to catch her, wrapping his arm around her before she collapsed. Standing over Peter, eyes dark and ruthless, Declan leveled his gun and put a bullet through the center of Peter's forehead.

When they heard pounding footsteps in the hallway, Evie jerked, gripping Declan's arm tighter. "It's okay. It's just Brogan and Finn."

"Son of a fucking bitch," Finn cursed, sliding into the doorway. "If that fucker isn't dead, I'll shoot him myself."

"He's dead," Declan said, holding Evie tightly.

"You're bleeding," Brogan pointed out. "There's a first aid kit in the kitchen, and I'll call the doc."

"Go with Brogan. I'll be right down," he promised when Evie only stared at him.

"I don't...I don't want to go without you."

Declan pressed his forehead against hers. "Okay," he said softly. "Finn, call McGee to come get that son of a bitch out of my house and clean up this mess. I want it to look perfect before the sun's up."

By the time they made it down to the kitchen, Evie had color back in her cheeks, and she felt a little steadier on her feet. Declan guided her to a chair at the kitchen table as Brogan went to find the first aid kit and call the doc.

"So you love me, huh?" he asked softly.

Her lips twitched at the corners. "Well, it's not how I wanted to tell you, but I guess it got the job done." When she looked up at him, her expression sobered, and she swallowed around the lump in her throat. "I love you, Declan."

Cupping her cheek, he leaned his forehead against hers. "I love you too."

Chapter Thirty-Five

They fussed over her and she let them. Marta insisted on working even though it was her day off, and Evie could tell she was worried. No harm in letting the woman keep her hands busy making breakfast for the steady stream of men that wandered in and out. Every so often she poked her head into the living room to see if they needed anything.

Declan wouldn't leave her side as much to be close as to keep her from going back upstairs to see for herself—to make sure once and for all—that Peter was dead. When McGee and his crew arrived, Declan had coaxed her into the living room, curling up with her on the couch.

Somewhere in the recesses of her mind, his overprotectiveness bothered her. She was sure of it. But for now, she was comforted by the warmth of him at her back and the lazy circles he drew up and down her arm with his fingertips while he worked from his phone with his free hand. Every so often he would take a break and press his cheek against the top of her head, almost as if he was making sure she was still real, still safe.

The incessant noise of drills and industrial vacuum cleaners had been going on for over an hour, and she knew they'd taken Peter's body out when she heard the metallic clang of a stretcher as it hit the hardwood floor. She tightened her fingers around her coffee mug at the thought, taking a sip to let the warmth spread through her. She was ok. She was safe. Peter was dead.

She'd been repeating that in the silence ever since Declan had cleaned and bandaged her scrapes, kissed her bruises. She'd known it would end in death; there was no other option. The thing that bothered her wasn't that Peter was dead or that she had watched Declan kill him. It was that she didn't feel nearly as bothered by it as she expected to be. She felt…free.

She looked to the door at the sound of her name, so faint over the noise that she wasn't sure anyone had really said it. She glanced at Declan to see if he'd heard it too. When she heard it again, he looked up. Okay, so she wasn't imagining it. That was good.

"I will not leave! You tell me where Evie O'Brian is right fucking now!"

Cait sounded distraught, near to tears as she argued with whoever was running security in the front hall. Evie pushed off the couch, setting her mug on the coffee table before going out into the hall.

"Cait!" Evie called, making her friend spin.

Sprinting toward her without a word, Cait launched herself at Evie, squeezing her with impressive strength. "Evie, thank God." Cait's voice was thick with tears. "Finn said you were okay and not to worry, but…but I had to see for myself."

Cait stepped away to look her up and down, eyes lingering on the purpling bruise around her neck where Peter's hand had squeezed.

"He—"

"I'm fine," Evie soothed. "He's in much worse shape. I promise you."

Cait wrapped her arm around Evie's waist and turned to Declan. "He'd better be deader than dead."

"Four bullets will do that to a guy."

Cait sniffed. "Good."

"I'm going to give you two a minute." He stopped next to Evie, leaning down to press a lingering kiss against her lips. "Stay put."

"Are we back to the prisoner thing again?"

He grinned. "Only because I love you."

Cait's eyes were wide as she watched Declan leave, and Evie reclaimed her seat on the couch.

"Okay, well, we'll come back to that. You're okay?" Cait asked, sinking into the spot next to her. "I mean aside from…" she fluttered her fingers at Evie's throat.

"My throat's a little sore, some cuts and scrapes on my side from the broken glass. But other than that, I'm fine."

"Okay. Good. That's good. I would have been over sooner, but I had to wait for my mom to come over to watch Evan. I'm so glad you're okay," she added, voice breaking.

"I feel like I'm maybe too okay."

"What do you mean?"

"I just watched Declan beat and kill a man. I would have killed him myself if given the opportunity and a clear shot. Why am I not more upset? More shaken?"

"You killed a murderer, Evie. A man who was hunting you, who wanted to destroy you. Maybe it says something about me, but I'm not going to be shedding any tears over the loss of that guy, and you shouldn't either."

She reached for Cait's hand just as they both heard running feet pounding down the hall. Evie tensed. Maybe she wasn't as fine as she thought. When Maura skidded into the doorway, she let out the breath she'd been holding with a huff.

"Maura? What are you doing here? Shouldn't you be getting ready for your wedding?"

"Oh, shut up," Maura said, rushing across the room and dropping onto the couch to throw her arms around Evie. "James told me what happened." She sat back, eyes wet with tears. "I've never been so scared in my life."

Maura's eyes dropped to Evie's throat, and she gasped, reaching up to trace the outline of a fingertip with her own. "That fucking bastard."

"He's dead," Cait confirmed.

"He'd damn well better be. What the hell happened?"

Evie took a sip of her now-cold coffee, setting it on the table before wiggling back against the cushions and waiting for Maura and Cait to settle in beside her.

"It's like it happened impossibly fast and excruciatingly slow all at once. The alarm woke me up out of a dead sleep."

"The security alarm?"

Evie nodded. "Shrill and screaming. Declan went to check it out and told me to stay put."

Cait squeezed Evie's arm. "Finn would have told me to do the same."

"When Declan left, I got up and got dressed. And when the alarm finally stopped, the house was eerily quiet."

"You don't have to tell us," Maura said when Evie rubbed at her forehead.

"No, I think it helps. I walked over to the balcony doors to look out the window, just trying to calm my nerves. It took me a minute to see his face, but he was right there. Staring back at me. He busted in the door, I'm not even sure how, and there was glass flying everywhere. And then he was there. And I was in the room alone with him."

Telling it was easier than she anticipated. Reliving it

helped her put it into focus. It helped remind her that it was exactly as Cait said—they'd killed a murderer who would have killed her without flinching if he'd gotten the chance.

"He did all that because he wanted to blame you for his wife's car accident?"

Evie nodded.

"Jesus, what a psychopath. You know it wasn't your fault, right? Her accident?"

"Actually, I do know that. He needed to blame somebody, to make them pay, and he convinced himself if she'd never met me, she'd still be alive."

"It's all very tragic, but we still hate him."

"We absolutely do," Cait agreed. "Now can we go back to the part where Declan said I love you?"

Maura's mouth fell open. "He what?"

"It's true," Declan said from the doorway, making them all jump. "But she said it first."

Evie shook her head, chuckling as her friends looked from her to Declan and back again. "I promise to tell you all about it sometime. But don't you both have a wedding to get ready for?"

"Okay," Cait grumbled, "fine. But I want a full rundown of all the details."

Maura pulled her phone out of her pocket as they stood to check the time. "God. Eight missed calls from my mother and one very shouty text message telling me I'm late for my hair appointment. Except I can't be late. I'm the bride!"

"Maura," Evie said, laying a hand on her friend's arm before she could leave. "If you want me to skip the wedding, I understand."

Maura's brows drew together. "Why would I want you to skip the wedding?"

"With the this." Evie gestured at her throat. "And the that." She pointed to the ceiling. "And we don't know how long it'll take word to get back to the Italians that Peter is dead and the bounty is useless. I don't want to ruin your day."

"The only thing that would ruin it is you not being there. So you better show up, or I'll sue."

Maura flashed a quick grin before skirting around Declan and down the hall.

"It's quiet," Evie said, noticing the stillness for the first time.

"They're done. You okay?" He wrapped an arm around her waist when she laid her head against his chest.

"Yeah. All things considered, I'm doing great."

"Did you ask Maura about the wedding because you don't feel up to going?"

She pulled back to look up at him. "I forget how well you know me sometimes. No, I want to go. I don't want Peter to take something else important from me. But I would feel better if we had some extra security or something."

"Love, it's a syndicate wedding. Every man in the room and half the women will be strapped," he said, making her laugh.

Chapter Thirty-Six

The sidewalk and front steps of the church were teeming with people when they drove up, and the nerves that had dissipated with a hot shower and the light lunch Marta insisted she eat suddenly returned.

"Maybe we should have driven separately."

Declan silenced his phone and slid it into the breast pocket of his tux. "Why?"

"Because…" she gestured out the window at the curious faces that were already looking toward the limo to see who might be inside. "You're royalty, and I'm—"

"Royalty's date?"

Evie snorted and rolled her eyes at his cocky grin.

"It's not like they haven't seen us together before."

"That was a lifetime ago."

"You're not scared, are you?"

Evie jerked around to pin him with a hard stare. "Your psychological mind tricks won't work on me."

He lifted a single brow, saying nothing.

"Of course I'm not scared!"

He flashed a quick grin and reached for the door. "Then there's no time like the present."

He rounded the trunk and helped her out, keeping a firm grip on her hand when she tried to wriggle free and then tucking it into the crook of his arm. The crowd parted as they made their way up the steps and stopped in front of the heavy, carved doors.

From this vantage point, she could see the black SUVs parked at either corner and the men who stood at the perimeter of the crowd, eyes alert.

"So you did put on extra security."

He brushed a curl off her face that the breeze had blown loose. "Well, it seemed important to you. And it made sense. I've got to go do groomsmen stuff. You going to be okay?"

"Yes. Go and leave me to fend off the horde of curious onlookers."

He laughed, and before she could stop him he leaned in and captured her lips in a quick, searing kiss that left her a little breathless.

"That should give them something to talk about," he said before disappearing inside and leaving her standing alone in the sunshine.

Evie ran a hand over her hair to smooth it in place and caught Helen's stare from the bottom of the steps. Her barely contained outrage lifted Evie's spirits, and she practically floated into the lobby to be seated.

People seemed to follow her lead, filing inside behind her, as much to take their seats as to get a glimpse of her. Being with Declan had always been this way. People were curious about him but too afraid to ask, so they had always asked her instead. She didn't imagine they'd be shy for long.

An usher led her to a seat in the second row, behind where the bride's family would sit, and she frowned.

"Oh no, this is a mistake. I'm sure I should be back there

somewhere," she insisted, gesturing over her shoulder with her clutch.

The boy, he couldn't have been more than seventeen, flushed under the collar of his tux. "Boss's orders, ma'am," he said before turning.

She slid into the pew to get out of the aisle and wondered if he'd meant Declan or Maura and hoped it was the latter.

The church was decorated exactly how Maura had described, with flowers in deep blues and purples filling large copper urns that lined the altar. More hung in pretty bouquets on the pews and speared up out of tall stands set in front of stained glass windows.

The last time she'd been in this building, she'd been burying her parents. Sometimes she missed them so much she ached with it, more than she ever had in the last ten years. The finality of it cut deeper, knowing they weren't a phone call away anymore, knowing she couldn't pick up the phone and hear her mother's voice or pop over to their house and walk in to the smells of baking bread.

But with their dying breaths, they'd given her something, something she couldn't even acknowledge she'd been missing a few months ago. They'd brought her back home, back to Declan. And she didn't want to waste this second chance with him. A second chance to make them proud.

Conversation faded to a hushed silence as the groom and his men filed out of a side door, lining up next to Father Charles dressed in his white robe and stole. She spotted Declan, who stood as James's best man. God, he looked good in a tux.

His eyes found her almost immediately, and he smiled, causing more than a few heads to turn. She noticed his crooked bow tie and mimed straightening it, watching as he did. She was really going to enjoy taking every single piece of that tux off him later.

When the processional music began, she shifted in her seat to watch Sean walk down the aisle with Alice, guiding her to the front row before taking his seat on the opposite side of the church. Alice turned in her seat to offer Evie a warm smile, leaning over the pew to squeeze her knee.

The flower girls followed next, dancing up the aisle, happily flinging blue and purple rose petals. Evan had to be nudged through the doors, clutching the pillow the rings were tied to in a death grip. Cait had been coaching him, but he looked nervous.

When he spotted his father, he took off down the aisle at a trot, halting in front of the altar and flinging the pillow toward the line of groomsmen like a frisbee before diving into a nearby pew with his grandparents. Evie stifled a laugh with her hand when Finn deftly reached out and caught the pillow with one hand, passing it to Declan.

Once the bridesmaids were in place, the bridal march began, and she rose with the rest of the guests. When the vestibule doors opened and Maura appeared, framed by large bouquets and supported by her father, tears pricked Evie's eyes.

She'd seen her in the dress at the fitting, but it paled in comparison to now in this moment with her hair done up and the veil cascading behind her and the radiant look on her face as she walked down the aisle toward James.

Evie peeked over her shoulder at James, who looked equally as entranced as his bride, and caught Declan watching her with an intensity that sent electricity racing along her skin and butterflies looping in her belly. It seemed somehow unfair that he could have such an effect on her with a single look.

Father Charles began the service, and she found something comforting about the ritual of it, about watching the depth of two people's love for each other take shape under vows and blessings. Watching Maura and James promise to love and honor each other forever had her eyes sliding to Declan. She'd eagerly awaited such a promise once.

When the priest pronounced them husband and wife, the congregation cheered, and as the recessional music began, she lost Declan in the crowd when he escorted Reagan down the aisle. Turning to join the crowd of guests making their way outside, she stopped short when she noticed Alice standing at the end of the pew.

Alice held her arms out and waited for Evie to step into them, giving her a tight squeeze. "I'm so glad you came. I hope Maura took my advice and gave you your own invitation instead of making you show up as a plus one."

Evie laughed softly, letting Alice tuck her hand into Evie's elbow and lead her from the church.

"She did."

"Good. It's time to let bygones be bygones between you two. You're good for each other, you three. As girls and now as women. Do right by each other."

"I promise to do my best."

Alice smiled, patting Evie on the hand. "That's all a mother could ask for. I've got to go find Tommy and haul him away for pictures. Don't be a stranger, Evie. My door is always open."

Evie watched Alice wander away, chuckling when Alice spotted her husband, Tommy, taking a quick nip from a flask people were passing around, hands on her hips in disapproval but her smile brighter than ever. She'd always loved Maura's parents and their casual way with each other.

She watched them disappear back into the church and spotted Nessa standing at the edge of a group of women, listening but not participating, and she wondered for the first time if her sister had any friends. She felt terrible that she didn't know the answer to that question.

Nessa caught her gaze and gave a halfhearted smile, moving to close the distance between them when Evie did the same.

"I wasn't sure you would be here after what happened with Peter," Nessa said. "Although I guess you and Declan are all the rage."

"It was a last-minute decision. You heard about what happened?"

"Owen told me this morning." Nessa shifted to point out her main security detail. "You really think he was behind all of it? Peter, I mean."

Evie nodded. "Who else would it be?"

"Good. I knew if you said it, it would be true. It's a relief knowing he's gone and my life can get back to normal. Will you be leaving soon? Heading back to New York?"

Evie saw Declan emerge from the side of the church. "I don't think so. I think I'm going to stick around in Philly for a while. Help you figure out what to do with the house and stuff."

"That'll be nice." Nessa peeked over her shoulder, following Evie's gaze. "Your friends miss you."

"I've missed them. Would you ever get married again?"

She hadn't even known she was going to ask the question until it left her mouth. She didn't know anything about Nessa's husband other than he had died young and they didn't have any children.

"Hmm?" Nessa twirled her wedding ring around her finger. "Me? No. I don't think I could after Michael. When you have your one great love, what's the point in trying to find second best?"

"Second best," Evie murmured, watching Declan pause to talk to a small group of guests.

"Well, I think I'm going to head home."

Evie dragged her eyes away from Declan. "You're not coming to the reception?"

"No, weddings are hard for me because…" Nessa cleared her throat. "Well, just because."

"Oh, Nessa, I didn't mean to—"

"Of course you didn't." Nessa smiled. "Don't worry about me. Really. Enjoy the party, Evie."

Nessa turned and fled before Evie could even say goodbye. Of course weddings would be hard for her sister after losing a husband so young. And she'd just casually picked at old wounds by asking if she'd ever replace him with someone else. Could she be any more insensitive?

"Was that Nessa?" Declan asked, stopping beside her.

"Yeah, she said she was going to go home."

"Everything okay?"

"Might have been better if I hadn't brought up her dead husband at a wedding."

"Ouch. Yeah, she doesn't come to many syndicate weddings. Don't worry about it, though." He rubbed a hand up and down her arm. "You couldn't have known."

"How did he die?" She stared in the direction Nessa disappeared.

"He overdosed on pain meds he was taking for a back injury."

"Oh, shit. Now I feel even worse."

"Why? You didn't kill him."

Evie turned to look up at him. "You know you can hurt people without killing them, right?"

"Can you? Killing them is more efficient."

She shook her head. "You probably shouldn't enjoy it so much."

He shrugged, but she caught a flash of a smile. "Probably. Have I told you how stunning you look today?" He nodded in appreciation at the pale pink dress that hugged her curves from breast to thigh before falling away in sheer billowy layers.

"Let me think...several times while you were trying to talk me back out of this dress earlier."

He grinned. "And I'm going to thoroughly enjoy taking that off you later."

"Hmm, that's funny. I was thinking exactly the same thing about your tux."

His blue eyes darkened, and he took a step closer so their bodies were nearly touching, making her breath catch in the back of her throat. "We could go now, skip the reception."

The invitation made her mouth water. "No, we can't."

He sighed. "Fine. A coat closet then."

"I'll be on the lookout," she replied, laughing. "Are you done with pictures already?"

"They cut me loose early. We could make out in the limo for a while."

She gave his chest a light shove. "You just want to get me out of this dress."

"Good. I was afraid I was being too subtle."

She did let his hands wander a little too far in the limo on the drive over to the reception but kept her dress firmly on, much to their mutual disappointment. She fixed the lipstick he'd smudged while the driver got out to open her door.

The 1920s era mansion Maura insisted on for the reception was stunning. Evie imagined it would be even more beautiful lit up at night. Maura hadn't done the place justice when she'd described it. Each room was carefully decorated with painstaking attention to even the smallest detail.

She accepted a glass of champagne from a passing waiter and wandered from one of the parlors into the library, moving to study the intricately carved marble fireplace that sat at the back of the room. She ran her fingertip over the relief of angels and cherubs, marveling at the craftsmanship. It had to be an original piece.

"See any coat closets?" Declan whispered loudly as he joined her, sipping a glass of whiskey.

She rose from her inspection of the mantel. "I think I saw a billiards room back that way, but no, no coat closets."

He glanced in the direction she was pointing. "I could make a billiards room work."

Laughing, she tilted her head when he leaned in to press a kiss to the side of her neck. "I'm afraid you'll have to wait."

"Well," he said when the library began to fill with other guests, "that wasn't a no."

Shaking her head, she scanned the room while people engaged him in conversation. She could see it, the visible shift in the man he was with her and the man he was with everyone else. He cared, no doubt about it, but he knew the power he carried and the respect he commanded and wielded them both expertly.

Reagan caught her eye from across the room and weaved between guests to reach them.

"I heard about what happened this morning."

"Seems word's been getting around," Evie replied. "Nessa asked me about it too."

"Need anything from me?" Reagan asked Declan.

"No, McGee's already been through, and we know what happened." He wrapped an arm around Evie's waist. "We were there."

Reagan nodded, studying them. "This looks nice. People are talking about this too." She wiggled her fingers at them. "Seems the consensus is about damn time. So I hope you're back for good, Evie."

Evie smiled. "Me too."

"Or the rabble might mutiny." Reagan grinned, excusing herself to follow a waiter carrying a tray of canapés.

Declan pulled her in tighter, squeezing her waist. She felt his gaze shift and spotted Finn carrying a teary-eyed, red-faced Evan in his arms, Cait trailing behind looking just as put out.

When Evan saw her, he squirmed in his father's arms and reached for her. Evie glanced at Cait, who nodded, before taking Evan and settling him against her shoulder.

"What am I," Declan ruffled Evan's hair, eliciting a small smile. "Chopped liver?"

"Sometimes aunties do it better." She rubbed small circles across Evan's back.

"I'm going to go check in with a few things. You ok?"

"I'm fine. How many times are you going to ask me that today?"

He leaned down to press a kiss to her temple. "A lot."

"Need me to take him?" Cait pointed at Evan once they were alone.

"No, but maybe we can…" Evie sidled over to a couch and sank down onto the edge, shifting Evan onto her lap.

"You are the hot gossip of the day, my friend."

Evie grimaced. "So Reagan said. I hope Maura's not upset about that."

"No, we've got a bet going."

"A bet for what?"

"To see how long it takes Declan to propose. I said by the end of the night, but Maura thinks by next weekend."

Evie blinked, setting Evan on his feet when he squirmed to get down. She hadn't thought quite that far ahead. She was just getting used to the idea of staying. Would she say yes if he asked her?

She was saved from having to answer that when a bell chimed and the waiters asked everyone to take their seats in the great hall for the bride and groom's arrival. Taking Evan's hand, Evie followed the crowd out of the library and into the ballroom with vaulted ceilings and chandeliers that sparkled like diamonds.

Someone had opened all the doors that led out onto the patio, allowing a light breeze and the sweet scent of magnolias to tease their way inside. She slid into her chair just as Maura and James made their entrance to thunderous applause, and everyone took their seats for the first dance.

It was sweet, the way they only had eyes for each other, swaying and talking as if they were the only two people in the room.

"What are you thinking about?" Declan whispered in her ear.

"I don't know if I should answer that considering what happened the last time I did."

His grin was quick and wicked, and she laughed. "I really should search harder for this coat closet."

The song changed, and Evie's gaze was drawn back to the dance floor and the father-daughter dance. A pang of sadness tightened her chest knowing she'd missed her moment with her own father, and Declan squeezed her thigh as if he understood.

"You ever come close to getting married in the last ten years?"

She met his searching gaze. "No. You?"

"Getting closer, I think," he said, and her stomach did a slow flip. "Dance with me."

"They're going to serve dinner in a minute."

He rose, holding his hand out. "I promise to make sure you eat."

When he didn't relent, she sighed, laying her hand in his and following him onto the dance floor. People made room for them, and he twirled her out and back as the song changed to a slow ballad.

"You couldn't have planned that better if you tried," she

said, letting their fingers twine as he wrapped his arm around her waist.

"I don't know what you're insinuating."

"I'm sure."

She swayed with him, allowed herself to get lost in the feel of his body against hers, the caress of his breath against her cheek, the warmth of his hand at the small of her back. She didn't want to think about the future, not yet. She wanted to be here in this moment with him for as long as possible.

She glimpsed Maura over Declan's shoulder, and her friend gave them two enthusiastic thumbs up. Evie chuckled.

"What's so funny?" Declan murmured against her hair.

"We have fans," she said, smiling as Declan spun them to see Maura, who waved.

"I've had no fewer than six people congratulate us."

She leaned back, eyebrows raised. "On what?"

"I don't know. I haven't asked you anything yet."

There was that flip-flopping in her stomach again. The song changed to an upbeat one, and they moved back to their table. Declan opened his mouth to speak but stopped short when Maura appeared at his elbow.

"There's only supposed to be one set of lovebirds at a wedding, you know."

"Sorry, I—"

Maura waved a hand in the air. "I'm just teasing. It's about damn time. Declan, I need to borrow her a minute."

Maura looped her arm through Evie's when Declan stepped back and gestured for them to go ahead. She led them out onto the patio, where the photographer waited with an impossibly large camera draped around her neck. How did she not fall right over?

"Please tell me he hasn't popped the question yet."

"He has not."

"Oh, what's that tone?" Maura stopped short and turned to face her in a rustle of skirts. "You wouldn't say yes?"

Evie puffed out her cheeks then blew out the breath. "Christ, Maura. I don't know. I'm just getting used to the idea of staying in Philly, potentially giving up my career. It doesn't sound all that appealing anymore knowing I could run up against another Peter. I haven't thought that far ahead yet. I'm not sure I'm even ready to."

"I get that. Plus, there's still whatever happened between you two in the first place."

"Yeah." Evie sighed. "That too."

"Well, you'll figure it out. But work it out by next weekend because I really want to beat Cait to that five hundred bucks."

Evie chuckled, posing for photos with the two women who meant the most to her in this world. Whatever happened between her and Declan, she would never again leave them behind. She'd lost too much already.

Chapter Thirty-Seven

As afternoon faded into evening, Declan watched Evie as she wandered, laughed, and made small talk with everyone who stopped her. Evan, all smiles, was captivated by her, and Declan couldn't help but smile himself as he watched them dance together, feet stomping and arms flailing.

Was it any wonder he was so in love with her? She fit in his world, she always had, and though he could still sense her hesitation at taking the next step, he could be patient. He'd let her take as much time as she needed to not spook her into running again. Especially since he had no idea why she'd run in the first place.

He'd wanted to ask a few times, but it never seemed like the right time to bring it up. Or maybe he didn't really want to know the reason. For now he was content to have her by his side, and they'd worry about tomorrow tomorrow.

"You're staring, brother," Finn said, joining Declan at the edge of the dance floor. "Which pocket is mom's ring in?"

Declan glanced at his brother, eyebrow raised. "It's in the safe at home."

"Cait will be disappointed."

"Why's that?"

"She and Maura have a bet going on when you'll propose. Cait thought you'd do it tonight, at the wedding."

Declan cast his eyes to the ceiling. "I didn't realize my love life was such a topic of conversation."

"Then you haven't been paying attention," Finn said, clapping Declan on the shoulder and leaning down to scoop up a giggling Evan, who raced over.

"Thanks for tiring him out," Finn said, bouncing Evan and eliciting more giggles.

"I think it's the other way around. I'm getting old."

"Nothing makes you feel older than a toddler with endless energy."

"Seriously," Evie agreed. "Where does he keep it?"

Finn grinned. "When I figure it out, I'll bottle and sell it. For now, I'm going to pass this guy off to the nanny to take home."

Declan glanced at one of the men he'd set up as security. "Send a—"

"Yep," Finn interrupted.

"Thirsty?" Declan asked, turning to Evie.

"Yes. Is there still cake?" she asked after a beat.

He laughed and took her hand, lacing his fingers with hers and kissing the back of it. "I think so."

"Oh my God," she groaned around a mouthful of cake when they were seated again. "Why is wedding cake so much more delicious than all the other cakes?"

"I have no idea."

Her eyes narrowed on his face. "I don't even remember seeing you eat cake. Have you not had any of this?" She held up a forkful when he shook his head. "Because it's you, I'll share."

"It's not bad," he agreed.

"Not bad?! I could eat this cake for breakfast every day and not get tired of it."

He shook his head, chuckling. "I don't really like cake."

She gasped, fork paused halfway to her mouth. "Well, more for me then, I guess."

He liked seeing this side of her. He missed it. She'd always been quick to tease or tell a joke when they were kids, and he liked knowing that playful spirit was still there under the rigid control she so often showed. More than that, he liked how the two twined together into a woman who always kept him on his toes.

"It's your time to shine," he said when he saw Maura step onto the dance floor holding her bouquet.

"What? Oh, no," she said, shaking her head when Maura asked all the unmarried ladies to gather for the bouquet toss. "Absolutely not."

"Oh, come on. You're not married. It's the rules."

"Evie. I see you," Maura called, shooting her friend a cheeky grin when Evie only glared.

"It's not fair when you gang up on me," Evie grumbled, tossing her napkin onto her chair and moving to stand at the very back of the crowd.

The look of stunned disbelief on her face when she caught it made him laugh, and he laughed even harder when she tried to gift the bouquet to someone else and they wouldn't take it. But he caught her sticking her nose into it more than once throughout the rest of the night, inhaling its scent with a dreamy look in her eyes.

It was late when the crowd began to thin, and he was glad that the entire day had gone off without incident. Brogan seemed to think the Italians had backed off and weren't actively pursuing Evie anymore after what had happened to Peter, but it was impossible to say. He wanted to keep Evie close a few more days until they were absolutely certain they didn't get a wild idea to do something stupid.

He watched Aidan wander out with a woman on his arm and shook his head. He needed to get that kid a wife or something. Settle him down with a family, and maybe he'd stop acting like such an entitled asshole.

When he realized Evie had disappeared, he went in search of her, finding her outside on the patio, staring up at the inky black sky. Without a word, he wrapped his arms around her from behind. She stiffened for a moment before realizing who it was and relaxing back against him.

"I didn't mean to scare you," he whispered against her ear.

"It's okay. I guess some things will still make me a little jumpy for a while. Party winding down?"

"Yeah, Aidan just left with someone. Finn and Cait went home about an hour after James and Maura left. And Brogan is currently trying to drink Rory McBride under the table."

"Brogan is totally winning that one."

"He is. Ready to go?"

"Yeah. Let's go home."

She stepped out of his embrace and slid her hand through his arm, swinging the bouquet at her side. She'd never know how much it meant to hear her call Glenmore House home.

Chapter Thirty-Eight

The buzzing of his phone on the nightstand roused Declan, and he moved quickly to silence it. What in the hell did Sean want at this hour? Christ, didn't the man ever take a day off?

Leaving it on the table, he rolled over and watched Evie sleep, flat on her stomach as she often did when he didn't have his arms around her. His eyes drifted down to the cuts on her side, and he frowned. Every time he saw them, he wanted to resurrect Peter and kill the bastard again.

Evie stirred when his phone buzzed a second time, and he groaned. No rest for the wicked. He rolled out of bed and sent Sean a quick text, only to realize he was waiting for him downstairs. He needed coffee before he sat through whatever disapproving speech his uncle surely had planned.

"What's wrong?" Evie murmured when he slid out of bed and pulled on a pair of sweats.

"Nothing," he whispered, leaning over to press a kiss to her shoulder. "Go back to sleep."

Closing the door gently behind him, he slipped a shirt on over his head as he made his way down the stairs in search of coffee and his uncle. In that order. He found both in the kitchen.

"You're up early," Declan said, accepting a cup of coffee from Marta and taking a deep drink. "I'm starting to think you work more than me. What do you need?" Declan asked once they were in his office.

"I just wanted to check in and make sure you weren't planning on doing anything stupid."

Declan raised a brow and set his mug carefully on the desk. He gave his uncle a lot of leeway considering their relationship, but even he had his limits.

"Explain."

The cool, clipped tone of his voice had Sean sitting back in his chair. "I meant to say I heard some gossip at the wedding last night and I wanted to see if it was true or not. Right from the source."

"You should know better by now than to trust syndicate gossip."

"So you aren't planning on proposing to Evie?"

"And if I was?"

"Well, we all know how that turned out the first time."

Declan drummed his fingers on the desktop. "What's your point?"

"My point is I know you were sweet on her when you were kids, but your father had his reservations, and frankly, so did I. And since he's not here now to tell you it's a big mistake, I'll have to say it for him."

"Oh, please. Go on."

Sean shifted in his seat. "She isn't good for this family, and she isn't good for you. She's a distraction. Just look at how you've been acting the last few months. Cutting back on your work, spending more time at the house, fumbling the DiMarco thing."

"Be very careful here, Sean."

"You need a woman who knows where she fits in the family. Like your mother did. Evie is not that woman, and she'll run this family off the rails if you let her."

"That's enough. Lucky for both of us, Evie is not your concern. I can handle her. As for the syndicate, have profits dipped? Have people reported being unhappy with their jobs? Have the cops been on our asses?

"No," he asserted when Sean remained silent. "They haven't. So I would appreciate it if you did your job so I can do mine. And while you're at it, keep your opinions about my love life and my woman to yourself."

"Dec—"

"You can go."

Sean shoved out of the chair so hard it fell sideways, and he stalked out without another word. Alone, Declan rubbed his forehead. He could handle opinions about his personal life, most of them he ignored anyway. What he would not tolerate were questions about his leadership or the way he ran the syndicate—from anyone.

Needing a minute before heading back upstairs, he went back to the kitchen for a refresh on his coffee and a second mug for Evie, waving Marta away when she offered to bring up breakfast. With any luck, he'd be able to tempt Evie into a long, hot shower.

What he got when he opened the bedroom door was a whirlwind.

"What are you doing?"

She barely spared him a glance as she continued to shove things haphazardly into her open suitcase.

"I'm leaving."

"What?" Panic squeezed his chest. "Why?"

Her laugh was bitter and cold. "Because you're exactly the same man now that you were then. Nothing's changed. And I was kidding myself thinking it had. I wouldn't settle for it when I was twenty, and I'll be damned if I'll settle for it now."

"Evie." He set the mugs down on a nearby table and crossed the room, gripping her shoulders to get her to stop moving for a goddamn minute. "What are you talking about? I don't understand what's happening."

The look she gave him was one of pure disgust, and he dropped his hands, taking a step back.

"I heard you," she spat. "So your innocent act is fucking insulting."

She disappeared into the bathroom, and he heard the clatter of bottles against the sink and tub. She came out with her arms full and dumped them unceremoniously into her suitcase.

"Do you remember the conversation you had with your father a month before our wedding?"

What the hell was she talking about? He fought to keep his voice even, anger rising as he watched her continue to pack. "You'll have to be more specific."

"I had come over to watch movies. We were finally going to have a night together where we didn't have to talk about wedding stuff, and I wanted to tell you about this awful conversation I'd had with my father that afternoon."

She moved to the dresser, yanking the drawers open and scooping out her clothes. Did she know she was ripping his heart out right now?

"You and your father were in the study talking about me, and your father told you to bring me to heel. Bring me to heel," she spat. "Like a fucking dog."

Shoving her clothes down, she slammed the top on her suitcase. "And I waited. I waited for the love of my life, for the man I was excited to marry, for the future father of my children to defend me, to stand up for me. For us."

She dropped the suitcase onto the floor with a thump and wheeled it to the door. "Do you remember what you said?"

She turned to face him then, and the tears brimming in her eyes tore at his heart. He remembered. He remembered because he'd uttered them again only minutes before.

"Evie, I didn't mean—"

"I can handle her." A single tear slipped down her cheek. "I can handle her," she said again, voice filled with anger and hurt. "I don't need to be *handled*. I wanted to be loved, to be cherished, to be respected. You weren't capable of it then, and you clearly aren't capable of it now. And I'm the idiot for thinking otherwise. God, I can't believe I let myself fall in love with you all over again."

When she turned to go, his heart beat thick in his chest. He couldn't let her leave. He couldn't lose her a second time.

"Wait…"

He caught her hand, but she turned and shoved him so hard he stumbled back a step.

"I'm done waiting for you to be the man I want and need you to be."

"So that's it then?" he demanded. "You're just going to run away again instead of staying and talking this out like adults? Instead of fighting for us?"

"All I ever did was fight for us! I fought for us every time every well-meaning syndicate wife told me I needed to remember my place or I shouldn't talk out of turn or I needed to defer to you. I fought for us every time my father told me our plans to reshape the syndicate were a pipe dream. I fought for us every time my mother told me I needed to concentrate on having babies and being a good wife."

She stabbed the air between them with her finger. "I fought for us against everyone who ever told me I wasn't good enough to be your wife because I was too much, too loud, too outspoken. And the one time you had to fight for us, you failed."

She took a step back toward the door. "You failed me, Declan. I left then because I deserved more than you were capable of giving me, and I deserve more now. I'm done loving somebody who only wants to handle me."

She sneered the word, and this time when she tried to leave, he didn't stop her. He listened to her suitcase drag down the stairs, clenched his jaw when the front door slammed, and sank down onto the edge of the bed when her car peeled out of the driveway.

He hadn't known. No one would have dared to say the things to his face that they had said to Evie, and she'd never told him. More to the point, he'd never thought to ask.

He had no intention of handling her. He wasn't sure it was even possible. They'd always meant to rule together, side by side. Not with her in the background like all the Callahan queens before her. Not like his mother.

His father hadn't liked the idea then; his uncle didn't like it now. So he said the one thing he thought would shut them both up. Except now he saw that for the mistake it was. He should have stood up for her, then and now, like she had stood up for herself. She deserved more from the man who claimed to love her. And now he'd lost her all over again.

No. He wasn't going to let her go without a fight. Not this time. Shoving off the bed, he crossed to the door. He could beat her back to her apartment if he left now and took the chopper. He dug out his phone to call the airfield and nearly ran headlong into Brogan, who'd come barreling down from the third floor.

"I have something you're going to want to hear."

"Not now, Brogan."

"Declan," Brogan said, and the tone in his voice had

Declan stopping in his jog down the stairs and turning to face him.

"What?" Declan snapped.

"Where's Evie? I should probably tell you both together."

"She isn't here."

Brogan's eyebrows shot up. "You might want to get her back."

"Well, I can't go after her standing here. So what is it?"

"There's no way Peter killed Evie's parents."

"That's not possible."

Brogan crossed his arms over his chest. "It is possible. His bank records show he was in Nebraska. Probably planning to come here because he was buying supplies. But he didn't even buy a plane ticket to fly to New York until a week after they were dead."

Fuck. The woman he'd just let slip away was still in danger, and he had no idea how to keep her safe.

Chapter Thirty-Nine

Evie didn't make it far before the tears overtook her. Easing her car onto the shoulder, she laid her forehead against the steering wheel and wept. Her heart ached at the thought of losing him again, but she had only herself to blame for letting hope take root there in the first place.

She was stupid for believing things were different this time, that they'd both changed enough to make it work. He was exactly who he had to be to live this life, and she'd become so much more.

Maybe she had always been so much more. She certainly deserved more than he was willing to give her, more than pretty promises to her face and ugly truths behind her back.

She'd go back to New York and figure out what was next, but she wouldn't lose touch with Philadelphia entirely. Cait and Maura were here, and if she'd learned nothing these past few months, it was that life was short and friendships were sacred. She'd move on with her life and let Declan move on with his.

He'd find somebody else and finally give the family a couple of heirs. The thought twisted like a knife in her stomach, and she shoved it aside. She'd have to work harder to wall that part of herself off again. She'd come back with too many cracks, vulnerable. Never again.

She took a deep breath to steady herself when her phone signaled. She ignored it. He didn't get to talk and plead his way out of this one. When it beeped again, she snatched it off the seat, ready to give him hell, but stilled when she saw the message flash across the screen. Not Declan, but an unknown number.

Can you get here in time to save her?

Fear raced up her spine. She thought of Cait, Maura, Nessa, their faces swimming into view. The next message had that fear pooling in her belly like a lead weight. Maura, bound to a chair, face wet with tears, a line of blood from a cut on her hairline trickling down her forehead.

She frantically typed a reply. *Where?*

When the address came through, she cycled through the map in her head, trying desperately to place it so she would know what she was getting herself into. That had to be out near Callahan warehouses. Who the fuck was this?

She put the car in reverse and turned back toward Glenmore House. Declan would throw the full weight of the syndicate at whoever had taken one of his own. Her phone dinged again.

Come alone or she dies.

She jerked to a stop, eyes darting up the road. It wasn't far. She could make it back in less than five minutes if she booked it. But she had no idea who she was dealing with or what kind of eyes they might have on her.

Going into this alone and without backup or even knowing who she was up against was stupid, but not showing up alone could potentially put Maura in even more danger, and she couldn't take that chance. Maura was supposed to be leaving for her honeymoon today. James would notice her absence and go right to Declan. She had to hope that would be enough.

Tick Tock.

With one last glance through the trees, Evie cut the wheel and sped off in the opposite direction. Her mind raced as she drove. If Peter was dead, who had kidnapped Maura?

The address was on the edge of the city, and she almost missed it, swerving into an unpaved lot, tires spitting gravel as she slammed on her brakes. The lot was empty save for a squat beige building that stretched from one end to the other.

It was a single-story, unused and run down from the looks of the flapping siding and paint peeling at the windows. It sat at the end of a row of similar buildings, most of them warehouses, some of them offices. The street was quiet, no signs of people or cars. It was eerie.

She gripped the steering wheel with clammy hands. James had to know by now that Maura was missing. Which means if he hadn't told Declan yet, he was on his way. If she could distract whoever had Maura inside long enough to give him time to catch up, Maura might have a chance. They both might.

She inhaled sharply through her nose, slowly blowing the breath out between her lips. Leaning over the console, she pressed the button for the glove box and pulled out the gun she'd been keeping there since coming back to Philly.

Flipping off the safety, she stepped out of the car. There seemed to be only one way in, and although it was impossible to tell how far back the building stretched from this angle, she didn't want to waste time walking the perimeter.

Resolved, she jogged across the lot toward the door,

slowly, quietly swinging the door open and stepping inside. It smelled musty, and every surface was covered in a thick layer of dust, more dust floating across the shrinking shaft of light from the closing door.

A single hallway branched off from what looked like a reception area, and she followed it, her heart pounding in her ears as she swept her gun through each room to clear it. Reaching the end of the hallway, she had the option to go right or left, and she cursed. She didn't want to waste precious time going in the wrong direction.

When a single shot rang out, echoing through the building, she spun toward the sound as terror squeezed her. She took off at a dead run to the left, her pounding feet kicking up more dust, choking her as she fought for air against the fear.

The hallway opened up into a big room that might have once been a storage area, but it was empty now. Only one chair sat at the far end of the expanse of concrete and carpet. Maura, arms and legs bound, slumped over in it, unmoving.

A choked sob escaped her lips as Evie raced across the floor, dropping to her knees in front of her friend. Oh God. Oh God. Please be alive. She reached up to feel for a pulse. There, that was it, wasn't it?

Maura groaned, and she trembled with relief. Still alive. But losing blood fast from a wound in her side. Evie whipped off her jacket, pressing it against the wound to try and stop the bleeding, and Maura groaned again.

"Evie," she said, her voice weak and thin. "Tell James I love him, okay?"

She shook her head. "You're going to be fine."

Maura attempted a smile, but it was more a grimace as Evie pressed the wound harder. "I won't. I'm an ER nurse, remember?"

"Maura, tell me what to do," Evie pleaded, tears slipping down her cheeks.

"I think we're well past that," Maura said.

"Don't say that. Hey, open your eyes," Evie said when Maura's head tipped forward. "Don't you dare die on me, Maura Elizabeth."

"Oh, leave her."

Evie jolted at the voice that echoed in the empty room.

"I did her a favor. Marriage is just another, slower way to die."

Rising, Evie reached for the gun she'd dropped to the floor, finger slipping to rest against the trigger. Slowly she turned to face her parents' murderer.

"Hey, sis." Nessa flashed a cold grin, taking a step forward. "Oh, man, you should really see the look on your face. You're all—" Nessa mimed anger and shock with a humorless chuckle.

"It's been you this whole time."

Evie stepped away from Maura as Nessa inched closer, running through everything that had happened, everything she thought Peter had done. Her parents' deaths, her flat tire where someone had watched and waited, the notes, the bounty on her head.

"Surprise! I admit I was getting a little annoyed that Peter was stealing my thunder, but I got over it. It was nice watching you squirm."

Evie eyed the gun tucked into the waistband of Nessa's jeans, trying to calm the storm of thoughts that raged in her head. She had to think. "Why?"

"Oh, as if you didn't know."

"I'm supposed to know why you brutally stabbed our mother and then shot our father in the head? Why you pretended to be a victim?"

"You always were their favorite. The oldest, the prettiest, the smartest." Nessa's laugh was cold, heartless.

"So you killed them?" Evie spat.

271

"You were the golden child. The perfect one. I was always compared to you, but I never measured up. Not with teachers or friends or good old Mom and Dad. Why can't you be smart like Evie? Why can't you be funny like Evie? Why can't you be good like Evie?"

"They loved you."

"Maybe." Nessa lifted her shoulders in a careless shrug. "But they loved you more. You were the one chosen by the prince, after all. After you left I thought I was finally going to get my shot at being seen as more than just the other twin. The other O'Brian girl. I was going to be the princess for once."

"That's why you told me not to come back." Rage ignited inside of her, had her hand tightening on the gun. "When I called a few months after I left. I wanted to come home. But you told me everyone was still mad. That I should stay away for a while until things calmed down."

"Oh, boohoo," Nessa sneered. "Perfect Evie didn't get what she wanted. Cry me a fucking river. I wanted my moment to shine. I wanted Declan to notice me for once."

"But Declan didn't want you." Evie shifted, inching forward.

Nessa's hands clenched into fists at her side. "No, he only wanted you. He pined for you." She spat the word, jabbing her finger at Evie. "He even went to New York looking for you, convinced that's where you'd go. It was disgusting."

"But you got married." She took another step closer. "Weren't you happy?"

"Ugh, Michael. I just needed to get out of the house. I figured he'd want to have sex a few times a week and then leave me alone. But he wanted an actual wife, someone to talk to. Jesus, he talked constantly—about everything. It was so annoying."

She ran a hand through her hair. "It was pure dumb luck that he hurt his back loading in a shipment at the docks. I started crushing up extra pain meds in his food so it looked like he was abusing them."

Evie's eyes widened in shock. "You killed him?"

"It's embarrassing how slow you are to catch on. Really. You're supposed to be the smart one. He was already addicted, but he didn't know it. One night I crushed up the whole bottle into a beer, and he just"—she waved her hand in the air—"never woke up."

"And now you play the grieving widow."

"In the beginning, pretending to be sad about it was the hardest part."

Nessa dissolved into a fit of fake hysterics that ended in wild laughter. Evie's stomach rolled. Her sister was a monster, cold and calculated.

"But after a while, no one knows what to say to the young widow. So you keep wearing your ring." She held up her left hand. "And giving sad smiles when someone asks you how you are. And they leave you the fuck alone."

"Why Mom and Dad?"

"That one was kind of an accident."

Evie's jaw clenched, and she had to force herself to relax. She had to keep Nessa talking, keep her distracted so she could get close enough to rush her sister before Nessa had time to draw her gun.

"How do you accidentally stab someone a dozen times?"

"I honestly don't think I could have planned it better if I tried. One day I was doing my obligatory visit where I'm forced to smile and nod and pretend like I care—so very exhausting, by the way—and Mom mentions that she'd recently spoken to you."

Nessa rubbed at her temple, eyes angry. "I didn't even

273

know you two were still talking. All she had to do was answer my damn questions. But she wouldn't. Your sister asked me not to. That's all she would say, over and over."

"You were the person I heard coming in when she said she had to go," Evie said. Oh God. She'd talked to her mother minutes before her murder.

"Oh, that was you she was on the phone with." Nessa's eyes lit with excitement. "Somehow that makes it even sweeter." She closed her eyes as if relishing this new piece of information. "No wonder you showed up so fast. Guess I shouldn't have sent that text. In a way, though, I'm glad you were the one who found them."

Evie raised her gun, aiming it straight at her sister's chest. "Give me one good reason, Nessa."

"Don't you want to hear the rest? Hmm." She tapped her chin with her finger. "Maybe it's not that interesting. I snapped. Even after ten years, I couldn't get away from you. She told me I was being childish for hounding her, and when she turned around, I grabbed a knife out of the block and shut her up. Forever."

Evie's finger flexed on the trigger. "And Dad?"

Nessa mimed holding a phone up to her ear. When she spoke, her voice was shaky, afraid. "Dad, I think Mom fell or something. She's not moving. You need to come home, quick!"

"And you waited for him."

"Yes, now you're following. And when he got there, I…" She mimed firing a gun.

"What was it for, Nessa?"

She shrugged. "I don't know, but it made me feel better. Until you showed up. Then you ruined everything. Again. I tried to get rid of you. With the notes and the tire, but you would not go. And then Declan had you under his roof, and what was I supposed to do then? Stroll up to Glenmore House and stab you to death?"

"So you put out the hit with the Italians knowing we'd think it was Peter."

"Yes. Clever of me, wasn't it?"

"A bit overdramatic," Evie replied.

Temper sparked in Nessa's eyes. "You never did appreciate my talents. It doesn't matter. I got to take one more thing you loved." Her eyes drifted over Evie's shoulder at Maura's slumped-over form. "And that's enough to last me for a very long time. Although killing you would be much more satisfying."

She grinned when Evie took a step closer. "You don't have the guts to shoot me, sis. I guess you really are the better twin."

Nessa reached for her own weapon, and Evie lunged forward, smacking it out of her hand. When her sister bent to retrieve the gun, Evie swung her foot up into Nessa's face, taking no small measure of satisfaction at Nessa's strangled scream. Gun forgotten on the floor, Nessa rushed her, stumbling forward when Evie danced out of the way.

"You're going to pay for that," Nessa spat, wiping blood from her mouth with the back of her hand.

When Nessa surged forward again, Evie rotated, ramming her elbow into Nessa's face, snapping her head back. Anger hummed through her body and, right or wrong, she wanted to see her sister bleed for what she'd done. She wanted to make her pay.

While Nessa struggled to regain her balance, Evie spun and kicked her in the chest, suddenly grateful for all of those self-defense classes she'd taken a few summers ago to pass the time while she cased a job.

She wasn't prepared for the way Nessa spun behind her,

though, gripping her hair and giving it a vicious tug, her other arm coming down hard on Evie's elbow and forcing her gun to the floor. Evie kicked back with her foot, hitting Nessa in the knee cap and stumbling forward when she released her grip.

Rotating, Evie narrowly missed landing a blow to Nessa's jaw but took a right hook that had pain exploding across her cheek. Her blood glistened on the ring on Nessa's little finger.

"What do you think I should do with Mom and Dad's house once I kill you?" Nessa spat blood on the ground. "Burn it for the insurance money? Oooh, you'd hate that, wouldn't you?" Nessa wondered when Evie's eyes darkened.

Evie vibrated with rage, rushing forward and landing first one, then two punches into Nessa's stomach until she doubled over, gasping for breath. Evie gripped Nessa's head and brought her knee up to her sister's face. Something deep inside of her delighted at the crack of bone, the rush of blood.

When Nessa straightened, face bloodied, Evie pivoted to kick again, swearing when Nessa gripped her foot and twisted. She stumbled forward, hissing out a breath when Nessa landed a punch to her shoulder and another to her kidney.

Eyeing the gun on the floor as she turned, Evie threw a fist into Nessa's jaw and then extended her leg so Nessa tripped backward over it, landing on the ground with a grunt. Before Evie could get clear, Nessa swept her leg out, knocking Evie to the floor. In anticipation, Evie rolled, fingers closing over the butt of her gun.

Panting, Evie pushed to her feet and loomed over her sister where she lay sprawled on the dirty carpet. Nessa's battered face grinned up at her.

"I always knew you'd be the death of me." She laughed, but it didn't quite reach her eyes. "Maybe you do have the guts after all."

"Go to hell."

Evie fired a single shot into the center of her sister's forehead, watching as her body relaxed into death. Suddenly she felt like all the air had been sucked out of the room, and she wheeled away from Nessa's staring eyes, doubling over to catch her breath.

Maura. She hadn't moved, and Evie had to force her legs to eat up the space between them. She tugged at the bindings on Maura's wrists and ankles with trembling fingers, carefully lowering Maura to the floor.

She felt for a pulse again. Was that it, or was it her imagination? She didn't care. She had to try. She couldn't let Nessa take someone else from her. She tipped Maura's head back as she went through the steps of CPR in her head. Thirty compressions, two breaths. Thirty compressions, two breaths.

She repeated it in her head over and over while she pumped her friend's chest, breathing life into her lungs. Why the fuck wasn't Declan here yet?

"Come on, Maura. You have to fight."

Blood oozed out in a pool on the floor, but she kept going, pushing through the fatigue. She couldn't stop. She had to keep trying. She couldn't just do nothing.

When she heard footsteps pounding down the hall, she grappled for the gun she'd tossed to the ground. Declan burst through the door, and she let out the breath she'd been holding, dropping the weapon and resuming CPR. Thirty compressions, two breaths.

Declan turned to speak to Finn, who had run up behind him, and Finn flicked a glance over Declan's shoulder before immediately turning on his heel and disappearing the way he'd come.

"Evie," Declan said, crouching down beside her. "You can stop now."

"No!" Evie said, voice breaking. "She's fine. As long as I… she'll be fine."

"Evie. She's gone."

His words arrowed through her, whispering through the haze of her frenzied rush to keep Maura's heart beating, and she stopped, sitting back on her heels to look down at her friend's lifeless body. Blood soaked her shirt and pooled under her. The diamond on her left hand was splattered with it.

She would have collapsed to the floor without Declan there to catch her, scooping her up and carrying her, sobbing, from the room. Evie saw James rush past them, his keening wail echoing down the hall.

When they were outside, she gulped fresh air into her lungs. The parking lot was dotted with people, and Declan carried her over to his SUV, sitting with her on the open tailgate, cradling her in his lap until her sobs faded into hitched breaths.

His fingers skimmed the cut on her cheek, tracing the sore spot on her jaw that must have been darkening into a bruise.

"Anything feel broken?"

She sat up, easing off his lap, and rotated her shoulder, hissing at the sharp stab of pain. "No. Bruised, maybe, but not broken. She killed her just to punish me."

Declan reached for her hand, squeezing it. "It isn't your fault."

"I know," Evie murmured. "But it hurts just the same. How did you find me?" she asked after a beat.

"Turns out technology really is magic. Evie…" His voice faltered. "I just need to…"

His words trailed off as he leaned in to capture her lips with his. His touch was gentle, the soft brush of his fingers across her jaw as he slid his hand back to cup her neck, the graze of his hand as it slid down to her waist.

Desperate to feel something that wasn't pain, wasn't grief, wasn't sorrow, she tilted her head up for his lips and let him take what he needed, give her what she needed in return. When he pulled away, pressing a long kiss to her forehead, she somehow felt steadier, like he'd lifted her back onto a solid foundation.

"Let me take you home," he whispered.

Chapter Forty

A week after Maura's funeral, Evie sat curled up on Declan's balcony in the gray, misty light of early morning. Sleep had been elusive, and when she did sleep, it was plagued with nightmares. Every time she felt like she was getting back on even footing, she woke up in a cold sweat, Nessa's haunting smile still fresh in her mind.

All the hours spent awake in the dark had given her time to think. Maybe too much time. She felt Maura's loss like an ache in her chest, constant and throbbing. Seeing James, numb and broken at the funeral, added guilt to the ache. She should have done more, tried harder to save her.

If she hadn't wasted so much time with Nessa, hadn't indulged her thirst for blood, would Maura still be alive? McGee insisted there was nothing she could have done, but it did little to absolve the guilt.

Most of all, she was angry. Angry at Nessa for killing three people she loved out of spite and petty jealousy, at herself for not seeing Nessa for who and what she was all along.

She existed in limbo now, back at Glenmore House, back in Declan's bed. Not quite sure where she wanted to go, but also knowing she didn't want to leave. They hadn't spoken about their fight since he found her in the warehouse, but he'd been there for every nightmare, holding her while she cried, whispering soothing words in her ear while he stroked her hair.

He demanded nothing, listened when she wanted to talk, sat quietly when she didn't. Sometimes she could feel the fresh, teasing tendrils of hope again, but she was scared to let them bloom. How did she know this time would be different?

The sun crested the horizon, peeking its way through the trees that ringed the property and dappling the balcony with light. William had called a couple of times. Once to ask about Peter and again to offer her a job, a lucrative one in Tokyo. She'd told him she'd think about it.

She should take it. That's what she'd been telling herself since William had called. Get back to work, use the jobs and the travel as a distraction, but it didn't have the same appeal it once did. Suddenly, she didn't want to be anonymous in a crowd of people. She wanted to be seen, to be known. She wanted to be loved.

She turned at the sound of the balcony doors opening and saw Declan standing in a shaft of light, chest bare, a pair of faded gray sweats riding low on his hips. Even in all her uncertainty, he tugged at her like a siren's call.

He crossed the balcony in bare feet, sinking down into the spot next to her. She surprised herself by shifting to lean back against his side. It wasn't that she didn't love him; it was that she didn't know if he could be the man she needed him to be. Loving him was the easiest part.

"Another nightmare?" Evie nodded. "You should have woken me."

"You can't baby me forever, Declan."

"Taking care of you and babying you are not the same thing." His voice carried a note of hurt in it.

"Well, then, you can't take care of me forever."

"Why not?"

She drew her legs up to her chest, hugging them tightly as his arm tensed around her shoulder.

"Why did you come looking for me ten years ago?" She turned her head to look at him, and she could see her question had caught him off guard. "Finn told me."

"Because I wanted to bring you home."

"Why?"

"Because I loved you."

She sighed, shifting away when his arm gripped her tighter, holding her in place. He inhaled, slow and deep.

"At first I was angry. I wanted answers your note didn't give. I wanted to know why and I had to find you to figure it out. But at some point, I'm not sure when, the anger dissipated. I didn't care why you left. I only wanted you back. I wanted to find whatever made you leave in the first place and make it better."

He loosened his grip, relaxing when she didn't move. "I figured you'd gone to New York, or I hoped you had, anyway. I went up to the city as often as I could get away, showed your picture to anyone who would stop long enough to glance at it."

He scrubbed a hand over his face. "I had Brogan combing security cameras for a glimpse of your face, hospitals, arrest records. If he could hack into it, I asked him to. Cait and I were at our wit's end. We didn't know what else to do, and one night she suggested filing a missing person's report for you."

He huffed out a sardonic laugh. "My father overheard that and finally put his foot down. No more trips to New York, no more wasting syndicate resources trying to find someone who didn't want to be found. Period."

"So you let me go."

His face was etched with hurt, with regret. "I didn't want to, but I had to. To survive. You left this hole in my life that I filled with work. I couldn't raise kids with you, so I raised businesses instead."

He sighed. "When my father died, I channeled even more of myself into my work, largely because people started asking me when I was going to get married and have kids. I couldn't even entertain the idea of doing that with anyone but you."

He looked at her then, eyes intense. "And then you were here again. Suddenly back in my world after all this time. I loved the girl I knew more than I thought possible. I love the woman you are now even more."

He reached up to brush his knuckles across her cheek. "I'm sorry, Evie. For ever making you think I wanted you to be anything other than who you are."

Tears pricked her eyes as she turned to face him fully, tucking her leg underneath her and scooting closer.

"Wait," he said when she started to speak. "Let me finish. I do not want to handle you. I think it might be physically impossible." His lips twitched up at the corners when she laughed. "I have only ever wanted you, exactly as you are. I would change nothing. And that's exactly what I should have told my father and Sean. I'm sorry I didn't."

"Are you done?" She swiped at her tears with her fingertips.

"Almost. I love you. I have always loved you. I will always love you. And I want you in my life. It doesn't matter how, as long as I can have you by my side. Married or not, I don't care. I want you in whatever way I can have you."

"No."

"No?" He dropped his hand, eyes searching hers before looking away.

"No," she said again, shaking her head. "Those terms don't work for me."

"Okay. Then I—"

"I want what you promised me ten years ago," she interrupted, reaching up to grip his chin and turning him to face her. "I want to stand beside you and not behind. I want to grow this family, this business, this empire with you. As an equal. I want to marry you. Those are my terms. Take it or leave it."

He watched her for a long moment, saying nothing. When he pushed to his feet and disappeared inside, her mouth dropped open and she hugged herself tightly. That was as much an answer as anything else. She rose just as he burst back through the doors, and she stopped short.

"Where are you going?"

"I thought your answer was pretty clear."

He stopped her when she moved to brush past him. "I had to go get something. I had to get this."

For the first time, she noticed the small black velvet box he held in his hand. He turned it over nervously in his fingers. Slowly he opened the lid, revealing a dazzling oval cut emerald encircled by brilliant diamonds.

"You are the only woman I've ever wanted to give this to. I've loved you since I was sixteen. It's always been you, Evie." He slipped the ring out of the box and slid it onto her finger. "I accept your terms. Evelyn O'Brian. Will you marry me?"

She'd worn this ring before, had been proud to wear it. It had been in his family for generations, and every Callahan queen before her had worn it.

Looking up at him, seeing all the love and longing in his eyes, she felt that whisper of hope grow in her chest and spread. It wrapped around her, warm and welcoming.

"I asked you first," she said.

He threw back his head and laughed, lifting her off her feet and twirling her in a circle. When he set her gently back on the ground, he reached up to cup her face in his hands, brushing his thumbs across her damp cheeks.

"Okay." He grinned. "I'll marry you."

When he brought his lips down to meet hers, she poured all her hope into that kiss and into the promise of forever with him.

A Note For the Reader

Dear Reader,

From the very bottom of my heart, thank you. Out of all the billions of books available to read you choose mine. I wrote this book because I had a story to tell and I am deeply grateful that you took the time out of your life to come along on Evie and Declan's journey.

If you enjoyed this book, I would really appreciate a little bit more of your time in the form of a review on Goodreads or Amazon or wherever you purchased it.

I couldn't do this writing thing I love so much without you, the reader. I'm so excited to share Brogan's story with you in Book Two of the Callahan Syndicate Series. Look for Bitter Betrayal coming in May 2022 to Kindle Unlimited and paperback.

If you'd like to stay up to date on what's next in the world of the Callahans, head to my website https:// meaghanpierce.com and sign up for my newsletter or follow me on TikTok for sneak peaks, updates, release dates, and more.

All my love,
Meaghan

tiktok.com/@meaghanpierceauthor

Acknowledgments

They say that writing a book is a solitary endeavor but I have to wholeheartedly disagree. The act of sitting down and pouring the words onto the page might be something I do all by myself but that's where it stops. The rest of my writing process is supported by a village of incredible women who never let me give up no matter how many dramatic GIFs I send them.

Endless thanks to Caoimhe and Paula, two of my very best friends who put up with my ridiculous author pop quizzes at all hours of the day and night. You are both always willing to offer your many opinions on a variety of subjects and you never fail to make me laugh, keep me going, and support me when it all feels like too much.

Kate and Ali. I am incredibly grateful we were introduced at the beginning of 2021. You have become such amazing friends and colleagues. Your advice and insight make my books better and your encouragement and dedication to your own craft keeps me going. You both inspire me every day.

Tasha, Kia, Erika, Sabrina, Jessica, and Veronica. I was scared to tell y'all I wanted to write a book but I shouldn't have been because you have been the best cheerleaders anyone could possibly ask for. I'm so grateful for your love and support on this journey.

A huge and unending thank you to Jill for tirelessly answering every single question I had about the beautiful city of Philadelphia. I wanted to get the details right and you helped me do it justice.

To my fabulous and brilliant editor, Mo. After only one book together I already feel like we're fast friends. I'm beyond grateful for your knowledge and expertise to polish up the prose while letting my story speak for itself. You are a blessing and I'm so happy I found you on the internet.

Last but not least, to anyone who offered their time, their skills, some words of encouragement, a listening shoulder while I gushed about this book and these characters, a helping hand, or just good vibes while I wrote and edited my little fingers off thank you to the moon and back.

Printed in Great Britain
by Amazon

10592372R00169